VEILE

HIGHL

BOOK THREE

BY HELEN HARPER

© 2016 Helen Harper

Chapter One

The rusting Fiat which Speck had managed to procure smelled of fish. Not in a fresh by-the-sea-with-a-tang-of-salt-and-wind-blowing-in-your-hair fish smell. More like a vat of rotting carcasses left in the hot sun for several days, and with several human corpses thrown in for good measure, smell.

'You'll get used to it!' he exclaimed cheerily, as we piled in and Lexie half retched. 'Just wind down the windows. In any case, fish is remarkably good for you. All that Omega Three.'

Brochan, who looked even greener than his merman skin normally allowed, reached over and tried to open the grubby window on his side. Given that his large frame was already hunched because of the cramped conditions, it wasn't a particularly easy manoeuvre. All the same, I craned my neck round and gazed hopefully at his contortions. The window didn't budge.

'Try your side, Tegs.'

I squeezed my hand down. With Lexie, Brochan and myself packed into the tiny back seat, it wasn't easy to get the space that I needed. As soon as I tugged on the handle it came away in my hand. Shite.

I held it up. 'No luck this side.'

'I don't think I can do this,' Lexie said. 'I can barely breathe.' There was a wildness about her eyes and it looked as if full-blown hyperventilation wasn't far off.

I patted her on the arm. 'Don't worry.' I bent down and pulled out my trusty hot-pink window tool. Before Speck could protest, I smashed the back window. The tinkle of breaking glass was drowned out by his cry of anguish.

'This car belongs to Tommy the Knock! He'll kill me if I return it like this.'

'He can bill me,' I said.

Taylor glanced round from the front passenger seat, his white eyebrows rising. 'And you'll pay him with what, exactly?'

I grinned. I'd been waiting for him to bring that up. 'You have all those winnings from the Games.' I shrugged. 'I'll just use those.'

He muttered something under his breath about ungrateful Sidhe. My grin widened. 'You auto know better than to rile me,' I punned.

'Tegs,' Lexie said heavily. 'It's over a hundred miles to the Adair Clan Lands. If I have to put up with your jokes as well as this smell and these conditions, I will kill you.'

'Don't worry,' said a muffled voice. Bob made his presence known and Brochan instantly sneezed into a spotted handkerchief. 'I'll do it for you.' He pushed himself up onto her knee and held up his tiny hand. Lexie mimed a high-five.

'Remind me again why we're doing this? Why we're not staying in Oban or, even better, moving back to Aberdeen?' Lexie demanded.

'Where's your sense of adventure?' I asked. 'We're going to reclaim my heritage, Lex. To right the wrongs of a generation and return Clan Adair to its formal glory.'

She blew out air through her pursed lips. 'Hurrah. Wake me up when it's over.'

Speck chose that moment to turn on the stereo. The car was so old that it actually took cassette tapes. As the booming tones of the Proclaimers deafened us, he turned round with a happy smile. 'Chill. This will be fun. I made us a mix tape for the journey.'

Lexie linked her fingers. 'Help me, Bob. Please. I'll wish for anything. Just make this stop.'

Bob's chirpy grin vanished. He jabbed a finger in my direction. 'Gotta wait till she's done with her other two wishes first.' Both he and Lexie turned to me with palpable hope.

'Nope,' I said.

'You promised, Uh Integrity!' Bob whined, his voice rising to the sort of pitch that would soon only be audible to dogs. 'Don't forget you promised.'

'Don't worry. I'll make that next wish soon enough.' As soon as I had figured out how to ask for something without bringing the sky crashing down on my head. I'd vowed to Bob that I would make my second wish within the next six months; the trouble was that genie wishes almost always had devastating consequences.

Bob subsided into a series of grumbles. With Lexie holding her nose, Brochan sitting with his arms folded, Taylor unfolding a newspaper to examine yesterday's racing results, Speck humming wildly and Bob in a sulk, we set off.

Despite the fishy reek and the less-than-enthusiastic atmosphere, I felt a swirl of excitement in my belly. I'd never even seen my Clan Lands before, much less been able to claim ownership of them. After my father, Gale Adair, had supposedly murdered every member of my Clan – my mother included – the Lands were salted and confiscated. I'd hoped to win them back by beating all the other Sidhe competitors at the Games. I didn't win but Byron Moncrieffe, who was the eventual victor, had asked for them on my behalf. That was after I'd stolen some of his magic and tried to explain to him what a prick his father really was. Byron didn't believe me on that score but the fact that he'd given up his chance of avoiding an arranged marriage with Tipsania Scrymgeour so that I could get my land back had to mean something. And of course, I didn't want him to marry Tipsania any more than he did.

I shook my head slightly. The thought of Byron might make my insides squeal and squirm but I couldn't let myself worry about him now. Easier said than done though.

From the get-go, Speck drove like a demon. For all his concern about what Tommy the Knock might do if his rust bucket wasn't returned in a decent state, he didn't seem to care about the suspension. We flew down the road with every pothole and bump making its presence painfully known. Before too long we were out in the open countryside surrounded by snow-topped mountains and moors; faint tinges of heather indicated the start of spring.

Cold air blasted in from the broken window and I tilted up my chin, enjoying the brisk breeze. I had no idea what the future might hold but it wouldn't be dull. I'd gone from accomplished thief to saviour of all the magic in the land to temporary mountain rescuer then competitive Sidhe; I certainly couldn't claim boredom and monotony as companions. Unfortunately, danger and excitement weren't usually good things either.

After a good thirty minutes, Speck muttered, 'Something's up ahead.' He turned down the music and peered through the windscreen. I jerked out of my reverie.

Taylor put down his paper. 'Is that a car?'

I twisted my head, trying to see. I caught sight of billowing black smoke and vicious flames on the side of the road in front of us as the screaming started. This was not good. Speck slammed on the brakes.

A woman, her clothes ripped and her face contorted in anguish, ran out in front of the Fiat. My anxiety rocketed tenfold. I tugged at the door, trying to open it. Curse this rusted piece of shite. Speck and Taylor were already out on the road and Lexie was trying to squeeze forward. With panic clogging my throat, I eventually shoved the door ajar with my elbow. I half fell, half ran out.

'What's happened?'

'My children!' she screamed. She pointed at the car. 'They're trapped inside. Help me! Save them!'

Children. My insides twisted. Brochan and Taylor tried to advance but the heat was immense.

'Back seat?' I yelled.

She covered her face in her hands and began gulping in air in huge ragged sobs. She was hyperventilating. Damn it.

I darted towards the back of the car where the fire was less intense. Even so, I had to shield my face and stay at least ten feet away. I wasn't going to waste precious time and risk debilitating injury until I knew exactly where the kids were. I had to be smart if they were going to be saved. If only there wasn't so much blasted smoke; it was next to impossible to see the vehicle's interior. I needed to make a decision.

Was that a small shadow towards the right? I couldn't tell. I tried to get nearer and it felt as if my very skin was being singed off. If those kids were still alive, they probably only had seconds.

Taylor appeared next to me. 'This is not good,' he muttered.

'Bob!' I yelled. I guessed he was going to get his heart's desire sooner rather than later; this was no time to play scared. 'I wish for the children in that car to get out safely!'

There was a flash of light and Bob appeared in front of me. 'Uh Integrity,' he said sadly. 'I'd love to help you out. I'd love to say that your wish is my command.'

I flung up my arms. What the hell was wrong with him? 'Then do it!'

He shook his head. 'I can't.'

'They're already dead?' Helplessness overtook me as I stared around. There had to be something we could do - it couldn't be over before we'd even started.

Brochan had given up attempting to reach the burning vehicle and was standing at the side of the road, chanting. No doubt he was trying to draw moisture from the air and bring about a rainstorm to douse the flames. Lexie was dashing round, doing what she could to peer inside the car.

'Something's wrong, Tegs,' Taylor said, his voice preternaturally calm.

Bob snapped his fingers in front of my face. 'The old man is right. Pay attention! I can't save them because they aren't there.'

I swung my gaze back towards him, confused. 'Eh?' Then my hackles began to rise. I looked at the children's mother who had stumbled over to join us. She tilted her head towards me and dropped her hands. The tears which had been streaming down her face were gone and she was breathing normally. She shrugged. 'Sorry. Not sorry.'

Realisation finally dawned. I was the worst kind of idiot. We all were. 'It's an ambush.'

And just like that, they were upon us.

It was a classic manoeuvre and one that all of us should have known better than to fall for. Draw the mark's attention by creating a diversion: the car. Even better, make that diversion create its own real smokescreen with the fire and smoke which obscured a large part of the banking to the side of the road. Then, when your mark is at its most vulnerable, attack.

I counted six. They were dressed like the worst kind of stereotypes: in black from head to toe with balaclavas covering their faces. They ranged in build from slight and wiry to squat and heavy. From the bulges, I reckoned they comprised two women and four men.

They'd planned this attack carefully. The two largest immediately ran at Brochan. With his size, he'd be the target to worry about the most – at least in terms of physicality. One woman headed for Speck and another for Lexie. That left two others – not to mention the so-called mother still standing to the side. Shite, shite and double shite.

I thought quickly. I still had some Gift residue lingering inside me. Telling lies from truth, the Gift which I'd nabbed from Kirsty Kincaid, was useless here as was what little remained of Morna Carnegie's magic that encouraged life from the ground. But I'd stolen from Byron too, even if I hadn't meant to, and his Gift was telekinesis. I hoped there was enough of that strange magical juice left inside me to do what was necessary.

The group had chosen their spot well: we were smack-bang in the middle of a steep-walled valley that effectively blocked us off from any escape beyond the road. That could work in our favour though – if I could get this right.

I flung my gaze towards the car, willing it to move. The wind was blowing the flames and smoke away from us. I concentrated hard. There was a loud creak and the car juddered upwards. Imagining my body as a magnet, I pulled it towards me. There was a strange feeling in my stomach and I knew I'd have to make this good or I'd be calling on Bob again out of sheer desperation.

I could already feel the magic draining from me. 'Come on,' I said through gritted teeth but the car didn't care that I was desperate.

Taylor, turning to the two men who were already upon us, did his best to shield me. 'Whatever you're going to do, Tegs, do it quickly.'

Sweat beaded my brow. 'I'm trying.'

As I tugged hard at the magic, the car heaved itself over, tumbling with ungainly somersaults. One. Two. Three... Bugger. I was losing control. I screeched, grabbed Taylor's arm and yanked him backwards out of the car's path.

Brochan, Speck and Lexie sprinted towards us in the nick of time, skirting past the flames so closely that I was terrified their clothes would catch fire. I forced the car to halt, creating a fiery barrier between us and most of the ninja-esque goons. One slipped through, however, and was already squaring up to us.

'We've got this!' Lexie yelled at me.

Between the flames and the angle the car was lying at, I'd bought us some time. Brochan, Speck and Lexie were dealing with the sneaky wanker who had made it through and I knew I could trust them to hold their own. Right now, my pressing concern was the fake mother. I spun round.

She wasn't Sidhe so at least I didn't have to worry about any violent Gifts rearing up to bring us down. She was, however, standing spread-eagled, with a shiny dagger clutched in each hand. There wasn't a scrap of emotion in her face; this wasn't personal for her. Somehow that made it even worse.

She gave a loud battle cry and leapt in our direction. Although Taylor tried to act as cover once more, it was clear that it was me she was interested in. She lashed out with one blade, slashing it against his arm, and then kicked him in the chest so he staggered backwards. As he gasped in pain, she continued her advance.

'Fucking Sidhe,' she hissed. 'You're all as bad as each other.' She lunged with her dagger again.

I held up my hands. 'Can we at least talk about this? I'm assuming you've been paid to attack us. How about we double that payment?'

She ignored me and swiped through the air. Taylor groaned and tried to get up but I spat out an instruction for him to stay down. He wasn't as nimble as he used to be and this would be easier without me having to worry about him. I danced to the side, avoiding yet another blow.

'We were told you didn't like to fight much,' the woman said with a cold smile. 'Perhaps you should revise your position.' From the expression in her eyes, I knew at least some of her buddies had managed to get round the burning car and were now at my back. That had been far too fast. These bastards were chillingly good.

There was a shriek from the far side of the car. Lexie - she was in trouble. Speck cried out and ran to her side but she pushed him off and gestured frantically at the ninja who was now taking on Brochan. Taylor was on the ground and bleeding. I could hear blood pounding in my ears and the continued roar of fire from the car. Even with the trickle of telekinesis which remained inside me, we were no match for this bunch: they were too strong and too determined. It was time for that last resort. Again.

'Bob! I wish...'

A huge hand appeared from behind and clamped over my mouth, followed by a tree trunk of an arm that encircled my chest and squeezed my ribs until it was painful to breathe.

Floating in front of my face, Bob shouted, 'You have to say the words!'

I bit down hard on the fleshy part of my captor's palm. He yelled but he didn't let go.

Bob threw himself forward, kicking and tugging. 'Let her go! Let Uh Integrity go!'

'Once you die,' said a rough voice in my ear, 'the genie is mine.' His arm left my chest. Before I could gasp in relief, his free hand wrapped round my throat and threw me to the ground.

'Tegs!' Taylor shouted.

I caught a glimpse of one of the attackers punching him in the side of the head and he collapsed like a sack of potatoes. Rage unfurled inside me and I kicked violently upwards in a bid to free myself. The woman was right: I abhor violence but dare to hurt one of mine and my rage is incandescent.

Anger wasn't going to help me, though. The grip round my throat tightened until my eyeballs bulged. The man fumbled at his side with his free hand and thrust a black object in my face. Gun, I thought dimly. That's a gun.

'You're not all that good after all,' he sneered. 'Say ta-ta.'

I couldn't believe it had come to this. After everything I'd been through and all my recent successes, I was going to end up as a corpse at the side of a quiet country road. Sorry, Dad. I tried.

There was a crunch of footsteps. A pair of booted feet halted by my side and a balaclava-covered face peered down. 'Integrity? Is that you?' a female voice asked.

I opened my mouth to speak but managed little more than a grunt. The figure gestured towards my captor and he released me. 'What gives?' he grunted as I rolled and coughed, my eyes streaming.

The woman muttered something in response. I tried to lift my head but the effort seemed too great. There was a loud curse and then I was hauled up by my armpits. The speaker pulled off her balaclava and I stared into a pair of arresting cat-like eyes. I half grimaced, half smiled. 'Chandra. Long time no see.'

***

It took us some time to re-group. With a series of malevolent glares, Brochan helped bring the fire under control while Taylor had his wounds tended. Lexie and Speck stood, arms crossed, both looking considerably worse for wear. Even Bob was in a huff and stayed as far away from Chandra's gang as possible.

I took a swig of water, wiped my mouth with the back of my hand and threw my one-time nemesis a suspicious look. 'So you're an assassin now?' I asked, unable to keep the sneer out of my tone.

'It pays well. And we're very choosy about our targets.'

I scoffed loudly.

'Sorry.' She didn't look apologetic at all. 'This was a rush job with limited time to carry it out.'

'Let me guess,' I said drily. 'You had between the Cruaich and the old Adair Lands to take me down.'

'Yup. All we knew was that you were a Sidhe. I should have twigged the truth. Who else would be interested in going to that place?' She looked at me curiously. 'Why *are* you going there?'

I ignored the question. This could be my chance to prove once and for all that Aifric wasn't the upstanding man everyone pretended he was. Byron's father, the Steward of the Highlands, was determined to see me dead. Knowing wasn't evidence though. If I could get

Chandra to give me proof that he'd hired her to kill me, then Byron would have to believe me. 'Who's your employer?'

'You mean who wants you dead,' she said. It wasn't a question. 'I have no idea. It was a dead drop. We advertise on the Dark Net and anonymity is assured for both client and freelancer.'

Shite. And thanks to the Gift I'd stolen from Kirsty Kincaid which, because I'd ripped it away from the hapless Sidhe in its entirety was showing no signs of dissipating, I knew she was telling the truth. 'There's no way you can...'

She shook her head. 'No.'

'I don't get it, Chandra,' burst out the man who'd thrust a gun into my face. He'd taken off his balaclava to reveal dark, swarthy skin, an impressive moustache and the largest set of ears I'd ever seen. He glared at her. 'Our job is to kill her. She's just a Sidhe, so why the hell don't we get on with it before she pulls more sneaky magic shit?'

'She's Clan-less, Ramsay.'

That wasn't actually true any more but somehow I didn't think this was the time to mention it.

'Bullshit. There's not a single Clan-less Sidhe in the whole of the Highlands.'

Chandra gave him a long-suffering look. 'This is Integrity Taylor.'

Ramsay started, more surprised than was sensible considering the gun he still held loosely in his hands. As he jerked involuntarily, it went off. Everyone jumped, apart from Speck. He screamed.

'You arse,' Chandra said to Ramsay. 'You could have killed someone. It's lucky that car was already set for the knacker's yard.'

I frowned and looked round, my heart sinking when I saw what she was referring to. The stray bullet had slammed into our fuel tank; a steady dribble of petrol was already leaking out.

'Brilliant,' I sighed.

Twitchy-Finger stared at me. 'Integrity Taylor is a myth.'

My eyebrows flew up as his words drew my attention away from the poor car. Before I could say anything, Chandra laughed. 'What colour is her hair?'

'White.'

'And is she old enough to have white hair?'

'She looks mid-twenties,' he said grudgingly. 'But she could have dyed it.' His lip curled. 'You women like to do that.'

Chandra rolled her eyes. 'Us women? Just remember who pays your wages, boyo.'

One of the others sidled up. 'You're really Integrity Taylor?'

I coughed. 'I hadn't realised I was so famous.'

'Infamous more like,' Chandra snorted. 'I keep telling them that I kicked your arse and broke your nose but they never believe me.'

'I was thirteen.'

She looked at me blankly. 'So?'

'You couldn't do that to me now.'

'Honey, we almost killed you about ten minutes ago.'

Okay, I'd give her that. I tugged at a loose curl, tucking it behind my ear, and massaged my neck. My skin was tender and I had no doubt that by tomorrow I'd be sporting some very unsightly bruises. 'Lots of people know who I am, Chandra. Why's he being so weird?'

'You've not been in Aberdeen for a while, have you?'

I shrugged. 'I guess not.'

'There are a lot of stories coming out of the Cruaich that you in-filtrated the Sidhe and stole the source of all their magic.' I frowned. 'Plus,' Chandra added, 'some people say you won the Games.'

'I didn't win.'

Chandra waved her hand in the air as if it didn't matter. 'Your old neighbour, Chump?'

'Charlie.'

'Well, Chump has been going around saying that he knows you intimately and that you've been using magic for years. He says you've sworn vengeance against the Sidhe for what they did to your family and that you're an amassing an army to destroy them.'

My mouth dropped open. I glanced round at Speck, Brochan, Taylor and Lexie. Formidable thieves they might be, but they were hardly an army.

'If you need some help,' Chandra said casually, 'then we'll offer our services.'

I gaped at her. 'Eh?'

She leaned in. 'The Clans have had a hold over us for too long.' Her eyes gleamed. 'It's time to start fighting back.'

'I don't fight,' I whispered. 'And I'm technically one of them.'

'No you're not.'

'I've taken my Clan name back,' I told her. 'I'm Integrity Adair. Not Taylor.'

Chandra lifted her chin. 'You're still one of us. You've still got the Clan-less in your heart.' She jabbed her finger at my chest. 'In your soul. You know what it means to be on our side of the magic.'

I did. But I wasn't a fighter. Then I thought of my true name, the one I'd received in the Cruaich's sacred grove: Layoch, meaning warrior. I shivered.

'You're not ready yet,' Chandra declared. 'But you will be. I can see why they want you dead. You should take care, Integrity Adair. Watch your back. You're damned lucky it was me who picked up this little gig. I'll spread the word, though, and make sure no one else takes up the contract. I can be pretty scary when I want to be.'

My thirteen-year-old self could attest to that. At least thanks to the stolen Gift running through my veins I knew she was telling the truth. 'Thanks,' I murmured.

She grinned and whacked me on the shoulder, sending me flying. 'Any time.' She pointed. 'We're parked over there out of sight. We'll give you a lift into Perth. You should be able to find someone to come out and do something with your ... car.' She said the last part dubiously as if she wasn't sure if such a rust bucket merited that title.

'Are you going to pay for the damage?'

Chandra flicked me a look. 'Well, sure,' she said easily. 'I reckon five hundred quid would more than cover it.'

I spotted Taylor wincing out of the corner of my eye. Great. He probably owed her money. And it was probably five hundred pounds.

'We should make a move before it gets dark. On the bright side though, it's Saturday night. There's a ceilidh on in the town hall.'

'I'd rather go to a rave,' Lexie muttered.

Chandra smiled then jerked her head. 'Come on, boys and girls.' Her team started trailing after her. One or two of them sent me suspicious looks while the others seemed to regard with me with awe.

I looked at my friends. 'We should go with them,' I said finally. 'That car's not going anywhere.'

'You mix with disappointing company, Uh Integrity,' Bob said. 'They are ... grubby. I don't like the way that Ramsay man looked at me.'

'And here was me thinking that you couldn't wait for me to make those remaining two wishes so you could get away from me.'

'The grass is not always greener,' he said patronisingly.

'It's pretty green on this side because we're fertilised by your bullshit.'

He stared at me. 'Is that a joke? That had better be a joke.' He rolled up his sleeves and formed tiny fists with his hands. 'Otherwise I'll break that pretty nose of yours again.' He danced from foot to foot and began humming *Eye of the Tiger*. 'I've seen every Rocky film. I will pulverise you, Uh Integrity. They will be picking bits of you up when I'm done.'

'Bits of me smashed into the green, green grass?' I enquired with a wink.

'You betcha! You...'

'How do you really know her, Tegs?' Lexie interrupted. 'Chandra, I mean.'

'We went to school together,' I said absently, turning my attention away from the genie. 'She was in the year above me.'

Speck cocked his head. 'You went to school?'

I smiled. 'Are you saying I come across as uneducated?'

'No. It's just that I'm having great difficulty imagining you dressed in a uniform and doing your homework. Did you have pigtails?'

'She only lasted six months before she was expelled,' Taylor said. 'I home-schooled her after that.'

'It's not my fault,' I protested. 'Living as a nameless Sidhe servant didn't exactly prepare me for the world of education.'

Taylor patted my cheek fondly. 'You did alright in the end.'

'It's not the end yet,' I grumbled. 'Let's grab that lift into town with Chandra. We don't need any more ... mishaps.'

We all began to move, apart from Brochan who remained immobile. I looked at him. 'You coming?'

'Isn't anyone going to point out the obvious? Raising an army against the Clans?'

'She was only talking, Brochan. It was just bluster.'

'It didn't sound like bluster,' he said. 'It sounded like hope.'

Something indefinable tightened across my shoulders. 'It's a really silly idea and you know it. Besides, the only really dodgy Sidhe who needs stopped is Aifric.'

Brochan rubbed his chin. 'Mm.'

I looked up. Chandra had already reached the top of the hill and was glancing back. She wouldn't wait around forever. 'Let's go,' I said softly.

Chapter Two

The mechanic, a loud, blousy woman with grease ingrained so deeply in her palms that I doubted it would ever come off, agreed to pick up the Fiat. She seemed doubtful about how quickly she'd get round to fixing it so we ended up buying yet another heap of a car so we could reach my Clan Lands before the month was out. Taylor was grumpy at the amount of money it cost but the last thing I wanted was to hang around Perth for days on end.

We were dangerously close to the Moncrieffe Lands here and it wouldn't take Aifric long to realise that he'd failed yet again in his bid to kill me. All the same, none of us were in the mood for getting back on the road just yet. I, for one, needed a drink to calm me down. Adrenaline was still firing through me and making me twitchy. Speck looked like he was about to pass out. We could wait until morning before continuing on our way.

Bob made a good effort to keep up everyone's spirits by jabbing light insults and flitting around us, but we were all shaken by what had just transpired. This was the second real attempt on my life – and there had been other half-hearted efforts too. It was a lot to take in. I was far from perfect but knowing there was someone out there who wanted me cold in the ground was definitely sobering. Especially when that someone was almost certainly the Steward. Even Brochan looked fed up.

'I was an assassin, you know,' I said, as we strolled towards the homely pub where we'd arranged to meet Chandra. 'I used to make a killing.'

Brochan grunted.

'Well, that's great, Integrity,' Speck said, his arms crossed as he marched alongside me. 'When Tommy the Knock puts a contract out on me for destroying his pride and joy, it will good to know that you'll be around to joke with him about it afterwards.'

'Don't worry about Tommy the Knock. I'll speak to him.' Besides, I seriously doubted that the Fiat was his 'pride and joy'.

'This is a bad omen,' Lexie said. 'We're not even at the Adair Lands yet and everything's going to shit.'

'You're not looking at this properly.' Taylor grinned. There was a lilt to his voice that put me on alert. 'We just escaped a serious assassination attempt. I'd say that's very a good omen indeed.'

I looked at Taylor then I looked around. By now, most of the high-street shops were shut and, this being a bitter Scottish February, it was already dark. Even so, there were people out on the street, mostly glammed up for a night on the town. I scanned each and every one of them. I didn't recognise anyone but that meant nothing. I knew from Taylor's expression that he'd spotted a way to gamble. Probably some old crony he'd spotted.

With a sinking feeling I cleared my throat. 'You're going to come to the ceilidh, right?'

He blinked at me innocently. 'Of course! I love a good ceilidh.' He grabbed hold of my hands and yanked me along. 'The Gay Gordons is my favourite.' He hummed loudly, cantering up and down the street. Then he stood on my foot.

'Ouch!'

'Oops.' He grinned. 'Sorry.'

I rolled my eyes and moved away. 'Look, there's the pub.'

'Praise be,' Lexie said. 'I'm parched.'

By unspoken consensus, we picked up speed, ignoring the wind blowing against us. A small group of Bauchans was hanging around outside. I guessed my supposed infamy hadn't reached these parts yet because one of them caught sight me and muttered to his mates, 'There's another fucking Sidhe.'

As soon as we reached them, all five made a show of curtseying. The action was far too deliberate and melodramatic; they swept the ground in a manner that suggested blatant disrespect. There were some Sidhe who would take great offence at that, though I wasn't one of those. Frankly, I'd rather be on the Bauchans' side than the Sidhes'. It wasn't a problem, though: I could match like for like and show them that we weren't all bastards. And I could have a little fun too.

I halted in front of the little group, pushed up my chin so my nose was in the air and held out my hand. 'Paupers,' I said loudly, in a posh, affected accent. 'Your manners do you well. I will permit you to kiss my hand in return.'

Four of them looked at me, aghast, apparently believing that I was taking myself seriously. The fifth, however, with a mischievous glint, did exactly as I asked. He bent across and began licking the back of my hand. Then he turned it over and began nibbling at the softer flesh on the other side. It kind of tickled. I remained perfectly still.

'I like your nail polish,' he said, between slobbery licks. 'Hot pink turns me on.' He grabbed his groin with his free hand. 'I'm already getting hard.'

I tossed back my hair. 'Kiss me more.'

His mouth twitched as he held back his laugh. 'My lady.'

I started moaning. Brochan, clearly put out by my display, hastily pushed open the door to the pub and disappeared. Speck followed, the tips of ears bright red.

'Have fun, Tegs,' Lexie purred, taking Taylor by the arm and propelling him inside.

My moaning increased. The four other Bauchans were backing away, shaking their heads. I threw my head from side to side in an almost perfect Meg Ryan imitation. 'Yes!' I cried. 'Oh yes! More!'

The Bauchan chuckled.

There was a flash of light. Bob appeared, floating behind the Bauchan's head and staring at me. 'Uh Integrity, what *are* you doing?'

I gave him a wink. Then I let out a tiny scream and pulled my hand back. I shook myself. 'That was orgasmic.'

The Bauchan smiled. 'And here was me thinking that the Sidhe didn't have a sense of humour. I'm Fergus, by the way.'

'Integrity.'

'Which Clan?'

I held his gaze. 'Adair.'

He raised his eyebrows and whistled. 'Seriously? I thought they were all dead.'

'Obviously not,' Bob said from behind, suspicion glazing his every word.

Fergus stared at him. 'Is that a genie?'

'Yep.'

'I've never seen one in the flesh before.'

'I can hear you, you know!' Bob flew in front of my face as if he was trying to protect me. Sweet, but really not necessary.

'You should be careful.' Fergus looked past Bob at me. 'It's not a good idea to ask a genie for wishes.'

'I got it,' I said drily.

His grin widened. 'Yeah, you seem like you can look after yourself.' He pointed at the pub. 'Can I buy you a drink?'

Tempting. He was good looking, even for a Bauchan, and I liked his banter and his way of thinking. It probably wasn't the best time, though. And he didn't have floppy golden hair or emerald-green eyes. 'I'm with my friends.'

He took the hint. 'Another time, perhaps.'

'Perhaps.'

Fergus bowed like a well-trained diplomat and left, sauntering down the street to join his gullible buddies who were still in a state of shock. He did, however, receive a slap on the back. I shook my head in amusement.

'Uh Integrity!' Bob hissed. 'What did you think you were doing?'

'Taking the piss.'

He recoiled. 'What? What piss? Do you mean urine? Were you taking that Bauchan's urine?'

'It's an expression. As an all-knowing supreme being, you should know that. It was just an act, Bob.'

'Did he know that?'

I sighed. 'Yes.'

He glared at me. 'Really? Because I think you were indulging in some very risky behaviour. I thought you were all lovey-dovey about Byron Moncrieffe.'

My eyes narrowed. 'And I thought you were more fun. Now get back into your letter opener unless you want to be bothered by every single person who walks into that pub.'

'It's a scimitar!' he yelled. 'You know fine well it's a scimitar!'

'Okay. Scimitar.'

He sniffed. 'That's better. And, for your information, I'm lots of fun.'

I stretched out my pinkie and ruffled his hair. 'Course you are.'

***

The second I entered the pub, I was whacked in the face with what appeared to be a bundle of cloth. 'What the...?' I spluttered.

Chandra smiled at me serenely. 'Come on, Integrity. You can't go to a ceilidh dressed like that.'

I glanced down at my jeans, warm jumper and sparkly hot-pink scarf. I didn't look that bad, surely? 'I have other clothes,' I said, gesturing at my bag. Chandra was well known for her appreciation of tight and revealing attire. Considering she was wearing bright green hot pants and a halter top and it was February, for goodness sake, I dreaded to think what was in the bundle she's thrown at me. I had no problem with getting dressed up but even I had limits. 'And since when were shorts *de rigeur* for ceilidhs?'

She raised an eyebrow. '*De rigeur*? My, my. Your vocabulary is coming up in the world.'

I stuck out my tongue and shook out the cloth. It was a tiny purple dress which glimmered with sequins.

'Pretty, isn't it?'

'I suppose,' I said grudgingly. 'But...'

Lexie appeared from the restroom in an electric-blue jumpsuit. 'I love this!' she squealed.

Chandra grinned. When Speck appeared wearing a similar get-up, I almost choked.

'Aw, Specky!' Lexie beamed. 'We look like the perfect couple!'

He looked like Elvis Presley on an acid trip. I flicked a look at Brochan who was still wearing his normal clothes. 'Are you...?'

'No.' His face said it all.

I stifled a smile.

Taylor's new clothes at least were slightly more sober, although his white suit with its giant lapels and shoelace-thin tie certainly weren't designed for a shy and retiring wallflower. I arched an eyebrow at Chandra. 'You just happened to have all these outfits lying around?'

'I'm branching out,' she said, flicking back her hair and adding a saucy wink which somehow still managed to be laced with danger. 'I can't be an assassin forever. It's murder on my knees.'

I couldn't begin to imagine what her knees had to do with it. It was probably better not to. 'You're going into fancy dress?'

'Fashion, darling.' She waved a hand. 'I designed all of this.'

'So you want us to be walking adverts for your new line?'

'Well, it'll be great publicity. You're not exactly inconspicuous, are you? Not with that long white hair.' Her eyes gleamed.

Without thinking, I touched my hair. Then I realised what I was doing and quickly dropped my hand. 'I'll try it on,' I told her. 'But I'm not promising anything.'

Bob coughed. 'Do you have anything in my size?' he asked hopefully.

Before I could see what Chandra might come up with for the fashion-conscious genie, I vamoosed into the bathroom. It was small, with only a single stall, a sink and a frosted window, but thankfully it was clean.

It was surprisingly difficult to get the dress on. I turned it this way and that. There was no zip. Under or over? I frowned. If I pulled it down over my head, I could probably manage to wriggle it on - if I breathed in. I stripped off, hanging my own clothes over the door to the toilet stall.

I found the right end of the dress, yanked it over my head and began an awkward shimmy to pull it down. Unfortunately for me, the dress somehow got completely twisted.

'This is what things have come to,' I said to myself, my voice muffled by the flimsy fabric. 'Chieftain of the Adair Clan stuck in a dodgy pub bathroom, half naked and with a dress wrapped round her head.'

Unwilling to yank too hard in case I ripped the damn thing, I carefully unwound it, ready to start again - except a bone-chilling scream from somewhere outside stopped me in my tracks. A dark, heavy shape fell against the window with such force that it shattered, spraying glass everywhere. I yelped and darted back, pressing myself against the wall. There was another scream and the shape collapsed. Shite, shite, shite. This day was just getting better and better.

I grabbed my shoes, hauling them onto my feet to avoid getting cut by the glass, and peered out of the window. An older-looking man wearing a bulky coat was lying on the ground outside. I couldn't tell whether he was breathing or not. I leapt out, scraping my side against some shards of glass, and bent down to check him. He was gasping, his fingers scrabbling at his face as he tried to suck air into his lungs. I grabbed the collar of his coat and dragged him up to a sitting position. From somewhere further down the street, there were several more shrieks.

'What's wrong?'

His face was turning purple. 'Can't ... breathe...'

Heart attack? I had some pretty good first-aid knowledge from my stint with mountain rescue but I was far from expert. I reminded myself to keep calm while I fumbled to unfasten his coat and loosen his shirt.

'Does it hurt? Your chest?'

He half shook his head then he half nodded. Damn it. Which was it?

People were spilling out of the pub door. Several idiots already had their mobile phones in their hands, no doubt more concerned with filming the action so their mates could gawp at it on social media than with the chaos that appeared to be descending.

'Taylor!' I yelled. 'Call an ambulance!'

He appeared by my side. 'What's wrong?'

'I don't know. Might be a heart attack. Might be a panic attack. Keep him calm and don't let him go into shock.'

'What are you going to do?'

I jerked my head grimly at the distant shouts and screams. 'I'm going to find out what the hell that is.' Without wasting any more time I took off, pelting down the street. I heard Taylor shouting behind me, something about 'underwear' and 'naked' but I ignored him. I wasn't any good in a fight but I was a Sidhe Chieftain. Keeping the Highlands safe was supposed to be my job, even if right now all I was capable of was telling truth from lies and growing pretty little flowers.

It wasn't hard to find the source of the problem - there was a trail of horror-stricken people to follow. As I rounded one corner, I grabbed a cowering guy who was close enough to reach. 'What is it?' I demanded. 'What is causing all that noise?'

He gaped at me. I wasn't sure whether it was because of what he'd seen or the fact that a white-haired Sidhe in her lacy underwear was standing in front of him. I didn't have time for this. I tried again, hardening my tone to encourage him to snap out of his daze. 'What is going on?'

He found his voice. 'Fomori demon,' he stuttered. 'I'm sure of it.'

For one long second, I stared at him. He was telling the truth; he definitely believed that was what he'd seen. If I'd been anyone else, I probably would have thought he was delusional but I'd been across the Veil and I'd seen thousands of the bloody things. I knew how distinctive they looked – and I could see the expression in this guy's eyes. I couldn't begin to imagine why one was here now after all these years, but I couldn't run away and hide either.

I spun round and began to run faster. I didn't feel the cold; I didn't feel anything other than the first vestiges of true panic. I splashed through dirty puddles and ignored the wind whipping round me. The streets were now almost deserted; everyone with any sense had already hurried inside for cover.

'Which way?' I yelled at an apron-clad shopkeeper who was standing, frozen, outside a small greengrocer's. Judging by the large set of keys he was holding, he'd been locking up for the night.

He didn't move, he was so terrified that he couldn't, but his eyes flicked slightly to the right. I took the hint and continued in that direction. When I rounded the corner and the River Tay came into view, I saw the creature.

There was no doubting it was a Fomori demon. It stood bow-legged by the side of the river, hairless and naked. Its skull bulged grotesquely and, where there might have once been ears, there were now only scarred holes. It hadn't seen me but its jaws were lolling open wide and its head was swinging heavily from side to side like a dog's. For a moment I was tempted to throw a stick and see if it would run panting after it. But this was no friendly Labrador - it wasn't even a trained, vicious guard dog. This was a thing of pure evil and I had absolutely no idea what to do.

I sidled closer, trying not to make any sudden movements which might draw the demon's attention. Unfortunately this part of Perth was fully pedestrianised; that was great if you were out shopping and having lunch but wasn't so helpful when you were hunting the most vicious beast known to man. I couldn't even be grateful that it was dark; from what little I'd gleaned from my journey beyond the Veil, the Fomori lived in semi-darkness. I'd probably have more luck sneaking up on it in broad daylight.

A thought struck me: I might not be able to wield any power over the sun but light was something I *could* manage. It was unfortunate that I'd left Bob's scimitar with the rest of my stuff and, in my virtually naked state, I didn't even have my phone. But there was a hardware shop directly opposite which was bound to boast powerful torches in its inventory. If I could break in, I should be able to find one. The trouble was, that meant leaving the Fomori demon on its own.

I had no idea why it had stopped moving but I bet that it wouldn't linger by the river for long. Surely the police would be on their way soon? Unless they were taking their time because they didn't want to get munched. Given that I was trembling with fear myself, I could hardly blame them.

I waited for the right moment to dart across the street. Now that I was no longer moving, I noticed the chill. My skin was covered in goose bumps; whether they were from fear or because I was standing in sub-zero temperatures in my knickers and bra, I wasn't entirely sure.

I prayed desperately that the demon wouldn't take off again. Fortunately, it lifted its head up and sniffed and an expression of what could only be puzzlement traced across its gaunt features. As it sniffed once more, I pelted across. I didn't look back again until I was safely on the other side of the street. I had no idea what scent the demon had caught but it was certainly finding it interesting. Interesting enough not to notice me.

Pressing my back against the glass of the shop front, I edged over to the door and wiggled the doorknob. It was too much to hope that it had been left unlocked and I cursed under my breath. The fastest way in would be to break the glass but that would alert the demon to my presence. I made a quick decision and pulled out a bobby pin from my now-less-than-perfect hairstyle. It would be a lot quicker with a real lock pick but my days of secreting one of those in my hair were long gone, more's the pity.

I kept glancing over my shoulder and checking on the demon. It was still sniffing the air and it still wasn't moving. I tried not to question my good fortune and concentrate on the matter in hand but it was bloody hard.

It took a few tries but eventually I heard a click and the lock slipped into place. I breathed a sigh of relief, opened the door and my gaze immediately fell on a large industrial torch on special offer on the front counter. I'd barely taken a single step inside, however, when the entire place lit up and sirens shrieked.

'Arsing hell!' What kind of shop had a crappy door lock that could be broken in less than thirty seconds but invested in a state-of-the-art security system inside? I twisted round, ready to throw myself on the floor in a last ditch bid to hide. It was too late; the demon was already there.

I'd been right about the light. The demon was covering its face and keeping its head down as if even electrical light would burn the skin off its sinewy body. It knew I was there, though; it couldn't fail to see me, illuminated as I was like a damned naked mannequin.

I lunged for the torch, grabbed it and flicked on the switch. Nada. It might have been on display but it didn't have any batteries. So much for running out of the shop blasting torchlight into the demon's eyes.

As I watched, the demon edged a few inches closer. It was still shielding its face but was showing a steely determination. I was relatively safe here within the light but sooner or later it would gain enough confidence to come after me. Or it would leave and I'd have no way of stopping it from whatever other chaos it decided to create.

I took a few steps backwards, wondering if there was something else that I could use. A range of expensive hammers hung along one wall. Despite the obvious danger of my current situation, I couldn't imagine myself using one to smash a hole in the demon's skull. Besides, as far as I could tell, the demon hadn't done much yet except look threatening.

It took another step, then another. My eyes travelled up and down its body as I tried to assess it for vulnerabilities. I spotted a dark shape on one arm – a tattoo just like the one I'd seen on May, the demon I'd saved in the Lowlands. It was also just like the concealed ornament I'd found in Aifric's quarters. Something about the design clarified my thoughts. There was only one thing left to do.

I wrenched the door open again and stepped into the street, facing the demon head-on. It stiffened and recoiled. Was it afraid? I lifted one arm behind my head, then thrust the other one forward. In my mind, I looked like Bruce Lee, ready to perform some outstanding kung fu. Or so I hoped. I needed the demon to fight me – and I needed it to use its Gift to do so. If it had been sent here from beyond the Veil, logic dictated that whatever magical skill it had at its disposal was violent.

It was still afraid of the light cascading onto the street from behind me and barely peeked at me from underneath its smooth arm. The siren continued to peal but there was no sign of the cavalry.

'It's just me and you,' I called out. 'Why don't you use your Gift? I know you have one, just like me.' I took a deep breath. 'Let's make this an even match. I'm Sidhe, you're Fomori.' I smiled humourlessly. 'It'll be like old times.'

I couldn't tell whether it understood me or not. It blinked once and I gritted my teeth. Come on, you bastard. Use your freaking Gift so I can steal it and throw you off balance. It'll hurt but it won't kill you. It'll be best for both of us.

The demon didn't move - I needed to do more to goad it. I took a tiny step towards it. It hissed in response and that's when I felt it, a light brush, nothing more than a probing touch against my mind. Psychometry. Just like Jamie Moncrieffe's Gift. The Fomori was looking into my very soul and assessing what I was. A shudder rippled through me.

Three things happened almost at once. I stared hard at the demon, wishing for its Gift; if I could wish hard enough, perhaps I could rip it from its body and make it collapse. As I did that, however, it turned to flee, a glinting expression I didn't recognise crossing its eyes. At the very same time, from out of nowhere, came a bloody fireball.

It slammed into the demon's back, sending it flying with a hard smack onto the concrete. The heat was almost as searing as Chandra's car trap had been. How many times was I going to be subjected to having my damned eyebrows singed off? I ran forward to the sprawled demon, averting my eyes from the massive hole that now gaped from its spine. Glassy dead eyes stared up at me. I grimaced and turned away, my stomach heaving.

Footsteps sounded from behind but I didn't look up. Somehow I already knew who it was going to be. His musky scent wafted over, intermingling with that of the demon's. 'I had that under control,' I muttered.

'It didn't look like it from where I was standing,' Byron said. His voice was tight and controlled. 'It looked like it was about to swallow you whole.'

I closed my eyes, blocking out the image of the curl of bronzed hair which fell across his forehead and the clinging cashmere sweater which was more appropriate on a Paris catwalk than on a dirty cold street in Perth. Violence with style. I shuddered and wondered if I should be happy that he was speaking to me. Last time I'd seen him, he'd done everything he could to avoid looking in my direction.

'I was taking its Gift from it so it would faint,' I said. 'Then it could have been captured alive.'

His expression went stony. 'Yes, stealing the magic essence of people is right up your alley, isn't it?'

He was pissed off about that? He killed the damn thing. I wouldn't have done that. I wouldn't resort to playground taunts either. Apparently Byron still had a streak of spoilt playboy running through him. I opened my mouth to tell him exactly that when another thought struck me. 'How did you know that Fomori demons have Gifts?'

He shrugged. 'I just do. Everyone does.'

I wasn't so sure about that. I filed it away and let it go for now and pointed at the demon. 'It was running away.'

Byron snorted. 'Bullshit.'

I twisted my head and met his eyes, the green searing into me with almost the same heat as the fire. 'Where did the fireball hit?' I asked.

He glanced down. 'It's a Fomori demon, Integrity. If you're going to suggest that it was cowardly to strike it in the back then perhaps you need to check your history books.'

I shook my head. 'The sins of the father. That's what it always comes down to with you lot, doesn't it?'

His jaw tightened. 'Are you suggesting that I should have been nice? Invited it round for tea, perhaps? With you standing there naked and vulnerable as it...' His voice trailed off.

I pressed my lips together and tried not to react. 'It hadn't hurt anyone.'

'There's an old man who's just been taken to hospital.'

'It didn't hurt him, Byron. That old man just saw it and had a panic attack. Or a heart attack. Or something.'

He stepped towards me. 'And that makes it alright?' He pointed at the body. 'A Fomori demon? Here? Next to my Clan Lands? Did you really think I'd just let that pass?'

I dropped my shoulders. He might be acting petulant and bristling with far too much self-righteous anger but he was right: a Fomori demon next to the Moncrieffe Lands couldn't be a coincidence. I pushed aside my own internal irritation. There were more important things than verbal tit-for-tat with Byron Moncrieffe.

'How did it pass through the Veil?' I asked. Three hundred years ago, we had created the magical barrier which separated the Highlands from the Lowlands to keep out the Fomori demons. Was it failing? I felt sick. Or was Aifric responsible for more than just the attempts on my life?

Byron shook his head. 'I don't know.'

He was telling the truth. I mulled it over. The demon must have been here on Aifric's behalf; Byron's father could have done something to let it cross. Out of everyone, he probably had the power to achieve such a feat. And the most to gain. Was he planning a secret meeting, some kind of alliance? Fear shivered across my skin. In any other scenario, I might have managed to keep my mouth shut. This, however, was too important. 'Where's your father?' I demanded.

Byron crossed his arms over his chest as his anger spiked once more. In fact, I had the distinct feeling that if I were just about anyone else the demon wouldn't be the only charred corpse around here. His glare intensified but I was determined to stand my ground. 'Why?' he said in an undertone so low I almost had to strain to hear it. He drew himself even closer. Furious tension sparked between us as he dropped his head towards mine. 'So you can accuse him of more wrongdoing? What if I told you that Taylor was a mass murderer?'

'I wouldn't believe you because he's not,' I said flatly. Byron gave me a pointed look and I sighed. I understood why he couldn't grasp that his own father was a villain but sooner or later he'd realise I wasn't lying or delusional. I might have been digging my own grave but my desperate need for Byron to see the truth wouldn't let me stay quiet. I tried a different tack. 'Aifric tried to kill me again this afternoon, Byron. Your beloved saint of a father wants me dead.'

Something dark flitted across his face. 'What happened?'

'He hired an assassin. We were attacked on the road.'

'Are you alright?' he demanded. The icy anger in his eyes was turning to incandescent rage. Whoa. Back up there a second.

'Obviously. But we got lucky.' I shivered. 'It could have been far, far worse.'

He scanned my face, as if trying to glean the truth. His gaze dropped to my body, drifting down as if to check I really was alright before relaxing ever so slightly. Then, because our strange slow dance wasn't apparently done yet, he stepped back towards me once more. Crowding me yet again. His actions were starting to seem very deliberate. 'How do you know it was my father?' he asked in a soft voice laced with steel. I opened my mouth then closed it again. Shite. Byron leaned in towards me. 'Give me proof. Give me one tiny scrap of proof that my father, the Steward of the Highlands, wants you dead.'

I had nothing and he knew it. 'Logically—' I began.

'Logically, nothing. You're full of shit, Integrity.'

'I might be shit out of luck,' I shot back, 'but I don't have shit for brains.' I'd gone too far. I could see it in the tightening round his mouth and I wished I could take back my words. Shite. He dropped his arms while I lowered my voice and tried to get him to see reason. 'Just think about it, Byron. Think about what I've said. It makes sense. I'm not lying.'

'It seems to me,' he said softly, 'that you're the one who's concerned with the apparent sins of other people's fathers.'

'I don't hate you for what he's done, Byron.'

He thrust his hands into his pockets and looked away. 'He's not *done* anything.'

I clenched my jaw at Byron's blinkered naivety. I wrapped my arms around my body for warmth, not for modesty. 'Have you told him about what I can do? That I can ... take Sidhe Gifts?'

'No.'

Relief ran through me and my veins buzzed with magic. He was telling the truth. That was something at least. 'Why not?'

He sighed. 'Because I know what will happen to you if I do.' I opened my mouth but he held up a hand to forestall me. 'Not because my father would see you hurt but because he would be hung, drawn and quartered for letting someone so potentially dangerous run around the Highlands.'

Oh, please. 'Aren't *you* worried about that? About dangerous little me?' I uncrossed my arms and revealed more of my bare skin.

He ran a hand through his hair and avoided looking down. 'Integrity, there are many things that worry me where you're concerned.' He raised his eyes heavenward and I wished I knew what he was thinking. 'I have to go. I need to tell my father, *the Steward*, the person who ensures the safety of every soul in the Highlands, about what just happened.' He pointed at the demon. 'And you're welcome for saving your life.'

I glanced at the dead demon once again. 'Oh, you're a real hero.'

He scowled. 'Yeah. I am. And that's because you're still alive thanks to me.'

'I was doing just fine without your help,' I pointed out calmly.

"You were about to be killed.' He said the words flatly and without inflection.

'Would that have really bothered you?'

He growled something under his breath. 'You know it would have. You know that despite what you've done, there's something between us. I wanted to pretend there wasn't but I can't.' Frustration twisted his features. 'You have to admit it as well. You need me.' To scratch a particular itch perhaps. Not for any other reason. Byron wasn't finished though. He leaned back slightly and eyed me with a mixture of what I could only define as both distaste and desire. 'Go and put on some bloody clothes. Why the hell are you naked anyway?'

'I'm not naked.'

'A couple of scraps of lace hardly count as clothing.'

I pointed at my shoes. 'Look. Trainers.' Then I pointed at my bra. 'Marks and Spencer's finest.'

He rolled his eyes. I thought he was going to leave but instead he shrugged off his jacket and put it round my shoulders. It was warm and snug and it smelled of him. Goddammit.

'Take this,' he said gruffly. His mouth twitched. 'I'm a heroic gentleman after all.'

We stared at each other. I rather he thought he was waiting for me to yank the jacket off and throw it at him. Instead I turned up the collar as if pretending to be cool. His mouth twitched again.

'Thank you,' I said. Why the hell did the villainous wanker of the world have to be *his* father?

Byron's fingers reached out and brushed away an invisible speck of dust from my shoulder as his expression softened.

'Look after yourself, Integrity. Please stop with the silly accusations.'

He jerked his head and two liveried Moncrieffe men appeared from out of nowhere. They paled at the sight of the demon but when Byron reached down and picked up its head, they swallowed their fear. One took the torso and the other the legs. Without another look at me, they walked off with their gruesome burden.

'They're not silly, Byron,' I whispered sadly. I pulled his jacket closer and inhaled. Then I trudged back in the direction of the pub.

Chapter Three

By the time I got back I was in no mood for dancing, despite Chandra and Lexie's assertions that it would 'warm me up'. Images of the dead demon kept flitting through my head. I knew it was a Fomori demon but surely executing it in that fashion should have bothered Byron, at least slightly. I pinched the bridge of my nose. Yet another reason why we were wholly incompatible.

I pulled on my clothes, downed a double whiskey, gagged when I remembered that I really didn't like the stuff and wandered off to an upstairs room which Taylor had had the foresight to get hold of. If I'd thought worries about Fomori demons and assassins would stop me sleeping, I was very wrong. I was asleep so fast I barely remembered getting into bed.

It was good to wake up surrounded by my half-comatose mates. I'd have time to get my head together before they emerged from their post-ceilidh fug. I didn't plan on wasting any of it. Leaving them to their slumber, I went downstairs, inhaled a large mug of tea and pulled out my phone. It rang several times before being answered.

'Yeah,' muttered Angus's sleep-fogged voice.

'Hi!' I said chirpily. 'It's Integrity.'

'It's six o'clock in the morning,' he grunted. 'Piss off.' He hung up.

Somewhat nonplussed at his grumpiness, given how polite and friendly he'd been towards me in the past, I waited a minute and tried again.

'It's you again, isn't it?'

I grinned. 'You're really not a morning person, are you? I just have one question then I'll let you get back to sleep.'

'Is it urgent?'

'Nope. But you're awake now.'

He groaned. 'I thought I liked you. Now I think I might throttle you.'

'You'll have to get in line,' I said cheerfully. There was an unfortunate ring of truth about that statement. 'What do you know about Fomori demons?'

'Ugly. Evil. Live on the other side of the Veil. What's there to know? There's not been one here in years, one that showed up at the Cruaich before getting slaughtered.'

'Actually, there was one in Perth last night.'

There was a moment of silence. Then, sounding much more alert, Angus asked, 'Are you sure?'

'Saw it with my own eyes.'

He swallowed. 'Shite.'

'Yeah.' I explained what had happened. 'The thing is,' I said, 'what I really want to know is what you know about Fomori Gifts.'

'Wait, the Fomori have Gifts?'

A knot of tension tightened in my lower back. That was pretty much all I needed.

'It does make sense,' Angus continued. 'I'd just never thought about it before. To be honest, I never really thought much about Fomori demons before. Does the Steward know what happened last night?'

'Oh,' I said drily, 'I imagine so. Thanks, Angus. Go back to dreamland.'

'I'm not sure I can sleep now,' he said. 'Stay safe, Integrity. Call me if you need anything.'

I smiled. 'Thanks. I appreciate that.' I drummed my fingers on the table. Angus was just one guy; he wasn't the only person I could call.

Unfortunately, it was a bit more complicated getting hold of the Bull. I had to go through several layers of people before I could finally speak to him. 'You have to give me your mobile number,' I instructed him when he finally huffed at me from the other end of the line. 'I need to be able to get hold of you quicker than an asthmatic snail can move up Ben Nevis.'

'I am not your slave.'

He seemed to keep forgetting that part. I reminded him helpfully. 'Actually, you pretty much are.'

'I don't have a mobile.'

I couldn't tell whether he was being truthful or not. It was interesting to know that Kirsty Kincaid's Gift only worked face to face. Either way, that kind of problem was easily solved. 'Get one,' I told him. I had the Bull's true name and he had to do what I commanded. 'And tell me what you know about Fomori demons and Gifts.'

'Eh?'

'Do Fomori demons have Gifts?'

I could picture him screwing up his face in response. 'How the hell should I know?'

I shook my head. 'Not good enough. Answer the question properly.' I paused and used his true name, 'Cul-chain.'

He let out a curse at which even Taylor would have raised his eyebrows. 'I do not know if the demons have Gifts. Alright?'

'Thanks.'

There was a pause. 'Why do you need to know that?' he asked.

'Nothing you need to worry your pretty little head about,' I said lightly and changed the subject. 'How are the wedding preparations coming along? For Tipsania and Byron, I mean. It has to be on the cards some time soon.' I realised I was holding my breath and cursed silently.

'It's not,' he said sourly. 'We are waiting for the Moncrieffes to make their move so we can announce the engagement. They are dragging their heels for some reason. The Steward is also disinclined to accept my requests for a private meeting.'

I scratched my nose. I might have been rather rash when I'd informed Aifric that I had the Bull's true name. Oh well. I couldn't change the past and it would be good if Byron and Tipsania got married. Then Byron would be off the table for good. Wedding rings were a serious turn-off. And Byron was not for me. I opened my mouth to tell the Bull to hurry things along then changed my mind. 'Well,' I said, 'you do the same when they get in touch. Drag your heels - for as long as possible.' I mentally slapped myself.

'This is because you want him for yourself,' the Bull spat. 'Byron Moncrieffe and Tipsania are in love and you're going to steal their happiness away from them. You -'

I interrupted before he could go any further. 'I have to go now. Bye!'

I hung up. The Bull was both right and wrong. No, Byron and Tipsy were most definitely not in love but yes, I did want him for myself, even with my serious doubts about him creeping in again. Crapadoodle.

***

The others roused themselves before midday, groggy and bleary-eyed. Brochan was the worst. When Taylor saw my look, he leaned over and whispered, 'Tequila shots. And a rather fetching mer-woman who insisted he dance Strip The Willow with her afterwards.'

I winced. Strip the Willow was a ceilidh dance that involved spinning. Lots and lots and lots of spinning. Poor Brochan. 'Are we okay to leave? We can delay if you guys need more time.'

'We should probably go now,' Taylor said with studied casualness. I looked at him suspiciously and he shrugged. He didn't even look guilty. 'There are a few selkies who came in from the river. They weren't very pleased when I fleeced them of their wages.'

He'd been gambling again. Big surprise. I might have been expecting it but the revelation still didn't make me happy. 'You can't keep doing that. You're an addict. You told me you'd stop.'

He grinned. 'No, *you* told me I'd stop. Besides, we need as much money as we can get. It wouldn't be so bad if people weren't try to kill you all the time, Tegs, but those Clan Lands of yours aren't going to get fixed up on their own. And if we have to keep buying new cars all the time...'

I held up my palm. 'Try to avoid making any bets for a while. Try it for a week.'

'I can stop gambling whenever I want to. How about I turn the tables? You stay away from Byron and I'll won't bet.'

Those were two completely different things. I shook my head. 'Come on,' I sighed. 'Let's get on the road.'

Our 'new' car didn't have the smell of fish that the Fiat had provided but it did bestow us with a series of alarming groans whenever Speck tried to change gear. He still managed to bring it up to an admirable speed, zipping out of Perth and back onto the road in no time. On the bright side, the stereo system was broken so we were treated to an unexpected and welcome silence.

As we settled in for the journey, we agreed that we wouldn't stop this time, even if Mother Theresa returned from the dead and asked for help. Enough was enough. Fortunately, the road was quiet and no one tried to interrupt our journey. I was lost in my own thoughts – and still wrapped in Byron's jacket - when we arrived at the gateway to the Adair Lands.

'We're here,' Speck said with obvious relief.

I looked up. A large sign was hammered into the ground. '*This land is off limits to all. By order of Aifric Moncrieffe, Steward of the Highlands.*'

'Stop the car,' I said softly.

I opened the door, got out, walked over to the sign then drew back my fist and punched it. Pain slammed through my hand. Taylor's door opened but I called out to him to stay inside. This was for me.

I kicked the sign, using as much force as I could muster. It creaked and the old wood splintered but it stayed upright, so I grabbed the edge of it and started yanking it, moving it back and forth until I could pull it completely free from the ground. I threw it down and slammed my heel onto it then I dusted off my palms and got back into the car.

'Feel better now?' Taylor enquired.

I shrugged and pulled out a splinter, sucking on the tiny wound. 'I guess. How far is it to the main house?'

'Only about a mile,' Brochan answered. I was glad that I'd sent him here before and that what was up ahead wasn't entirely unexpected. I gave him a satisfied nod.

'Are you sure you're up to this?' he asked.

I considered the question. 'What lies at the bottom of the sea and shivers?'

'I know that one!' Bob yelled. 'A nervous wreck! Ha! Got it! You can't pull the wool over my eyes! There's no kidding a kidder!'

'Well done. Now look at Brochan. Does he look scared?'

'Nope.'

'Because there's no sea near here. So there's no need to shiver and no need to be scared. Hell, yes, I'm up for this. Home sweet home.'

'It'll be fine, Tegs.'

'Yeah,' Lexie said. 'We're all here with you.'

My shoulders sagged. 'Am I that obvious?'

She grinned. 'Yeah, kind of.'

Speck put the car into gear and we drove on slowly. I stared out at the land. It didn't look like a place of evil. There wasn't anything growing but then I already knew that would be the case, given the salting that had taken place after my father's alleged murder spree. It was barren but sun was splintering down from the clouds and the resulting light was soft and welcoming. Off in the distance, however, there was a lone, desolate tree. For some reason that single sign of life struck at my heart more than anything else.

Gravel crunched under the wheels as the road curved to the left. That was when I caught my first sight of what had once been the Adair stronghold.

It was far larger than I'd envisaged, a grand building which must have housed the entire Clan very comfortably. Even from this distance, though, it was clear that it was a state of incredible disrepair. Moss and lichen crawled up one side of it; on the other side it looked as if some of the stonework was loose and crumbling. The heavy door at the front gaped open and there were scorch marks across it.

I breathed in and reached inside myself, detaching the childish part of me that still occasionally wished all this was a mistake and that at any moment my parents would jump out from behind a corner and yell 'surprise'. I wasn't a child any more. I had to deal with this.

Speck parked at the front. I got out, craning my neck and gulping in every detail. Lexie came up beside me and grabbed my arm. Taylor took the other one.

'It's not as bad as I expected,' I told them. 'I'm alright. It's just that...' I shook my head. 'I don't know. Something seems off.'

'It's because it's so quiet,' Speck said. As soon as the words left his mouth, I realised he was right. There was the faint sound of wind echoing through the building but there was nothing else – no voices, no wildlife, not even any birds. I swallowed and took a step forward, then another and another. Before long I was standing on the threshold. My father had passed through here, my mother too. Maybe he'd gone with tradition and carried her over the threshold in his arms. They'd both have been laughing. Loving. I shook my head. These ghosts were of my own making. There was nothing here.

Drawing in air and holding it in my lungs, I moved inside, passing through a large entrance area which was covered with rotting wood and piles of what seemed to be old fabric. I caught sight of some ancient bloodstains and hastily looked away. I didn't need to see those.

Beyond the entrance area was a large open courtyard. A chill descended across my body and I bit my lip hard, drawing blood. A dark patch covered the dirty flagstones and, feeling my chest tighten, I walked over to examine it. I bent down, trailing my fingers along its edge.

'What is it, Tegs?'

My hands shook. 'It was here,' I said in a whisper. 'I'm sure it was here.' It didn't make any sense but somehow I *knew*. Apparently some invisible tie linked me to the past in ways I couldn't begin to understand.

Bob buzzed over. 'What? What was here?'

'Shut up,' Taylor told him, not unkindly. 'Your parents?' he asked me.

I laid my palm flat on the spot, feeling the cool stone radiate against my skin, and nodded. 'They died here. Both of them.' I didn't have any tears, just a hard knot in my chest that seemed to expand. I stood up and walked away, breathing quickly.

Taylor followed me and touched my arm. 'We can still turn round and walk away.'

I pressed my lips together. 'No. Let's do this.'

Averting my gaze from the patch, I looked at the rest of the courtyard. It was in a very sorry state. Weeds poked up here and there, nature asserting itself over our arrogant attempt to claim the land. There were numerous other dark splodges, old cracks and piles of rubble.

Discounting the main entrance, there were three other doors leading into the dark maw of the interior. 'Eeny meeny miny mo,' I muttered, before raising my chin and striding towards the first one on the left. I'd barely stepped inside when there was a strange rush of air. Speck shrieked. A heartbeat later, dozens of bats came flying out, wheeling round the open courtyard then exploding into the air. I ducked to avoid them.

'My hair!' Speck screamed. 'They're in my hair! Help me!' He cowered, his hands covering his head. 'Bats. Hate bats. I'm okay, I'm okay, I'm okay.'

Brochan ambled over and yanked Speck to his feet. 'You're okay,' he said gruffly.

Speck slowly dropped his arms. He looked around. 'They've gone?'

I smiled. 'They've gone.'

He shuddered.

'You're such a wimp,' Lexie told him.

'Bats are dangerous,' he replied, his voice still high. 'They carry rabies, you know.'

'Yeah. And if one bites you, you'll turn into a vampire. Then, hard as it is to believe, you'll be even paler than you are now.'

He stuck his tongue out at her and she grinned back. 'Now I, on the other hand, would make a fabulous vampire queen. I'd dress in blood red and swan around Aberdeen making everyone my bitch.'

'Everyone's already your bitch,' he mumbled.

She patted his cheek. 'No. Only you.' She sauntered away from him.

Leaving them to it, I peered through the open doorway. 'Hello?' I called, not expecting an answer but hoping that any other wildlife would hear me and get out of the way. This time only silence answered me so, ignoring the faint hammering of my heart, I stepped inside.

I was in a long and surprisingly wide corridor. It was dark and dingy, with wood panelling and heavy green wallpaper which felt furry to the touch. Here and there I saw old paintings, most of which were covered in so much grime that it was impossible to see what they were of. The place smelled heavily of guano.

Taking the first door, I pushed it open. Something was blocking it from the other side so I used my shoulder against it. It opened enough to allow me entrance. Now at least there was some light; whatever this room was, it was well designed in that respect. Windows lined one side and, although the majority of the panes were smashed and brocade curtains fell across a large portion of them, this was no dingy cave.

A long-dead fireplace that was probably larger than my first bedroom stood at the end. Hanging over it was a grimy and dust-laden emblem. I squinted: it could only be the Adair coat of arms. How long was it since that symbol meant anything other than death and disaster? I traced over it with the tip of my finger, blowing off the dust, then pulled back. My father had stood here, my mother too. They'd gazed at the emblem just like I was doing, except their emotions were probably proud. I wished wholeheartedly that I could feel the same.

The wall along the right was filled with book-lined shelves. Abandoning the coat of arms, I stepped gingerly across an old armchair and pulled out one dust-laden tome, blowing at it so I could examine its title. *Midwifery for the Modern Household*. My jaw tightened and I quickly returned it to the shelf.

The other rooms were very similar. Signs of decay and creeping mould, not to mention the destruction that had happened so long ago, were visible everywhere. Thankfully there were no bodies. No doubt whoever had been here after my father's purported massacre had cleaned them up.

I took my time exploring, memorising the layout. With four storeys and rooms galore, it took a long time. I found it hard to imagine myself growing up here. Even in this sorry state, it seemed a world away from the childhood I'd actually experienced.

When I finally emerged into the courtyard, Brochan was busy pulling up weeds. Speck, Taylor and Lexie were in a huddle. There was no sign of Bob.

'This place is a real mess,' Lexie said quietly. 'Just cleaning it up will take years.'

'It's huge too,' Speck agreed. 'Can you imagine us rattling around here with only ourselves for company?'

The blue-haired pixie waggled her eyebrows at him. 'Well, there are a lot of bedrooms. We could christen each one. Just you and me, Speck. A different position in each...' He gave her a small shove.

'Will you two cut it out?' Taylor grumbled. 'Tegs needs this. We're going to be here for her no matter what.'

'Yeah? And what exactly are we going to eat?' Lexie demanded. 'We can't just wander down to Tesco. There's no Wi-Fi, no phone, no electricity. We're miles from anywhere that—' Speck hit her arm as he caught sight of me listening in. She faltered. 'Oh. Hi, Tegs.'

A smile tugged at my mouth. 'Don't stop on my account.'

She had the grace to look embarrassed, which wasn't my intention at all. 'What do you call a power failure?' I asked.

Her head drooped. 'Don't know.'

'A current event.'

'Ha ha,' she mumbled. 'I suppose I deserve some cheese.'

I was only just getting warmed up. 'What do you call cheese that is sad?'

She glanced at me through her fringe. 'Haven't I suffered enough?'

I smirked. 'Blue cheese.' I pulled out a scrunchie and tied back my hair. It was time to get down to business. 'Now let's get serious. You don't have to be here. I'm not going to hold it against you if you want to leave.'

'It's not that. It's just...' Her voice trailed away.

'Getting this place into shape is going to be more work than any of us realised.'

Lexie bit her lip and nodded. 'Yeah.'

'I have the money I won from the Games. I could use it to hire some Clan-less. Get enough of them and we can clean this up,' Taylor said.

'We'll run through that cash far too quickly. But it would be good if you could work on getting some power down here. Even that will cost a pretty penny. They must have had electricity at some point so it shouldn't be too hard. It's not as if my parents were around in the dark ages. Wi-Fi though...'

'I'll get on it,' Taylor said.

I smiled at him gratefully. 'As for cleaning up, I have an idea. We can get one of the other Clans to help us. I promised Chieftain MacBain I'd retrieve her uncle's body for her.'

Lexie paled. 'The one beyond the Veil?'

'Yep.' I bit my lip. 'You know I have to go back. I have to find out whether the Fomori are keeping people like us as slaves.' The evidence had certainly pointed that way when I'd breached the Veil before the Games to retrieve Dagda's Harp. It wasn't a thought I wanted to dwell on but I couldn't forget about it either.

'You told Aifric. He's the Steward, he should send a team to find out,' Brochan protested.

I met his eyes. 'We all know that's not going to happen. Besides,' I added, trying to make light of the situation, 'it shouldn't be too hard. Matthew MacBain's remains are in an abandoned house on the fringes of Glasgow. I can scout around on the outskirts and look for evidence of others while I'm there. It's unlikely I'll even see a Fomori demon.' Given the events of last night, my words sounded hollow even to myself but I soldiered on. 'And in return I'll ask Chieftain MacBain for some help with sorting this place out. She promised me a favour for retrieving her uncle's body and she's got minions coming out of her ears.'

'You know,' Brochan rumbled, 'you did promise the genie another wish.'

I winced. 'Yeah, but I don't want to waste it on something we could probably manage ourselves with a bit of elbow grease. If I wish for this place to be returned to its former glory, we'll probably end up in the middle of another massacre. You know how wishes work.'

'That didn't worry you when your old mate Chandra attacked us.'

'Saving lives is a whole heap of different. Speaking of which, that's what the rest of you need to do.' I paused. 'If you choose to stay, that is.'

'What?'

'Find a way to reactivate the magical border. We need to know that we'll be safe within these Lands, if nothing else.'

'We can do that,' Lexie said quietly.

'Thank you.'

'Is all this going to be worth it?'

I looked round at the high walls and tried to envisage what the place could be like. 'Yeah,' I said, wishing I could convince myself. 'I'm sure it will be.'

***

By unspoken agreement, we moved out of the mansion for the night. Until the place was cleaned up and sparkly new, it was too damned spooky to sleep in. Taylor settled into the back seat of the car and Lexie, petite as she was, curled up in the front like a cat. The rest of us pulled out some old blankets and bedded down on the ground. It wasn't the epitome of luxury and we had to snuggle together to keep out the cold but it was quite romantic being outside and staring up at the dark night sky. I bundled up Byron's jacket and used it as a pillow, telling myself that it was because it was bulky and comfortable; the fact that I could smell him every time I twitched had nothing to do with it.

Stars twinkled down at us. I stretched my arms behind my head, ignored the loud snores coming from either side of me and trailed my eyes across the dark expanse. Despite the long day, I didn't feel in the slightest bit tired; my mind was too busy, flitting from problem to problem. Aifric. The Perth Fomori demon. My ability to steal magic. The Adair Lands. What might be happening beyond the Veil. The truth about my parents. On and on and on and on.

A faint buzzing rose up in my ears and I slapped at myself absentmindedly. Damn midges, they were the bane of every Highlander. It was hard to believe they were alive at this time of year; surely it was still far too cold. Then I frowned and sat bolt upright.

I scanned the horizon. Everything was dark but I could make out the shape of the lonely tree off to the right and, if I craned my neck, the looming hulk of my ancestral home. There wasn't a sign of anything else but if Aifric was sending more would-be assassins after us, this was where they'd arrive. Until that magical border was up, we were vulnerable.

I was too jumpy. I had to be imagining things but the buzzing was getting louder. I pushed off the blankets and stood up, trying to avoid disturbing Speck and Brochan. I stepped over their sleeping bodies and tensed my muscles.

A strange, keening cry came from the distance. I whipped round, eyes narrowed to try to see what manner of beast this could be. Another demon?

'Yeeeeeeeee...'

I tilted my head. That sounded like...

'...haaaaaaaaaa!'

I did a double take. No, strike that: it was more like a triple take. From round the far corner of the Adair mansion came Bob's tiny figure – and he wasn't alone. Instead he was perched on a glowing orb of silvery light which was hurtling towards me at immense speed.

Convinced that it was going to smash into my face, I ducked. The sound, which I couldn't believe I'd mistaken for a cloud of midges, grew louder. It wasn't a buzz though, it was more of a happy hum.

'Uh Integrity!' Bob yelled. 'Are you playing hide and seek? Because that's not a very good hiding place. Just because you can't see me doesn't mean I can't see you!'

I lifted my head. Hovering directly above me was Bob, clad in full cowboy gear complete with tiny leather chaps, a battered Stetson and spurs. And he was sitting astride the Foinse – the source of all Scottish magic which no one had seen since I'd freed it from its mountain prison.

'Wow,' he said. 'You need to go see a good dentist. I can see all your teeth and, sister, they ain't looking good.'

'Bob,' I said faintly, closing my mouth so I no longer looked like a guppy. 'You're riding the Foinse.'

He beamed. 'I know! I think Foinse is a daft name though. I'm going to call it Draoidheachd instead. That's Gaelic for magic,' he said knowledgeably. 'I've been practising the spelling. You Scottish people don't half make life difficult for yourselves. Anyway, let me tell you, having this kind of power between my legs makes me realise why all those women love me so much.' He flung an arm up into the air. 'Giddy up!' The Foinse didn't move. Bob frowned. 'Come on. Let's go that way!'

Rather than flying in off in the direction Bob wanted, the Foinse gently lowered itself down and brushed – or, truth be told, nuzzled – my cheek. It felt oddly warm and pleasant.

'What is it doing here?'

'Uh Integrity,' Bob said patiently. 'I am a magnificent being with powers you can only dream of. I have told you this many times. How-

ever, the source of all Highland magic does not speak, even to a won-
drous personage such as myself.'

The magic in my veins buzzed. I scratched my head. 'Kirsty's Gift
still works,' I said quietly. 'In fact, it feels stronger than normal.'

'So?'

'The last time I encountered the Foinse...'

'Draoidheachd,' Bob prompted.

'Dree...' I rolled my eyes. 'I can't even begin to pronounce that.
The last time I encountered the Foinse, being close to it nullified all
Gifts. This is different.' I gave the orb a suspicious look, as if it were
some kind of imposter.

Bob's expression turned serious. 'You of all people should understand just how powerful freedom can be. Truth, liberty and justice for all.' He glanced sidelong at me. 'I helped write the American
pledge of allegiance, you know. I wanted it to be truth, liberty and
cake for all but they seemed to think justice was better. Ha! Goes to
show what *they* knew.' He snapped his fingers and produced a cup-
cake, then buried his face in its icing and made sounds of approval.

'It's free,' I said quietly.

'I already said that,' Bob told me through a mouthful of crumbs.

'It's happy.' I reached out a hand, thought better of it and with-
drew it. 'So the magic is stronger.'

'Freedom,' Bob agreed. 'George Michael was right when he sang
about it.'

'Careless,' I whispered back with a wink.

The Foinse pulled back and started to shake. Bob tossed the remnants of the cake away and hopped off, landing on my shoulder. Still
agog at its appearance, I continued to watch it. 'I wonder if it's been
here all the time since I freed it from the box in the mountains.'

'None of those Sidhe would have thought to look for it here,'
Bob agreed.

I felt a sudden gnawing worry. 'Some of them thought I'd stolen it to keep it for myself. Even Chandra thought that.'

'They didn't really believe it, though. They just don't like you. They wanted something they could hang that hatred on to,' Bob said with surprising insight.

I pointed at the Foinse. 'It's here, on my land. If anyone finds out, everyone will think I really did nick it.' My insides tightened. 'With Aifric's assassination attempts failing, he's going to do the next best thing.'

The genie nodded wisely. 'Go on a booze cruise in Ibiza.'

'No, you idiot. He's going to discredit me.' The Foinse hummed louder. 'And if anyone finds out the Foinse is here, he won't have to try very hard.'

'You're being paranoid.'

I shook my head. 'No. I'm not.' I bit my bottom lip. 'There's a reason it took four Clans to unlock the way to the Foinse in the first place: nobody wants anyone else to have more power than they have. The Foinse is the source of all magic; it provides more power than most people could ever dream of. The Sidhe designed a system to keep it away and keep the Clans honest. If it's here on these Lands, it will look like I'm trying to grab all that power for myself.'

Bob pondered this. 'Well,' he said slowly, 'there's probably only one thing you can do.'

'What?'

He shrugged. 'Grab all that power for yourself.' I rolled my eyes and he sighed patiently. 'Then no one will want to get angry about it because you'll zap them. It'll be like you have your own phaser. Instead of setting it to stun though, you'll use it to kill.'

'As much fun as it would be to have a phaser if we were on the Starship Enterprise, I can guarantee that right now you and me would be wearing red shirts.'

Bob winced. 'Red really isn't your colour.'

As if bored of all this talk, the Foinse shot up into the air, doing a dramatic loop-the-loop and then shooting off back the way it came. It disappeared round the far side of the mansion, its silver shimmer swallowed up by the inky night.

At my feet, Speck stirred. 'Wha...?'

'Shh,' I said. 'Go back to sleep.'

He murmured something, turned over and his snoring started up again.

'Out of sight, out of mind?' Bob asked.

I stared off in the direction the Foinse had flown. More shite to worry about. 'If only, Bob,' I sighed. 'If only. If this sort of thing keeps up, I'm going to be making apocalypse jokes like there's no tomorrow.'

Chapter Four

The next morning, as we breakfasted over a delectable mix of stale rolls, salt-and-vinegar crisps and Irn Bru and I tried to think of a way to gently break it to my friends that we were harbouring the root of all Scottish magic, I spotted Speck flexing his fingers and looking confused.

'What's up?'

He pressed his lips together. 'I dunno. I feel ... strange.'

Lexie leaned over and caressed his cheek then her fingers trailed teasingly down his body. He jerked away. 'You're right,' she said with a grin, 'you *do* feel strange.'

'Piss off.' He scowled. 'It has to be the effect of sleeping out in the open. It's playing havoc with my sinuses.'

Somehow I bet it was a lot more than that. 'Speck,' I said slowly, 'when was the last time you tried a spell?'

'Hogmanay,' Lexie said, answering for him. 'He tried to do those fireworks, remember?'

'That wasn't my fault!' Speck protested. 'The average person can only concentrate for a maximum of twenty minutes and the display you wanted involved a lot more than that!'

I grimaced. Oh yeah: instead of pretty explosions of light, we were treated to an out-of-control Catherine wheel that burned off Taylor's eyebrows. Speck was a warlock but, truthfully, that didn't mean much. Few warlocks could control their magic and they tended to err on the side of dismal failure. In fact, many of them were so clueless that they often died young as a result of magical experiments that went horribly wrong. When Speck was at his best, he could conjure up enough magic to bust open a padlock; at his worst, he burnt down entire buildings when it all went tits up. The Sidhe might be limited to whatever their own personal Gifts dictated but at least they had absolute control over what they could do.

I decided to throw caution to the wind. 'Try now,' I said.

He stared at me. 'You're inviting me to do a spell?'

Brochan put down his cup carefully, stood up and backed away. Even Taylor looked alarmed. 'Tegs, I don't think...'

'Shhh.' I twisted round. 'You see that window up there? On the right? It's about the only one that's not been broken.'

'I see it,' Speck said warily.

'Can you open it? With your magic, I mean?'

He paled slightly and swallowed. 'Sure.'

I glanced at the others. 'Maybe we should all move away. Just in case.'

'You realise he might blow up your ancestral home?' Lexie whispered loudly. Speck threw her a nasty look.

I shrugged, trying to appear nonchalant. 'It's one way to sort out the mess inside.'

Speck wiped his mouth and stood up. Lexie squeaked and ran behind Brochan. I stayed where I was. Speck closed his eyes and pointed upwards. 'Aperio!'

I held my breath as we all stared up at the window. Speck opened one eye and squinted. 'Huh,' he grunted. 'Nothing happened.'

'Thank the Highland heavens!' Lexie stepped out from her temporary cover just as there was a sudden creak.

I kept my eyes trained upwards. With what appeared to be a mighty effort, the window swooped open. Unfortunately it also swung round and smacked itself against the stone wall, immediately shattering into a thousand tiny shards which tinkled to the ground.

Speck blew air through pursed lips. 'Almost.'

Hm. I yanked my gaze away and looked at him. 'How do you feel?'

I received a suspicious glare in return. 'Why are you asking?'

'Humour me.'

He twitched. 'Fine.'

'Any different to normal?'

An awkward expression crossed his face. 'Yeah,' he admitted. 'I feel more ... tingly than usual.'

'What's this all about, Tegs?' Taylor asked.

I took a bite out of my roll. It really was almost inedible. I chewed vigorously for a moment then swallowed and, without further preamble, told them. 'The Foinse's here,' I said.

Speck flung his head around wildly. 'Where?'

'It's not *here* here,' I tried to explain. 'It's just ... here.'

'On these Lands?' Brochan rumbled, understanding my garbled attempt at an explanation.

I nodded. Taylor whistled. 'That's amazing! We can sell it off for more money than any of us have ever dreamed of! Forget the Sidhe, I've got a few contacts in China. I bet they'd be keen to part with a considerable amount of yuan. Or there was that dodgy American businessman I met at...'

'Taylor.'

He pasted on an innocent expression. 'What?'

'It's a free agent, not a slave to be bought and sold.'

'It's a thing. It's not a person.'

I looked up at him. 'Frankly, we don't really know what it is. Besides, it belongs in Scotland.'

'Yes, but just think of all that money!'

I tutted.

Brochan was still watching me. 'You want to know if the Foinse being here is affecting Speck's magic.'

'Yep.'

He didn't move a muscle. 'Is it affecting yours?'

'I don't have much magic left in me to experiment with other than truth-telling and its presence isn't blocking that.'

'Speck tried. You should too.' He pointed at the distant tree. 'You've still got that Carnegie woman's Gift, right?'

'A bit of it. I think.'

'Then,' Brochan said quietly, 'make the tree grow.'

'I think it's already dead.' I paused. 'What's wrong with the lonely fir tree? It's pining to be poplar.'

Nobody smiled. 'Go on, Tegs,' Lexie said. 'What's the worst that could happen?'

I wagged my finger at her. 'Don't say that. Don't ever say that.' I ran my hand through my hair, teasing out the ends. 'Fine.' I stood up and walked towards it.

It was further away than it looked and, when I finally reached it, it was in an even sorrier state than I'd realised. I touched the gnarled bark; it felt cold and dead. This was never going to work.

'Think positive,' Taylor said from right behind me.

I jumped. 'How can you do that?' I complained. 'How can you always know what I'm thinking?'

His eyes were warm. 'I know you.'

I muttered something uncomplimentary and stared back at the tree. I reached down inside myself, feeling the tug of Morna Carnegie's nature-based Gift. Then, not knowing what else to do, I flicked my fingers at the tree. 'Grow,' I commanded. Needless to say, nothing happened.

'I don't think that's how you do it,' Lexie said.

I grimaced at her. 'Any suggestions then?'

Speck cleared his throat. 'Look inside the tree itself. If there's a spark of life left in it, you can focus on that.'

I bit my tongue to avoid snapping that I didn't have X-ray vision. Instead, I nodded and tried it. I screwed up my face and hunched my shoulders, focusing all my energy on the tree. 'It's not working. Nothing's happening.' Morna's Gift swirled through me. 'Nope,' I declared. 'It can't be done.'

'Tegs,' Taylor said. 'Look.'

I opened my eyes properly. 'What?'

He pointed to the furthest branch. 'Right there.'

I sucked in a breath. He was right: at the very tip of the long, skeleton-like branch was a single little bud. 'Oh.'

'That's power over life and death,' Speck breathed.

I could taste something unpleasant on my tongue. 'No. It's not. It's just...' I cursed. 'I don't know what it is.'

Brochan nodded. 'She's right. It's hardly a scientific experiment. She might have been able to do that without the Foinse.'

'*She* is standing right here,' I muttered.

Taylor slapped me on the back. 'And *she* needs to stop over-thinking and get going. Tree or no tree, you've got a Chieftain to sweet talk.'

I watched the bud for a moment. It was a tiny splash of green against the almost black tree. Extraordinary. Goose pimples danced along my arms. 'Yeah,' I said finally. 'It's time to go.'

***

The one good thing was that the MacBain Clan Lands weren't far away. The MacBains were lucky not to be located as dangerously close to the Veil as the Adair Lands were. I managed to reach them before it was time for a mid-morning snack. I took Bob with me for company but, after his night flying around on the Foinse, he was inside his letter opener and refusing to come out. All the same, I kept him close to me, attached to my belt for quick and easy access if necessary.

I halted at the border, which was signified by a monstrous flag-pole displaying the MacBain colours. Unlike the Cruaich, which was open to all Sidhe, the magical border here wouldn't permit me entrance unless I already had permission. The different Clans were too wary of each other's machinations to let just anyone wander in.

I stepped up and pressed my palm against the border and received a mild electric shock in return. Hopefully that would be enough to alert any nearby guards. Then I hopped onto the bonnet of the car and waited. It didn't take long. A figure appeared from a distant guard house, marching down the road towards me. Troll. That figured; the Sidhe always used trolls as guards.

'What do you want?' he snarled. He was dressed in ridiculously formal livery. Chieftain MacBain seemed to think she was living in the eighteenth century. It didn't help that, of all things, he appeared to be carrying a spear.

I smirked. 'Nice togs. Are you going to a fancy-dress party?'

The spear shook. 'No.'

Okay then. I stared at him and he stared back at me. Eventually, growing bored, I sighed. 'I'm Integrity Adair. I'm here to see Chieftain MacBain.'

'I wasn't informed. There are no visitors due today.'

I held up my palms, trying to get him to relax. It didn't work. 'It was a loose invitation. She wants me to help her retrieve something.'

'If your name's not on the list, you don't get in. I don't care who you are.'

I smiled pleasantly. 'Why don't you phone up and check? I'm sure when she knows I'm here, she'll want to see me.'

The troll's lip curled. 'Rules are rules. Without her permission, you have to stay out.'

I jumped down from the car. He waggled the spear at me in what I assume he thought was a menacing fashion. 'Keep back!'

'You're right,' I said. 'Rules are rules. It's very important to stick to them.'

He sniffed. 'I'm glad someone agrees with me.'

I nodded wisely. 'Not everyone understands how important security is.'

He stood up a little bit straighter. 'Yes! They complain to me all the time. Demand to be let in when they're late. Forget to log out when they leave. It's my job to make sure this area is secure! It's me who'll get in trouble when something bad happens.'

I noted he said *when*, rather than *if*. I murmured soothingly, 'People just don't get it, do they? They'll learn when a marauding band of Fomori demon come marching through.'

He snapped his fingers. 'Exactly!' His gaze softened as if he was starting to think we were kindred spirits.

'You're a troll to be admired. Not all security specialists are as dedicated as you.'

He bowed. 'Thank you.'

'What's your name?'

'Sorley.'

I clapped my hands. 'Great name!' His cheeks went slightly pink. 'Anyway, Sorley,' I said, 'I'd be so grateful if you could tell Chieftain MacBain that I'm here to see her. Don't break any rules. It's very important that you stick to them - I wouldn't want your security compromised in any way, shape or form. Honestly, I wish my Clan had as good a set up as this.' I dropped my voice in a conspiratorial whisper. 'Don't tell anyone, but we don't even have a proper border in place.'

Sorley looked utterly horrified. 'What did you say your name was again?'

'Integrity Adair.'

'Adair? But...' He clicked his heels together. 'I see.'

See what? Before I could ask, hooves clattered up from behind. I turned in time to see a lordling I vaguely recognised pull up on a monster of a horse. Admittedly, all horses looked like monsters to me.

'Sorley,' he barked. 'What's the problem?'

'Her name's not on the list.'

The lordling, who had more muscles than I'd seen in a long time, leapt off the horse and landed on both feet. I glanced down and realised that his torso might be the size of an oak tree but his legs were more like puny saplings. I had to bite the inside of my cheek to stop myself laughing. Someone hadn't been doing their exercises properly.

He cast a long look over me. He seemed rather wary. 'Don't you know who this is?' he demanded of Sorley.

I winced.

'I do now,' Sorley replied shortly. 'She's Integrity Adair.'

'Chieftain Adair,' the lordling said.

'Makes no difference,' the troll mumbled. 'Her name's not down on my list.'

'And your dedication is admirable.' I broke in before the increasingly irate Sidhe let out a barrage of expletives. I smiled. 'I really would appreciate it if you could check with Chieftain MacBain and then...'

The lordling clicked his fingers. 'Let her in.'

The troll looked at him then back at me. 'I cannot.'

'You will do what I say or...'

I rolled my eyes. 'I will wait here until Chieftain MacBain agrees that I can enter. Alright?'

Sorley threw a smug look at the lordling, who seemed very put out. 'I will tell her you're here,' the lordling said huffily. Then he clambered back on his horse and cantered through.

Sorley checked his watch. He looked a bit upset.

'Don't worry about him,' I told him. 'He's just another Sidhe wanker.'

Sorley's eyes shot to mine and he coughed. 'It's not that,' he said stiffly. 'He said he'd be back at 10 a.m. It's 10.12. I'll have to log that and write a report. He should be more punctual.'

I pressed my lips together hard. 'Mmmm.'

I was expecting Chieftain MacBain to make me cool my heels for some time. It's what Aifric would have done - anything to make sure I knew my place. Surprisingly, less than fifteen minutes passed before she appeared followed by a large retinue. She strode down the long driveway at such a brisk pace that her hangers-on struggled to keep up. I guessed that, for all her mistrust of me, Chieftain MacBain believed in manners.

'Ma'am,' Sorley said as she reached us.

She looked at him coldly. 'How many times have I told you to address me as Chieftain?'

He shuffled his feet. 'Ma'am, Stuart MacBain was twelve minutes late. I really do think you should have a word with him about...' Her glare intensified. Sorley noted it but kept on going. '...about punctuality. What if we'd sent a search party out for him? It's simply not good enough. You put me in charge of security.'

'Enough of this nonsense.' She said it quietly but there was more menace in her tone than the Bull could have managed with an ear-splitting bellow.

'Chieftain Adair,' she said, turning to me.

I almost fell over. That was the last way I'd expected her to address me. I recovered quickly, however, and inclined my head as if I was completely used to being treated as a highborn Sidhe noble. 'Chieftain MacBain,' I returned.

'I was not convinced you were going to keep your word.'

I stood my ground. 'I told you I would do as you asked and retrieve your uncle's body.'

'So where is he?' She obviously wasn't in the mood to waste time.

'I don't have him yet. Our agreement was that I would receive a favour from you in return.'

'Yes, yes,' she said impatiently.

'Fifty people,' I said, plucking a number out of thin air. It sounded like a lot to me. 'I would like to borrow fifty of your people to help me clear the Adair Lands and make the mansion habitable. They need to be strong, capable workers.'

Something akin to relief crossed her face. I wondered what she thought I was going to ask for - the soul of her firstborn? 'How long for?' she asked with a sniff.

'Er ...' I tried to calculate how much work would be involved. 'Three weeks?'

'Done,' she said, snapping her fingers.

I blinked. Shite. I should have asked for a lot more. 'Thank you.'

'They will travel to you as soon as I receive the body.'

I nodded. That was good. It would give me time to impress upon the Foinse that it needed to stay hidden. Although how on earth I was going to tell it that was beyond me at the moment.

Chieftain MacBain stared at me. 'Is there anything else?'

Sorley shuffled his feet. No one looked at him. I shook my head and tried not to appear too grateful.

'Good. Then I have a demand of my own.'

Uh oh. 'Go on,' I said cautiously. I'd listen to her 'demand' at least.

'I do not know you, Chieftain Adair,' she said, 'but I do hear certain things. I appreciate that I may have been too hasty in believing you stole my necklace at the Games. However, there is little about that you is trustworthy.'

I didn't like where this was heading. 'I can assure you that I will not go back on my word,' I said, stiffening.

She didn't blink. The woman was like a damn lizard. 'And, strangely, I believe you won't. But you did present me with a gold ring which was found near my uncle's body.'

'It was *on* his body,' I said through gritted teeth. I was starting to understand. 'He must have been wearing it when he died.'

'Perhaps there was more than just his ring. When he left us, he was carrying a considerable amount of money.'

I couldn't imagine why; I didn't think the Fomori cared much for Sidhe cash. 'If I find any money, I will bring it back and give it to you.'

'Of this I am not so convinced. You are a thief, are you not?'

'I *was* a thief.' I tried to smile. 'Surely everyone should get the chance to turn over a new leaf?'

Her mouth turned down. 'Please do not use clichés in my presence. I simply abhor language of that ilk.'

I shouldn't have done it but I couldn't help myself. 'Well, this worm has turned. I've moved onto bigger and better things, and I think even my harshest critic would say that I've come on in leaps and bounds.'

The expression on Chieftain MacBain's face suggested that she was screaming inside. 'You are not amusing in the slightest.' The Gift I had stolen from Kirsty Kincaid informed that she was telling the absolute truth. Before I could throw another quip at her, she continued. 'I would like someone to accompany you. Someone from another Clan that is not your own. Someone Sidhe.'

My heart sank as I thought of the rude lordling who'd stopped earlier and I tightened my jaw. 'Someone from Clan MacBain? I think it's my turn to show my mistrust, Chieftain MacBain. How do I know you won't order them to stab me in the back once I've led them to the bones?'

She drew back with an incredulous shiver. 'How dare you? A MacBain would never act in such a manner!'

Okay. Enough was enough. 'So you won't trust me,' I said icily, 'but I should trust every single one of you?'

Two spots of colour appeared high on her cheeks. Apparently Ma MacBain had suddenly realised how rude she'd been. She'd want to save face and not back down entirely, but I'd already learnt enough about the premium she placed on manners to wonder what she'd do next.

'Then we compromise,' she said finally. 'You may choose someone from the main Clans. The important ones.'

I raised my eyebrows. The important ones? 'You mean Darroch, Kincaid or Moncrieffe,' I said.

'They can all be trusted.'

I almost laughed aloud. This lady was more nuts than I'd realised. 'Look, I...' I paused. Hang on a minute. 'Okay,' I said. 'I'll accept those terms. I nominate Byron Moncrieffe.'

Her eyes narrowed suspiciously. 'Why him?'

Because Aifric would hold off on the assassination attempts if his son was hanging around. Of course that was the only reason. Definitely. Absolutely. One hundred smackeroony percent. 'I know him. He's a hero.' My eyes gleamed. 'And as the Steward's son, he's beyond reproach.'

I watched MacBain's reaction carefully but all she did was agree with me. 'True.' She nodded. 'I'll send word immediately.'

'Great. I'll depart for the Veil as soon as he arrives.'

'Excellent.' She turned to go.

'Aren't you going to invite me in for a cup of tea?' I called after her, checking how far I could test her civility.

She didn't respond but Sorley coughed loudly. 'Ma'am.'

'Chieftain!' she snapped again, over her shoulder.

'Please...'

She sighed dramatically and turned round. 'What?'

He looked at me. 'She needs security.'

I was slightly taken aback. 'Er, yeah.' A lot of security probably but I wasn't going to admit that in front of his boss.

He faced her. 'I would like to tender my resignation and go with Ms Adair. I don't feel that my skills are appreciated here and you have other trolls on your staff to take care of your needs.'

Chieftain MacBain raised her eyebrows while I took an involuntary step back and swallowed. Say what?

Sorley gave me a hasty glance. 'If you'll have me, of course.'

'Sure, I'll have you.' What else was I going to say?

She addressed me. 'He counts as one. You only get another forty-nine.'

Was she displeased or ecstatic at this development? I couldn't tell. I shrugged in resignation. 'Okay.'

She nodded again and strode off. I glanced at Sorley. 'That was, uh, a bold move,' I said finally. 'I thought once you swore fealty, you were with a Clan for life.'

'Trolls don't swear fealty - but neither do we all wish to be completely Clan-less. A group of us struck a bargain with the Sidhe decades ago.' His expression made it clear that he thought the Clans had got the best deal.

Ah. That explained his refusal to call her Chieftain. I scratched my neck. 'I don't have much money at the moment to pay you.'

'That is not a problem. I can wait.'

For someone who was such a jobsworth, he was remarkably laid back about remuneration. Taylor would love him. I sighed and pointed at the car. 'Come on then.'

He smiled suddenly, a wide grin that spread from ear to ear. Then he stepped across the border and got in without once looking back. I had the feeling I was going to regret this – but at least Sorley was happy.

Chapter Five

Regardless of how gruff Sorley was while on duty, now he was in the car he proved to be quite the garrulous troll. He rambled on for almost the entire journey, barely pausing to take breath. I heard about the merits of magic versus machinery in keeping out larger species of wildlife; a treatise on punctuality; details about some failed key-card system which apparently the MacBain Clan had instituted in a bid to rid themselves of the trolls. At one point Bob roused himself, appearing in his usual flash of light. Sorley didn't falter; he just kept on talking. It took Bob all of twenty seconds to decide that he was going back to sleep.

It hadn't occurred to me that I'd be glad to see the Adair Lands but when we approached their border, I exhaled with relief. Sorley was well-meaning but even I had limits.

'So you see, if you take a combination of an interlocking system and add it to a linear magic fold, then you'll— Stop the car!'

'Eh?'

'I said, stop the car!'

I slammed on the brakes. 'What is it?' I hadn't even finished the question when he leapt out and ran over to where I'd flung down Aifric's old sign.

There was another blinding flash of light. 'Charming fellow. Is it safe to come out yet?'

'He takes security very seriously, Bob.'

'He needs to get out more.'

Rather than involve myself in a pointless argument, I got out of the car too and joined Sorley. He had picked up the old sign and was gazing at it with disgust.

'It's defunct,' I told him. 'I've been given back the Lands.'

He wrinkled his nose and glared. 'Desecration,' he hissed.

Er... 'Well,' I said, folding my arms, 'not really. The Land was confiscated after Gale Adair - after my father supposedly killed the entire Clan. But, like I said, it's been given back to me. The sign no longer holds.' I tried not to sound antagonistic; I didn't succeed.

'That's not what I was talking about,' Sorley snapped. He twisted his squat body and flung the splintered wood away. It hurtled some considerable distance through the air.

I blinked. 'Have you ever considered taking up the javelin?' I enquired.

Sorley ignored me. He knelt down and began scrabbling at the dirt with his long, yellowing fingernails.

'Look,' said Speck, appearing over a small hill with Brochan who was carrying several large, heavy books. 'The line is here.'

'I am not disagreeing,' Brochan said. 'But the magic is not.'

'How would you know? You're just a merman.'

'*Just* a merman?'

Speck caught sight of me and took advantage of my presence to change the subject. 'Integrity! Hey!'

I waved up at them. 'Wotcha doing?'

'Trying to sort out the border,' Speck called back. He jogged down, leaving Brochan to glare after him as he shifted the pile of books in his arms and lumbered down in Speck's wake.

'Any luck?'

Speck clicked his tongue. 'Nada. In theory, it shouldn't be that hard. We simply find the right spot and turn it on and, hey presto. Except we can't find the spot and we don't know how to turn it on. I'm also starting to feel a bit queasy. It's all these open spaces. Without the comfort of a city, I just don't feel right.' He pushed his glasses up his nose and looked at me anxiously.

'I knew you were claustrophobic,' I said, 'but I didn't know you were agoraphobic as well. Isn't that some kind of weird oxymoron?'

He shrugged. 'I'm a walking mess of contradictions. I can't help it.' He glanced down at Sorley. 'Did you know that there's a troll wearing a peculiar outfit digging into the ground beside your feet?' he asked in exactly the same tone of voice.

'This is Sorley.'

'Why is he here?'

Sorley straightened up. 'To sort out your ridiculous mess of a security system, you dunderhead.' He jerked his head at me. 'Do these two have clearance?'

Brochan finally reached us. He stared at Sorley as if he'd never seen a troll before. 'Clearance?'

I took Sorley by the arm and pulled him to one side. 'We only arrived yesterday. We've not had time to put a proper system in place. Why don't I leave all those details to you?'

An odd light appeared in his eyes. His mouth twitched and he began scratching furiously at a spot on his arm. 'To me?'

'Yeah,' I shrugged. 'You're the security expert.' I decided against mentioning that my life as a thief meant that I knew quite a bit about security myself. I just didn't have a clue about magical borders.

'Er, Tegs?' Speck said from behind. 'Can I have a word?'

'What is it?'

He glanced at Sorley but the troll wasn't listening. He still seemed awestruck by the fact that I'd given him complete control. He stared around him as if he couldn't quite believe what was happening.

'Security expert?' Speck asked.

I nodded. 'Yep. He was working for Chieftain MacBain but he chose to leave and join us instead.' I pasted on a big grin, hoping to encourage Speck to welcome the troll rather than just continue giving him the nasties with his eyes.

'Tegs,' he said plaintively, 'we're thieves.'

'We *were* thieves,' I corrected. 'Anyway, so what?'

'Security expert? Thieves? Oil and water come to mind, don't you think?'

'I worked with a troll once,' Brochan broke in. 'Good guy.'

Sorley shook himself back to the present. 'You are referring to the one who shall not be spoken of.'

I stared. 'Voldemort?'

Sorley gave me a funny look. 'No.' He glanced round as if he was afraid he would be overheard then dropped his voice. 'Harris.'

'Harris?' Speck asked loudly.

'That was his name,' said Brochan, remembering.

'Sssshh! We don't talk of him. He brought us great disrepute. He took everything we taught him and used it against us.'

Brochan pursed his lips and nodded. 'He was a very good thief.'

'Scum.'

Brochan pulled himself up. 'Now just hang on a minute—'

'Whoa! Let's all calm down!' I stepped between them. 'Let's agree to disagree, shall we?'

'Integrity,' Brochan snarled, 'the damn genie is bad enough. You are dreaming if you think I'm going to get on with this ... this...'

'I had a dream last night!' I said desperately. 'I dreamt I wrote *The Lord of The Rings*! I was Tolkein in my sleep.'

It wasn't my best effort. Brochan's lip curled but a strange sound escaped Sorley and we all turned to look at him. He clamped one massive hairy hand over his mouth, his eyes were filled with mirth and his shoulders shook. He was definitely giggling – and in a surprisingly girlish manner. We exchanged looks.

'I tell you what, why don't we leave you here to inspect the border, Sorley?' I said. 'I'll check in with our other two companions. Then you can, um, report to me later.'

Sorley nodded. Tears were starting to pour from his eyes. It should have been gratifying that he found my joke funny but I was slightly concerned by his dramatic reaction. 'If a Moncrieffe shows up, bring them up to the mansion,' I instructed. Speck looked alarmed. I shook my head. 'Strike that. If Byron Moncrieffe shows up, bring him up to the mansion. Try to keep everyone else out.'

Swallowing hard in a bid to compose himself, Sorley nodded to show he understood.

'I didn't think he had a sense of humour,' I whispered to Speck and Brochan as we got into the car and drove up to the mansion.

Brochan threw me a look. 'He obviously doesn't,' he sniffed.

I checked the mirror. Sorley was still chuckling to himself. I grinned. 'I think this is going to work out great.'

***

We sat down together outside the main door to touch base. I explained what had happened with MacBain and Lexie shook her head in dismay. 'You should have asked for Jamie. That would have had your Byron sprinting here in his place.'

Speck looked confused as I rolled my eyes. I had enough going on in my life as it was; I didn't need to play silly games.

Brochan reiterated what they'd discovered about reinstating the magical border, which was nothing useful. Taylor had also not had much luck. He'd driven more than fifty miles to get a phone signal only to be told that the electricity company might be able to get to us by April. If they could squeeze us in.

I whistled in dismay. 'That's ridiculous. What about running water?'

He shook his head. 'Sorry. They said they might get that to us by the summer.'

'It's those bloody Clans. Aifric must have done something. He'll be behind the scenes pulling the strings.'

'You don't know that for sure.'

'It's an educated guess,' I said sourly. My earlier good mood was quickly disappearing.

'I found a well,' Lexie said, trying to be helpful. 'But the water is pretty rank. There was something floating in it. Old clothing maybe. Perhaps someone died in there when...' Her voice trailed away.

I grimaced. 'Perhaps.'

'There is one thing I don't understand,' Taylor said. 'You're pretty certain that it wasn't your father who killed everyone.'

'The vision I had in the Cruaich grove suggested that,' I agreed.

'Well, if the magical border only disappeared when the land was confiscated and it was up and running when the massacre took place, how did the actual killers get in? There must have been a lot of them to take care of everyone here.'

My mouth turned down. 'It must have been someone my father trusted. Someone who'd already been invited in.'

'You mean someone like Aifric Moncrieffe.'

'Plenty of people don't like me,' I pointed out. 'But he's the only one who's tried to kill me.'

'The Bull tried to kill you.'

I nibbled my lip. I'd almost forgotten about that. 'True.'

'And there might be others that we don't know of.'

I gazed into the distance. 'I'm still convinced that Aifric is behind all this. I don't have proof, I don't even have circumstantial evidence, I just...' I sighed. 'I just think it was him.'

'Well,' Taylor said cheerily, 'it's a good thing you're not in love with his son then, right?'

I scowled. 'I'm not in love with him. I...'

'Want to get into his kilt? Wear his clothes? You need to get over it, Tegs. I understand you can't help how you feel but it could end up getting you killed.'

My cheeks reddened. I sat on my hands to stop them plucking at Byron's jacket, which I was still wearing. Keen to change the subject, I focused on Lexie. 'Speaking of the grove, did you find the Adair one?'

Her eyes danced. 'I thought we were speaking of Byron Moncrieffe.'

I rolled my eyes at her. 'Lex...'

She flashed me a grin before sobering up. 'There's nothing that I could see. Just that one tree that we've already been to.'

We turned to look at it. Silhouetted black against the sky, it was like some post-apocalyptic vision, tiny bud on one branch or not. I shivered.

'So,' Brochan said, 'the Adair sacred grove is all but dust. The mansion is overgrown with weeds and bats and goodness knows what else. We're not going to get any power or running water for months. We can't work out how to kick start the border that'll keep us safe – and even if we did, we're not sure whether it *will* keep us safe.' I opened my mouth to speak but he held up a palm. 'Your theory about what happened with your father and the Clan is speculation, Tegs. Sorry. And,' he flicked a look up at the grey clouds overhead, 'it's about to rain.'

'I hate rain,' Speck said.

'You hate everything.'

My shoulders sank. Shite. I hated it when things went wrong like this. I liked sunshine and early mornings and cheesy jokes and optimistic science fiction that made no sense. I didn't like glumness.

I got to my feet and dusted off my jeans. 'There is one thing we can solve.'

'What?'

I grabbed Bob's scimitar from my belt and slid it out of the sheath. After I gave the blade a quick rub, he appeared in a flash of light. 'Where's the troll?'

'Not here.'

He looked round suspiciously. Brochan sniffed then cursed.

'You should see a doctor,' Bob informed him. 'You always have a cold.'

Brochan glared. 'I'm allergic to you.'

'Well,' Bob said, 'I'm allergic to you. You bring me out in hives.' He showed us his forearm. 'Look!'

'There's nothing there.'

'That's because your eyesight isn't good enough.' He flew into Brochan's face and thrust his arm out. 'Look harder.'

Brochan sneezed with such violence that Bob was sent spinning backwards in the air. Spluttering and wiping his face in disgust, he shook his fist angrily. 'You did that deliberately!'

'I can't sneeze on cue.'

'You disgusting merman!'

This wasn't the usual good-natured banter; there was a definite edge to it. I wasn't sure that what I was about to do would improve the mood but at least it would provide us with a different focus. And it would answer one very salient question.

'Bob,' I said loudly. 'I'm ready to make that second wish.'

Everyone turned, slack-jawed. 'Tegs, I'm not sure that's a good idea.' Taylor looked troubled. 'You were right before. You shouldn't go wishing for things we can get on our own. We could try breaking into the nearest power station to see what we can do about electricity. Wish for it and we'll end up blasted by lightning.'

'He's right,' Lexie agreed reluctantly. 'Much as I'd like to take the easy way out, you can't trust the genie. Sorry, Bob. No offence meant.'

'Huh!' he blustered. 'Lots of offence taken! Ask for that wish, Uh Integrity!' He puffed out his chest. 'I am here and I am ready. Wish, wish, wish.' From nowhere he produced a banner with the word WISH emblazoned across it. As he waved it in the air, it lit up in neon pink. 'I made it pink just for you,' he added.

'The MacBain woman is sending people,' Speck said. 'You really don't need to do this.'

'I promised Bob that I would and I'm not going back on my word. And anyway, this isn't something that can be done by hand.'

'I don't suppose anyone knows if Tegs' father built a bunker?' Speck asked, looking round.

'If he did,' I said simply, 'we're about to find out.' I drew in a breath and looked at Bob. 'I wish to know what happened here on May 5th, 1989. More specifically, what happened when the Adair Clan was massacred?'

Lexie and Speck drew in breath simultaneously. Brochan rubbed his cheek vigorously and Taylor went completely still.

For once Bob was completely serious. 'Integrity Adair,' he said, 'your wish is my command.'

There was a crack like thunder and the atmosphere suddenly felt heavy and oppressive. Lexie swung her head from side to side, alarmed. I remained perfectly still.

Speck watched me. 'Do you know? Did the knowledge, like, just pop into your head?'

'She doesn't know yet,' Brochan said.

'How can you tell?'

'I just can.'

I waved my hand at them. 'Back up.'

Speck frowned. 'Huh?'

'Back up,' I hissed. I moved several feet away just as the hairs on the back of my neck started to rise and several ghostly forms appeared from the main entrance. They were wispy and transparent but their identities were clear, even with more than twenty-five years separating us.

'Is that a fucking ghost?' Lexie whispered.

Bob shook his head. 'It's what she asked for. It's a memory.'

Aifric Moncrieffe, his face unlined and his step jauntier than I'd ever seen it, smiled into the distance. The other men beside him wore faded Moncrieffe colours. I didn't recognise any of them but their expressions were grim and set. I realised my legs were shaking but I pulled back my shoulders and walked up to Aifric, passing a hand across his face. He didn't blink. I reached forward to touch him.

'Don't,' Bob called out.

I drew back. 'What will happen if I do?'

'I don't know exactly but this is a wish. And you know there are consequences to wishing.'

It was the first time Bob had ever directly admitted that. Wisely, I did as he suggested and stepped to the side once more.

A couple walked up from behind the others. I held my breath. I had seen these two before in the grove at the Cruaich when I'd received my true name. My parents. I drank in the sight of them hungrily. My mother was petite and pretty, with an elfin delicateness about her features. The same couldn't be said for her belly, however. It was massive, protruding like a taut drum. One hand rested protectively over it as she smiled warmly at Aifric. By her side my father was tall and muscular; the brilliant shock of white hair which I'd inherited was visible even through this opaque vision. There was a faint slump to his shoulders and a pained look on his face although he was smiling through it. My stomach tightened. Was this it? Was this a hint of the madness that everyone said had caused the destruction of my Clan? The vision I'd seen in the grove suggested otherwise and that was what I'd believed. There was always a tiny kernel of doubt, though. Always.

My father strode forward, embracing Aifric in a tight hug. They clapped each other on the back and their mouths moved as they spoke.

'What are they saying?' I burst out desperately. 'Why can't I hear them?'

'I have no control over this, Uh Integrity,' Bob said. 'This is the wish. I can only promise that it will fulfil what you asked for.'

I balled up my fists and glared at the camaraderie between the two ghostly men. It took everything I had to keep my greedy eyes away from my parents and focus on Aifric. I had to see what he did. He was here. Despite the fatigued, sickly look on my father's face, this had to be the moment when Aifric gave the order for slaughter. To believe otherwise might kill me.

I watched every twitch and every movement but Aifric didn't do a damn thing. He kissed my mother's hand and gestured at her stomach – at me – then simply left.

A choked sob escaped me. Taylor came up and put an arm round my shoulders, squeezing me tightly. 'It has to be him, Taylor,' I whispered. 'It has to be Aifric.' Aifric was already disappearing down the road, however, vanishing out of sight as it curved away.

I shook my head. My mother turned to Gale, my father, and touched his cheek, murmuring something. He put his arm round her waist, his tenderness making me catch my breath once more. She brushed her hand against her belly again and grinned at him in a way I recognised; there was an impishness that I had seen in myself in the mirror. My father returned her smile with an expression of fear, hope and joy.

He passed a hand across his forehead and nodded, then turned back inside. I followed immediately, barely aware of my friends behind me.

Gale left my mother in the courtyard and disappeared through a doorway to the left, trudging heavily up the stairs to where the bedrooms were located. As I watched, he walked into one, fell heavily onto a bed, turned onto his stomach and closed his eyes.

I screamed in frustration. 'What are you doing? You have to realise what's about to happen!' He didn't stir. Of course he didn't stir. 'It's the middle of the fucking day. Why is he sleeping?'

'He doesn't look well, Tegs,' Speck murmured. 'Maybe he was sick.'

Brochan sighed. 'He's not sick. He's hungover.'

I exhaled loudly. It made sense. His old buddy had spent the night and they'd probably been carousing until late. I could understand the action but I couldn't condone it. Not knowing what I did.

'He slept. He fucking slept while everyone was being murdered.' Something stabbed at my heart and I spun round, pushing past the others to sprint back downstairs.

The courtyard was empty. Where had my mother gone? I ran left into the vast room with the gigantic fireplace, searching desperately. A group of Sidhe was clustered there, joking and laughing, while a servant tidied up a cluttered mess of whiskey bottles and glasses. My mother wasn't there. I ran to the next room, then the next. By the time I reached what was once the dining hall, I was getting desperate. 'Where is she, Bob? Where did she go?'

The genie fluttered up and placed one tiny palm on my cheek in a gesture he'd never made before. 'Be patient. The wish will show you what you need.'

My mouth twisted in frustration. The wish wasn't showing me a fucking thing. My father was comatose upstairs, my mother had vanished, and here were dozens of Adair Sidhe who I didn't know filing in for their lunch break. This wasn't what I needed to see.

'Cheese freaking sandwiches?' I yelled. 'Who the hell cares?' I watched a group of laughing women toss back cups of water poured from large flagons and gritted my teeth. 'This is ridiculous!'

'Look.' Brochan said it quietly but there was an urgency in his voice that made my tantrum subside immediately.

'What?'

'The far end of the table. The woman.'

I followed his gaze. One of the older women, dressed in servant's clothes, was turning purple and choking. Without thinking, I darted forward. Taylor grabbed my arm, pulled me back and reminded me that what we were watching had already happened. There was nothing I could do to change things.

Bit by bit, her companions started to notice. A burly warlock hauled her out of her seat and thumped her on the back. When that didn't work, he wrapped his arms round her body to start what could only be the Heimlich manoeuvre. Even if he could have pulled if off, it wouldn't have worked. As it was, he began having breathing difficulties. He released the woman, whose eyes had already rolled back into her head, and doubled over in agony.

Lexie pointed at the group of laughing women. They weren't having fun now. Several of them had been sick, a pool of their vomit spreading across the long wooden table. At least one was already dead.

Watching this terrible scene unfold in total silence made its horror even more wrenching. These were my people - and they were all dying.

'It was poison,' I said, turning away, unable to look any longer. 'It wasn't my father who killed them. It was poison.'

Taylor nodded grimly. 'And we already know Aifric has form for that method of disposal.'

I tried to think clearly though it wasn't easy. 'It's still circumstantial. There's no actual proof that he did this.'

'Who else could have?'

I didn't have an answer. I wanted to feel relieved that it wasn't my father who'd committed such a heinous act but, until I knew for sure who was culpable, I couldn't relax.

My mother appeared in the doorway, right in front of my eyes. She was sweating and pale but there was a smile on her face. She was clutching her belly and obviously looking for help. Labour, I thought dully; she was in labour.

It was the expression on her face that made me start crying my own huge, silent tears. Her eyes darted round the dining hall, her smile slowly disappearing as first confusion, then horror followed quickly by terror filled her face. She ran forward, a few stumbling steps made all the more awkward by her size and condition. Then she seemed to think better of it; perhaps she realised there was nothing she could do. Maybe she wanted to get my father. To fetch help.

She spun round and ran out. We went after her. She fell into the courtyard, threw back her head and screamed, her mouth wide open.

A shadow flitted in the corner of my eye. Lexie cried out and so did I. But we couldn't warn Coira Adair. She couldn't see us. She saw the archer though, and turned to him just as he loosed the shot. His eyes were dull and pained as he melted away again but right now, it wasn't him I cared about.

Whoever he was, his aim was true. The arrow struck my mother in the chest, embedding itself deep in her body. Without realising it, I clutched at the same spot on my chest. There was another flutter of movement as my father appeared, running towards her and scooping her into his arms. The anguish on his face filled the entire courtyard. He yanked open her simple peasant's blouse, his fingers touching the arrow, pulling away and then touching it once more.

'He can't decide what to do,' Speck said softly. 'Should he pull it out or leave it in?'

I didn't answer. I wasn't capable of speech.

My mother wasn't dead. She grabbed at my father, her lips moving. He shook his head and she tried again. He was crying but her eyes were clear as she told him what she wanted. She was a warrior right up till the end when her body jerked violently just once before going still.

I collapsed to my knees; I could barely see what was happening through my tears and I wiped furiously at my face. My father seemed frozen for a long moment, staring down at her as if willing her to wake up. Then he sprang up and ran to a bag hanging from a nail. He drew out a knife with a long sharp blade and went back to her.

I knew what he was going to do and the last thing I wanted was to see it but I had to. I owed both of them that much; they deserved that I bear witness to this terrible event. It was, after all, what I'd wished for.

Brochan knelt down beside me and took my left hand; Lexie did the same to my right. I felt both Taylor and Speck at my back and Bob on my shoulder. They were there with me. I wasn't alone.

My father cut through my mother's flesh, slicing through it as his own body shuddered in pain. There was blood everywhere. It seemed to take an age and I could sense him withdrawing into himself. There was just him and his gory task; nothing else remained. When he pulled out the tiny red baby, her face contorted and her umbilical cord still linking her to her mother, I felt as if I was being stabbed in the heart over and over again.

'That's you,' Taylor said. 'That's actually you.'

Coldness descended across my shoulder blades. 'And that's Aifric Moncrieffe.'

The Steward strode through from the main entrance, his hands gripping a sword. My father didn't even notice. Aifric sliced the sword through the air, once, twice, and then he smirked. A heartbeat later he plunged it into his old friend's back.

My father spasmed and crumpled, falling as my baby self fell with him. Moncrieffe hands took me from him as Aifric stood over his failing body and grinned from ear to ear.

I stopped looking at my father's killer; instead I focused on my father. 'I'm with you,' I mouthed.

He blinked slowly. He knew he was dying, it was there in his eyes and in the way his body relaxed. He didn't fight death; it was almost as if he welcomed it. A world without Coira, his wife and my mother, wasn't worth lingering in. I saw the light leave his face and his jaw slacken.

And then the ghostly vision disappeared and I was looking at the old dark patch and the few forlorn weeds still pushing up from the ground.

It took me a long time to move. At some point I was aware that my tears were drying and my heart was still beating. I got to my feet and slowly walked over to stand on the spot where my parents had breathed their last.

'That's how he did it,' Speck said. 'Aifric. That's how he beat the magical border. He pretended to leave but didn't. Probably killed whoever was guarding it and simply waited for the poison to do its job. Then he came back to mop up.'

'It's a miracle he didn't kill Tegs too.'

'She was a baby. An innocent baby.'

'Everyone else in Clan Adair was innocent too,' I said aloud. My voice rang out more steadily than I thought it would.

Lexie murmured something as I walked away. I loved my friends like family but right now I needed to be alone.

'What about the consequences of the wish?' I heard Speck ask.

'You're looking at them,' Bob said. 'The consequences of fulfilling the wish are already consequences enough.'

I kept walking.

Chapter Six

I sat under the tree for the rest of the day, watching both the real shadows and the imaginary ones. The others were sensible enough to leave me in peace. I'd like to say my thoughts were coherent but there was little other than pain. For now I didn't plan or scheme or plot, I just let myself feel. I was entitled to that much.

The sun had fallen when Taylor eventually approached. His hands were in his pockets and he ambled slowly, giving me plenty of advance warning. When he reached me, I looked up. 'You drew the short straw then?'

He gave a crooked smile. 'I wanted to come.' He held out his arms, ready to envelop me in a hug. There was no denying the anxious light in his eyes.

I shook my head and stood up. Enough wallowing; I was supposed to be a warrior, after all. 'No. I'm good now.' There was just the slightest tremor in my voice.

'Integrity...'

'I'm okay, Taylor.'

He searched my face, trying to ascertain the truth. Then he nodded and dropped his arms. 'Good. The, um, troll. Surly?'

'Sorley.'

'Yeah, him. He's causing some kind of ruckus. He's not very ... happy.'

'You mean he really is surly?'

Taylor's smile grew, albeit tentatively. 'Yeah. I'm not sure he's going to fit in. He's very stressed. About everything. What if he decides to go back to Chieftain MacBain and tells her about how pathetic our security is?'

'Well,' I said slowly, 'we'll just have to cross that bridge when we come to it.'

Taylor looked at me. I looked back innocently.

'You know,' he said, 'that joke doesn't actually work. He's not a bridge troll.'

I smiled. 'You still got it though. Come on. I'd better go see what he wants.'

When we reached the courtyard, I dared myself to look at the dark patch for a moment. Pain lanced through me. I could feel Lexie, Speck and Brochan watching me anxiously. None of them said a word. Get a grip, Tegs.

'I'm alright, guys,' I said, when the silence became too uncomfortable.

Lexie bobbed her head. 'Course you are.'

'We'd expect nothing else,' Speck agreed. They kept on sending me sneaky looks though, when they thought I wasn't looking.

Brochan cleared his throat. 'I thought...' He coughed again when Speck nudged him. '*We* thought that this would be a good time to swear fealty to you.' He got down heavily on one knee and the others did the same.

Alarmed, I stalked over. 'Get up!'

'We need to do this, Tegs.'

Nope. Not happening. I shook my head vehemently. 'No, you don't. Anyway, I'm not accepting your oaths so don't even bother.'

Lexie lifted narrowed eyes. 'You'll take the crazy MacQuarries but not us?'

I sighed and put my hands on my hips. 'You're my family.'

'We agree,' Taylor interjected. 'That's why we want to make it official.'

'I appreciate it, I really do. But I'm still not accepting.'

'Tegs...'

I held up my hand. Fealty would change everything between us. I was not going to set myself apart from the only people who mattered simply because of my blood. I paused. Hang on a minute. 'There's another way.' I cast around, looking for something I could use. Eventually my gaze fell on the Swiss army knife which hung loosely from Taylor's belt. I pointed at it. Confused, he unhooked it and silently handed it over.

Concentrating, I slid out a small blade and nicked my forefinger. A bead of blood appeared on my skin. I raised my eyebrows at Taylor and he understood instantly and grinned. He took the knife from me and did the same to his own thumb then we pressed them together.

'Now your blood runs in my veins,' I said softly. 'And vice-versa. We're officially family.'

Lexie arched an eyebrow. 'Does that mean he has to change his name? That we can't call him Taylor any more because he's Adair?'

Speck waved an irritated hand at her. 'Hush.' He stepped forward and we completed the ritual. He had to look away and bite his lip to avoid the sight of his own blood but he still did it. I squeezed his shoulder hard.

Brochan moved up. 'This is an honour,' the merman rumbled, bowing his head.

'It is for me too,' I told him honestly. Even if it made me feel like I was six years old and playing around with a few mates.

When we were done, I glanced at Lexie. 'You don't have to do this. No one will hold it against you.'

'I will!' Speck said.

I glared at him.

Lexie tossed back her hair. 'You think I'm going to let you lot keep me out of the inner circle?' she scoffed. 'As if!' She sliced open the tip of her thumb, making more blood gush out than she'd probably intended. Speck gave a tiny whimper then, just as with the others, we made a blood bond.

We stood there for a moment, absorbing the solemnity of the occasion.

'We should come up with a secret handshake,' Speck said finally.

Lexie rolled her eyes. 'In case we can't recognise each other, you mean?'

'No. But it would be cool. All the best societies have secret handshakes.'

'If you want a secret handshake, then you can have one,' I told him.

He beamed and stuck his tongue out at Lexie. Brochan threw me a long-suffering look. If Speck could bear the sight of blood for this rite, then Brochan and Lexie could bear a few silly rituals. Let's face it – we all needed a little silliness.

Sorley was slumped in the corner, his head in his hands. I guessed his 'ruckus' had faded away. I smiled to reassure the others and walked over to him. 'Sorley,' I said gently, 'what's the matter?' He muttered something about desecration. 'You said that before, when we arrived at the border. What do you mean?'

He raised baleful eyes and gazed at me. 'Who did this?'

I swallowed. 'Who did what?'

He gestured round at the mansion, with its crumbling walls. 'This.'

I looked away. 'Aifric Moncrieffe.'

'The Steward?'

'Yes.'

Sorley stood up, stretched his legs, cracked his knuckles and started to stride away.

'Whoa! Where are you going?' I shouted.

'Isn't it obvious?'

Not really. I quickened my pace to try and catch up with him. For a troll with short legs, he was remarkably fast. 'Sorley, wait.'

'He cannot be allowed to get away with it.'

I was puzzled. 'I agree with you, of course I do. This was my Clan. But why are you so upset about it?'

He stopped in his tracks and turned slowly, disbelief colouring his swarthy features. 'Why am I so upset?' he repeated. 'Why am I so upset?'

I held up my hands to ward him off. 'Er, Sorley, I...'

'Blasted Sidhe. Think they're the centre of the universe,' he muttered. 'Bunch of dunderheads who wouldn't know if the sun fell from the sky and struck them on the nose.'

Clearly I wasn't the only person having a bad day. 'You're going to have to spell it out for me,' I told him. 'I'm not that bright.'

'Got that right,' he mumbled. 'Come on then. I'll show you.'

He set off again, marching out of the mansion and down the driveway towards the border. We followed him, trooping behind him in a ragtag formation. I exchanged a look with Brochan who shrugged. Apparently the ways of trolls were a mystery to us all.

When we arrived at the spot where the sign had stood, Sorley halted. There was a mound of earth that reached up to my waist; as there was no sign of any tools, I could only imagine that the troll had dug it out with his bare hands.

'For those of you who are uneducated fools,' he said, 'this is the most important place in the whole of your godforsaken Clan Lands.' He pursed his lips. 'It's no coincidence that the Steward placed that sign here.'

When we stared at him blankly, he rolled his eyes. 'This is the conduit for the border, the border that lets you sleep at night without fear of attack from fell beasties.'

Speck flinched visibly. 'What beasties?'

Sorley ignored him. 'When you came to the MacBain Lands, what was the first thing you saw?'

I thought about it. 'A flag?'

'Is that a question or an answer?'

I counted to ten in my head. 'I saw a flag. A MacBain flag that was large enough and ostentatious enough to be seen for miles.'

'Exactly.' He crossed his arms.

I tilted my head. 'So?'

Sorley spluttered. 'So?'

Taylor leaned forward, agog. 'What you're saying is that the source of the magical borders around every Sidhe Clan comes from a single spot, just like this one? And it's marked by a flag?'

The troll threw his hands up into the air. 'Finally, someone who has more than a single brain cell! Yes! The Clan sustains the magic but we guard the spot.'

'Do you realise how important this information is?' Taylor breathed. 'We've never broken into a Sidhe stronghold for one very good reason.'

'Tegs was hiding from them,' Speck said. 'That's why.'

Taylor squinted. 'Okay, yes. That too. But also because when you don't know where the lock is, you can't pick it. Now we know.' He beamed triumphantly. 'Folks, this opens up a whole new world. We'll be the most successful thieves in history. They'll be writing songs about us a thousand years after we've gone. We'll...'

The sour expression on Sorley's face made Taylor falter. The troll rose another notch in my estimation; there weren't many people who could make Taylor forget what he was saying with just one look. 'Knowing this is the conduit doesn't do anything. You still couldn't break in,' Sorley said. 'Not without inside help.'

Taylor's face glowed. Inside jobs were his favourite. I quickly shushed him before he got carried away. 'So you're saying that after the massacre, Aifric had the Adair flag taken down for more than just symbolic reasons.'

Sorley's face tightened. 'Yes,' he said, turning his head. For some reason he wouldn't look directly at the hole. 'The Clan members' deaths would have weakened the magic to the point where the border was only hanging on by a single thread.' He glanced coldly at Taylor. 'So massacre several hundred people all in one go and you might be able to break into any Clan Lands that take your dunderheaded fancy.'

Taylor's scheming expression vanished. 'Aifric Moncrieffe is a monster,' he whispered.

'Monster' didn't begin to cut it. There wasn't a word invented that came close to describing that wanker. Sorley, however, seemed momentarily appeased. He nodded. 'And I'm going kill him.' He turned and started walking away again.

'If he's going to walk all the way to the Cruaich,' Taylor said, 'it'll take him weeks.'

Brochan scratched his chin. 'He really does take security seriously, doesn't he? That's a bold move for what's really just a gate. A pretty cool gate but...' His voice trailed away.

I followed Sorley's progress for a moment or two before calling, 'Wait!'

'Maybe you should let him do it, Tegs,' Speck suggested. 'The worst that can happen is that he fails.'

'I don't want Aifric dead.'

Even Taylor looked surprised. 'He killed your father with his own hand. He ordered the deaths of your mother and all of your Clan. He—'

I interrupted him. 'I know.'

'Tegs, I realise pacifism is your thing but you can't let him get away with all that.'

I narrowed my eyes. 'I'm not going to. Believe me, Aifric Moncrieffe will get his come-uppance – but not through death.' I tried to explain. 'Death is quick. It's the end. And everyone dies. It's not punishment because it's inevitable.'

Bob winked into existence beside us. 'You still have a wish left. You can make his death the longest and most painful event the world has ever seen.' He seemed almost gleeful.

I looked at him suspiciously. 'You've been eavesdropping?'

He looked slightly guilty. 'I wasn't sure how you'd react after the wish. People have been known to try and shoot the messenger, you know. It's happened before. It seemed prudent to stay ... hidden for a while.'

Exasperated, I gazed at them all. 'You all know I hate violence. Did you really think that I'd let Aifric Moncrieffe compromise my morals and my beliefs on top of everything else he's done? He'll just win again if that happens.'

No one said a word. Bob, looking downcast, flew up to my ear. 'You're the most amazing person I know,' he whispered. Then, abashed, he pulled back.

'Aifric can't get away with what he's done, Tegs,' Lexie said.

'And he won't. I can steal his Gift from him, I can humiliate him, I can do any number of things to him - but I won't stoop to his level. I won't kill him. There are far, far worse things than death.' My voice shook with angry promise.

Speck put his hand up in the air like a schoolboy. When I frowned at him, he spoke up. 'You're pretty scary when you want to be, Chief.'

I wrinkled my nose. 'Don't call me that.'

Brochan cleared his throat. 'Who's the leader of the hankies?'

'The handkerchief,' I answered automatically. Then I stared at him. 'Did you just make a joke?'

He lifted his massive shoulders in a shrug. 'The situation seemed to call for it.'

I turned to Taylor, worried that he'd be upset at losing his role as de facto leader of our little group. Not only did he seem blithely unconcerned, he was fixated on Sorley's hole. I edged over to get a better look then sucked in a sharp breath. Where the Adair flagpole had once stood, there was now a collection of bones.

'There must have been trolls guarding this spot back then.'

'And Aifric killed them, along with everyone else, and flung their bodies here.' I glanced at Sorley's retreating back. 'No wonder he's so pissed off.' I squeezed my eyes shut for a moment and then ran after him. 'Sorley!'

As soon as I reached him, I grabbed his arm. He yanked it away. 'Leave me alone. I have things to do.'

'You can't go after Aifric.'

'You can't stop me.'

I drew in a breath. 'No, I can't. But you know that he'll kill you first. You probably won't even get within a hundred feet of him.'

He straightened up. 'I won't be alone. There are more of us than you realise.'

'Trolls?'

'Yes.'

'He's Sidhe,' I said simply. 'And he's the Steward. It doesn't matter how many of you there are.'

'He's responsible for the deaths of my kinsmen!' Sorley yelled, bunching up his fists. 'Then he sullied their memory and ensured their souls would get no rest by burying them there! In that spot!'

The location obviously held some important religious significance for him. I bit my lip, trying to show that I understood at least some of what he was feeling. 'I'm going to get revenge on him,' I promised. 'Just not like this.'

A fat tear rolled down Sorley's cheek. 'They have to be avenged.'

I put my hand on his shoulder. 'They will be.' I bent my knees slightly so that we were face to face. 'What happened to them is my responsibility,' I said. 'I'm Chieftain Adair and they were working for the Adair Clan when they died. I will take care of it.' In that moment I believed absolutely that I would. There was no other choice. 'Will you come back with me? We should remove their remains and bury them properly. I know the grove doesn't exist any longer but there's one tree left.' I smiled bitterly. 'It's only half dead now. Will you help me lay your kinsmen to rest there?'

Sorley's eyes widened. His nostrils flared and he took several steps backwards. It suddenly occurred to me that I'd made a horrible mistake. Of course he wouldn't want trolls buried on Sidhe sacred ground, especially not on Sidhe sacred ground that was tarnished with the blood of hundreds and all but laid to waste. Shite.

'I'm sorry, I...'

He bowed before I could finish my sentence. 'Thank you, Chieftain. That would be an honour.' He wiped away his tears with the back of his hand while I scanned his face, unable to decipher what he was thinking. He took a deep breath and an expression of calm descended. He cleared his throat. 'Such a ceremony would normally be conducted at sunset. We mirror the going down of the sun with the laying of our fallen comrades.'

Nice symmetry. Relieved that Sorley wasn't mortally offended and that he'd realised going up against Aifric would be useless, I tried to smile. 'Tomorrow then?' I asked, glancing upwards. We'd already missed today's sunset.

He bowed again. 'There are no words,' he said simply. I blinked, still confused by his demeanour. He turned and looked back. 'I shall ensure that the border is reinstated. Clan Adair will have the strongest gateway that Scotland can provide. It will help that the Foinse is here. We can draw on its magic.'

I started. 'You know it's here?'

He nodded. 'Of course. I can feel it.'

Okay. That wasn't great. 'Can you maybe keep that to yourself?'

His heavy brow creased. 'It is a great honour having the source of all magic reside here.'

'A great honour which other Sidhe might be, um, jealous of.'

His expression cleared. 'I understand.' He met my eyes. 'I shall leave the dealings with those other Sidhe in your hands but I am available for you to call on should you require further help.' His sudden formality was surprising.

'Thank you,' I murmured, not entirely convinced I understood all that had just happened.

He inclined his head and together we returned to the others.

***

Sorley refused to abandon his post at the border so, in deference to him, we all stayed there for dinner. Taylor produced a few tins of beans which we heated up over a small fire. No one said very much but I thought it was less out of awkwardness and more because we needed time on our own to absorb the day's revelations. Once the tins had been scraped clean, however, the lack of conversation began to grate on me.

I was just about to try and engage Sorley in small talk when he raised himself up slightly from his cross-legged position and farted.

Taylor raised an eyebrow. 'I can do better than that,' he declared. He proceeded to do so.

Lexie got up and backed away, holding her nose. 'You guys are disgusting.'

'Oh come on, it's perfectly natural.'

'You don't have to be so ... so ... blatant.' She sniffed. 'At least my farts smell pretty.'

Even Speck laughed at that. 'Pretty?'

'Of course. Like roses. Or a fresh sprig of lily of the valley.'

Bob looked at her archly. 'I am a magnificent being – but even my bodily emissions do not smell like that.'

Brochan leaned over to me. 'This would be a good time for a joke, or in about sixty seconds flat we're all going to be sniffing each other's arses.'

I grinned. 'You want a fart joke? Really?'

'Lesser of two evils.'

I opened my mouth but, before I could speak, there was a squeak. Speck looked at Lexie. 'So not only do your farts smell like flowers but they sound like mice?'

'That wasn't me!' she huffed.

We turned to Bob. He threw his little arms up in the air. 'What? Just because something strange happens, you automatically think it's me?'

There was another squeak. The smile disappeared from Sorley's face and he leapt to his feet. 'It's an intruder. It has to be.'

'Mate,' Taylor drawled, 'I understand you take your job seriously. But we don't have to worry about rodents sneaking in. We can't worry about every furry creature or we'll go even crazier than we already are.'

Sorley ignored him. He was in full attack stance, his legs splayed and his head darting from side to side. 'Sorley,' I said gently, 'it's alright. It's not a monster. And it's not going to hurt us.'

He whipped round a full one hundred and eighty degrees. A tiny ball came hurtling from out of the darkness and crashed against his leg before hopping manically upwards. Everyone jumped about a foot.

'Kill it!' Bob shrieked.

I sighed. 'Bob...'

Sorley lifted one massive foot. Alarmed at what he was about to do, I lunged forward and grabbed the fur ball with both hands. It squeaked again and wriggled, trying desperately to get free.

Taylor peered at it. 'What the bejesus is that?'

I held it up. 'It's a haggis.'

Lexie nudged Speck. 'I knew it,' she said in a loud whisper. 'It was only a matter of time before hanging around with all those Sidhe made Tegs lose her marbles.'

'Uh Integrity,' Bob said. 'Haggises are not real. Not unless they're on a plate anyway.'

Brochan pursed his lips. 'Isn't it haggi?'

I held the squirming creature towards them. 'Whatever the plural is, it really is a haggis.' I shrugged. 'Something to do with Morna Carnegie.'

'The flower woman?'

I nodded. At the Games, she'd used her Gift to give life to the most stunning display of heather that I'd ever seen. I was on a promise to visit her and gain control over my Gift. Considering I'd stolen part of her Gift – whether unconsciously or not - and she hadn't censured me for it, it wasn't a promise I wanted to break. 'They get all over the place. The haggis, I mean. I've seen their tracks everywhere. It's probably just lost.'

Sorley glared at it. 'I don't like it.'

'It won't hurt you.' I crouched down and released it. It ran straight back to him, leaping up at his leg once more. I laughed. It wrapped one of its three legs round Sorley's ankle and nuzzled him. He tried to shake it off. 'Vermin!'

'It's not doing any harm.'

'How do you know? You should be wary of anything linked to the Sidhe.' He shook his head vehemently. 'Giving life to a ... a ... thing like that is not natural.'

'I think it likes you.'

Speck nodded. 'Looks like love to me.'

Sorley shuddered. He started to bend down but the haggis suddenly let out a loud yip and yanked itself away, disappearing into the night just as a set of headlights appeared in the distance. Whoever was out there was heading directly for us.

'We're not ready! The ground needs to be re-consecrated. The border isn't in place.' Sorley flung out his words. 'Get to your places!'

Lexie scratched her head. 'What places?'

He started stamping out the small fire. 'Like a bloody beacon,' he muttered. He slapped himself around the face. 'Idiot.'

'If it was someone dangerous,' I pointed out, 'they would have kept their lights off.'

'It could be a diversion. There could be others coming from different directions.'

I watched the vehicle approach. 'Nah. Don't forget I'm expecting a visitor.'

Lexie twirled a blue curl in delight. 'You think it's...?'

I smiled. A couple of butterflies made their presence known to my stomach. 'Yes.'

We turned and watched as the vehicle pulled to halt about fifty feet away. The engine and lights were turned off and the door opened. Sorley tensed but I put my hand on his arm. 'It's alright. Really.'

Despite my words of reassurance, I was still relieved when the figure silhouetted against the moon was unmistakably Byron's. My eyes travelled across his broad shoulders. His hair was edged in silver from the moonlight, although his face remained shadowed.

'I don't get it,' Speck muttered. 'I know you like Byron Moncrieffe but his father is our mortal enemy.'

Sorley drew himself up. 'Moncrieffe?'

'It's alright,' I soothed. 'He's not like his father. And I told you he might be coming.'

The troll threw me a suspicious look but he didn't rush Byron and try to stab him in the chest or cut out his heart, so I felt things weren't going too badly.

'Sorley,' Lexie said patiently, 'Byron likes our Tegs too.'

He was still confused. 'But the Steward...'

'Aifric's trying to kill me,' I pointed out, 'but Byron still thinks the sun shines out of his arse. Either he'll avoid another assassination attempt while his son is here and we're all safe or...'

'Or he'll try again and Byron will finally see the truth.' Lexie nodded. 'Of course, it helps that you like him. A lot.'

Brochan growled under his breath.

I shrugged. 'He's a good guy.'

Lexie smirked and shook her blue hair. 'Sure.' She winked. 'You still should have asked for Jamie, though. Nothing works better than a bit of old-fashioned jealousy.'

'Are girls always so manipulative?' Speck asked plaintively, appealing to Taylor.

'Apparently so,' I muttered, as Byron walked round the car, opened the passenger door and another figure appeared. 'Because Tipsania Scrymgeour has managed to invite herself along with him.'

Two other shapes extricated themselves from the back seat.

'And,' Brochan grimaced, 'he's brought back-up.'

Chapter Seven

The butterflies, which had been reaching a delicious crescendo, evaporated in an instant. Byron took Tipsania's arm and the pair of them strolled towards us, flanked by their companions. As they drew closer, it was apparent that the back-up consisted of two trolls. I resisted the urge to shoot a questioning look at Sorley and forced myself to look relaxed. I'd brought this down on my own head and I could blame no one but myself. The least I could was to disguise my annoyance. Taylor had taught me well.

I waved enthusiastically. 'Hello! Have you broken down? Do you need help?'

Something glinted deep in Byron's eyes but Tipsania merely looked at me as if I was deranged. 'No,' she said flatly. Her gaze drifted to the still-smouldering embers of the fire. 'Is this the best that the Adair Lands have to offer? A few sticks to rub together?'

I tried my best to smile. 'You should have been here five minutes ago. The entertainment was ... ripe.'

'And,' Lexie butted in, 'we had haggis.'

Tipsania recoiled. 'I don't like haggis. Sheep's stomach and oatmeal? My tastes are more cultured.'

I battened down the urge to call the haggis back and order it to attack her. Instead I turned my attention to Byron. 'So what can we do for you this evening?'

'Don't play coy, Integrity,' he said. It was more of a purr than an accusation. Apparently Byron's ego had been massaged by the fact I'd asked for him. Whether that was a good or a bad thing, I wasn't entirely sure. 'You know very well why we're here.'

I tapped the corner of my mouth thoughtfully. 'You're delivering your wedding invitations by hand?'

Funnily enough, both their expressions soured. 'No,' Byron said, a muscle throbbing in his cheek. 'I'm here as the designated hero.' He placed emphasis on that last word. 'Apparently you require help to travel beyond the Veil and retrieve the body of Matthew MacBain.'

I think I made a good show of frowning prettily. 'Oh? But it's scary and dangerous. You don't have to come if you don't want to.' Byron glowered at me. I shrugged. 'Beggars can't be choosers,' I said cheerily. 'I suppose you'll do. Why don't you come in and I'll give you the grand tour? We can't leave for the Veil just yet, no matter how keen you are to meet some Fomori demons.'

Sorley coughed. 'If they must be permitted entrance, they cannot be left unattended at any time.'

I rubbed my chin as if thinking about it. 'You're right, Master Sorley,' I said. I beamed at our new guests. 'I'm sure you understand that we can't take any chances.'

Byron shrugged, giving every impression that I could rip off my clothes and prostrate myself on the ground with legs spread for his personal delectation and he wouldn't care. Tipsania, however, was less impressed. 'What do you take us for?' She waved an elegant hand around. 'Do you think we're likely to steal a piece of wood?' She nudged one of the empty tins with her slippered toe. 'Or a piece of your rubbish? We're not thieves like you, you know.'

I reminded myself that I was a pacifist; throwing her in the dirt and rubbing her face in it would go against my beliefs. 'Oh, Tipsy, you have no idea what delights await you inside. You might not be able to help yourself.'

Her lip curled. 'I can hardly wait.'

I glanced around. 'Brochan,' I said, 'you are not to leave darling Tipsania's side.'

He bowed. I was so surprised – and amused – that I almost fell over. 'My pleasure, Chieftain,' he intoned.

I snuck a look at Tipsania. She was not happy at the deferential treatment Brochan was bestowing on me. Her mouth tightened and she folded her arms across her chest. Given that when we were kids, she'd treated me as little better than a slave and now I was Chieftain of my own Clan, she must be feeling put out at the way the tables had turned. I shrugged inwardly. She was on my turf now.

'Speck,' I said, pointing at the troll on the left, 'take this one. Lexie,' I added, gesturing to the other troll, 'take that one.'

They aped Brochan's movements, bowing so dramatically that at one stage I thought Speck would topple over, then flanked each of the burly guards. I noticed that the troll next to Lexie was staring hard at the hole in the ground where Sorley had discovered the remains of his kin. It wasn't a friendly look.

'Er, Chieftain,' Sorley interrupted.

'Yup?' I coughed. 'I mean, yes, Master Sorley?'

'I can look after the trolls here.'

Byron stiffened but the expression on Sorley's face was so earnest – and Speck looked so relieved – that I agreed. At least then he could explain that it wasn't me who'd desecrated the bodies by dropping them here. 'Very well.'

I went over to Byron's parked car, reached for the keys and tossed them to Taylor. 'It's a pleasant night. Why don't we walk up to the main house? Taylor will drive your car up.'

Tipsania glowered. 'Who's looking after Byron?'

'Excuse me?'

'If I'm to be guarded like some dirty Clan-less...' Her voice faltered slightly at my look and she started again. 'If I'm to be guarded and the trolls are to be guarded, why isn't Byron going to be babysat as well?'

I smirked. 'Oh don't worry. He's the Steward's son so it's only fitting that I take care of him personally.'

She looked like she'd swallowed a sour plum. Byron remained silent; whatever he was thinking, he was hiding it well. I skipped up to him and hooked my arm through his. I felt his bicep twitch almost imperceptibly but, other than that, he was motionless.

I raised an eyebrow at Tipsania. 'Can you feel the air crackle?'

'No,' she snapped.

I pursed my lips. 'Hm. I'd tell you a chemistry joke but I probably wouldn't get a reaction.'

Byron exhaled loudly, as if under great sufferance. 'I'd tell you a joke about sodium but you probably wouldn't get it.'

'Try me,' I said.

He gave me a long look. 'Na.'

I grinned. 'Does this mean we're friends again?'

Something flashed in his eyes and his amusement vanished. 'We were never friends, Integrity.'

True. I pulled my arm away from his, feeling more hurt than I had any right to. 'Then you shouldn't have come here.' I marched away. He could follow me if he wanted to or he could stay here. His choice. I quashed down the relief I felt when I heard the crunch of his footsteps behind me.

The car engine revved and Taylor drove past, slamming on the horn in acknowledgment as he did so.

Sorley started to laugh. 'Sodium. Na. That's funny.' He laughed harder.

Byron caught up with me. 'Your troll is laughing at *my* joke,' he said with an air of competitive smugness. 'Not yours.'

'He's not my troll.'

'He called you chieftain. I've never heard a troll do that before.'

I paused in mid-step. Byron was right. I shook myself; considering what he now knew about Byron's father, Sorley probably did it for show. 'If you really don't want to be here, you can leave,' I told him, ignoring the lurch I felt.

'You need me. As I told you in Perth.' He dipped his head. '*You* asked for my help. Here I am.' He paused. 'Milady.'

I exhaled all my breath in a rush. 'One minute you're not talking to me. Then you're arguing with me. The next minute we're bantering and...'

'Flirting?' he inquired.

'If you want to call it that.'

He raised a lazy shoulder. 'I find you attractive. And manipulative as hell.'

That stung. Even if he was right. Before I could respond, however, Tipsania hissed right behind us. 'Stop treading on my heels, you lumbering merman!' Tipsania hissed.

I smirked, which was unfortunate because at that moment I got my toe caught in a small pothole and went flying. Byron lunged and grabbed my arm, only just keeping me upright. 'I guess,' I said somewhat breathlessly, 'I just can't stop myself from falling at your feet.'

He rolled his eyes. 'Don't you ever stop with the jokes?'

I blinked innocently. 'Why would I?'

He muttered something under his breath and clicked his fingers. 'It's dark out here.' The air fizzed. A glowing ball of fire coalesced in front of our eyes, hovering about a foot away and throwing long flickering shadows onto the ground.

'Pyrokinesis is a handy Gift to have, Integrity,' he said softly. 'Don't you want to steal it from me?'

'It doesn't work like that,' I said honestly. I started walking again. The little ball of fire kept pace, lighting up the road beneath our feet.

'Then how does it work?'

'I don't know. It's not deliberate, Byron. I tried to explain that to you before.'

'Explain it to me again.'

So he could take all my secrets to his damned murdering father? No chance. Byron might have kept quiet up until now but that didn't mean I was going to be reckless. 'You just said we weren't friends. Why would I want to confide in you?'

'You are determined to misunderstand me, aren't you? You know what I meant when I said that. I also said I'm attracted to you. Crazy and criminal must be the new sexy.' His eyes glittered with what I could only interpret as smoky promise but wariness still lurked there too.

Oh. Well, okay then. *Now* I knew. If I was honest, it was a large part of the reason why I'd nominated him for this little venture. I sighed and pushed back my hair. Byron's eyes followed the movement. 'We don't trust each other,' I said finally.

'That's a given.'

'We have nothing in common.'

He leaned his head down to mine. 'That's not entirely true.'

This was a mistake; I should never have brought him here. 'Sex,' I told him. 'We need to have sex and then we can clear the air and be more professional.'

Byron didn't smile. 'I'm game if you are.' He looked round the darkened landscape. 'Right here? Because we should probably let Tipsania and your merman go up to the buildings first. Unless you'd like an audience.'

Was he joking? I was tempted to call his bluff and find out. I massaged my shoulders. There was no doubt that things would be very different without the spectre of Aifric hanging between us.

'I'm sorry,' I said. It was far less dramatic than throwing him to the ground and ripping off his clothes but it would do for now.

'For what?'

'Everything,' I answered softly. 'And nothing.'

I wasn't sure he'd understand but I should have given him more credit. 'Yeah,' he said. 'Me too.' And with that, we walked the rest of the way in silence.

***

With Byron's Gift to light the way, I gave Tipsania and Byron a cursory tour. 'The bedrooms are up there. There's a kitchen through there. This is the courtyard.'

'It's not exactly luxurious, is it?' Tipsania sniffed.

Brochan rounded on her. 'It's been lying empty for a generation. What did you expect?' The venom in his voice was unusual for him.

Fortunately, before Tipsania could respond with a stinging retort of her own, Byron got involved. 'Actually, Tipsy, you're not seeing it properly. The craftsmanship and stonework are quite extraordinary.' He whistled through his teeth. 'This place was built to last. I'd have expected its condition to be far worse.' He looked round. 'And this courtyard is magnificent.'

I had no right to feel proud at his words but I did. 'We've not been spending much time inside,' I said gruffly. 'Not until we get it all cleaned up. Last night we slept in the car.'

'In the car?' Tipsania shrieked.

Byron took her hands and murmured something while Brochan sidled up to me. 'Why do you think he brought her?' he asked quietly.

'Damned if I know.' I watched them, ignoring the tug of jealousy at the way he soothed her with just a few words and at the sight of his thumb caressing the back of her hand.

She nodded, turned around and walked back out through the main entrance. Brochan nodded to me, then followed her.

'Tipsania's tired,' Byron said, as if that explained a lifetime of bitchy selfishness. 'She's gone to lie down in our car.'

I shrugged to indicate that she could do whatever she wanted. He looked at me for a long moment as if trying to decide something. Eventually he ran a hand through his hair and I pretended not to notice the way it flopped silkily across his forehead. I wasn't a sex-crazed Sidhe who was turned on by nothing more than the faint smell of shampoo and pretty golden locks. Nope.

'Have you had a chance to look over the rest of the land?' he asked, his tone somewhat less stiff now.

'Not really. There's not much to see. Everything was salted so nothing is growing, apart from the tree where I think the grove used to be.'

'Will you show me?'

I was probably supposed to say something along the lines of, 'Hell, no. It's sacred Adair Land, boyo!' I knew that in his own way he was holding out an olive branch though. I chose to take it. So sue me. I nodded and led the way out. Let's face it, at this point, it was pretty much just a half-dead tree; maybe it would look pretty in the firelight from Byron's Gift. The little fireball was still bobbing around in front of me like an overexcited puppy tugging at its leash.

Tipsania was already back inside Byron's car. I lifted a hand to Brochan, who had perched himself on top of its roof. Taylor was leaning against the nearby wall with Speck, Lexie and Bob surrounding him in a suspicious-looking huddle. As soon as Byron and I drew close, they threw us gigantic fake grins and stopped talking. I narrowed my eyes but their smiles widened.

'Your friends are ... interesting,' Byron commented, once we were out of earshot.

'They're the best people I know,' I said simply.

'I wasn't trying to put them down.'

'I know.'

Byron sighed. 'We always seem to be at odds with each other, Integrity. This isn't how I intended things to go. I could have handled things better but you...' he exhaled, 'you don't tend to encourage my rational side.'

I passed a hand across my face. 'Why did you give me the Adair Lands? You won the Games, Byron. You could have asked for anything.' He could have got himself out of his relationship with Tipsania; it was only manufactured to help the Moncrieffes with their appalling financial situation. Instead he had helped me – and that was after he'd discovered I'd stolen part of his Gift and accused his father of murder.

He was a silent for a moment before answering. 'I was blistering-ly angry with you. I still am. But the look on your face when you...' He heaved in a breath. 'Does it really matter?'

'Yeah,' I said, frankly. 'It does.'

He scratched his chin. 'However I felt towards you at the time, you deserved the win. But I also feel like you and I have unfinished business. I suppose I wanted to have you in my debt.' His eyes glittered. 'I wanted you to owe me a favour even if I couldn't face talking to you at that moment.'

I was taken aback by his honesty. 'Is that why you came here? You want to call in that favour? Just because I named you to Chieftain MacBain doesn't mean you have to follow.' I paused. 'I would have understood if you'd stayed away.'

He snorted. 'You didn't really think I'd cower in my castle, did you? I want to see the Lowlands for myself. And keep an eye on you. Besides, despite everything, I know the real reason you asked for me.'

I raised my eyebrows. 'Do you now?'

There was a gleam of mischief in his eyes. 'You're still wearing my jacket.'

I immediately began to shrug it off but he held up his hands. 'Keep it. It suits you better than it does me. Anyway,' he added with a lightness of tone I'd not heard for some time, 'it proves that you have feelings for me.'

This was one of those occasions when I should have remembered to think before speaking but, rather than maintaining the banter, the words fell thoughtlessly from my mouth. 'Right now, most my feelings are centred around frustration that you won't see the truth about your father.'

He stiffened. Just like that the moment was gone. I. Was. An. Id-iot. I damned myself for it.

'You're delusional.' He said it quietly, and with less anger than be-fore, but there was no denying that he believed I was fantasising. 'I can understand it, Integrity, believe me, I can. You've been shat on from a huge height for most of your life. I agree that my father should have done more to help you when you were a child and we've had words about that. He recognises that he could have done things dif-ferently. But he didn't try to kill you. You're jumping at shadows.'

I stopped walking and folded my arms. 'Do I seem damaged to you?' I enquired. 'Yes, my childhood wasn't the greatest but I'm okay. I sleep well at night. I'm generally a pretty happy person.' I thought about it a bit more. 'In fact, I'd say I'm a very happy person consid-ering how many times I've had brushes with death recently. A lot of that is to do with those four people back there. I'm not leaping at shadows because my mind is warped from maltreatment.' An im-age of Aifric thrusting his sword into my father's back flitted into my mind and pain lanced through me. 'I'm hurt,' I said softly. 'And I'm angry. And maybe I want revenge for what happened here to my Clan. But don't ever mistake that for irrationality or insanity, Byron.'

'My father is a good man, Integrity.'

Byron was blind. Desperation clawed at me. What could I do to get him to see the truth? 'How did you know that the Fomori are Gifted?' I asked, repeating my question from Perth.

He frowned at me. 'Why do you keep asking that? What do you mean?'

I sighed and pushed back my hair. 'No one else knows that the demons have Gifts, just like the Sidhe. I checked. How did you know? Did your father tell you?'

He stared at me like I'd lost my mind. 'Are you seriously trying to suggest that he's in league with the Fomori?'

'I know it sounds implausible but hear me out. Your father—'

'For goodness' sake! Can you even hear yourself?'

All I'd succeeded in doing was making Byron think I was even crazier than he'd realised. But I'd started so I'd finish - what choice was there? 'Your father has an emblem hidden in his room,' I said. 'I saw the same emblem tattooed on a Fomori demon.'

'So what you're trying to say is that my father, the Steward, is working with the demons.' His eyes turned to cold chips of icy emerald. 'Maybe he's a time traveller. Maybe he's actually three hundred years old and he conspired with them to annexe the Lowlands.' Byron crossed his arms over his chest. 'Maybe he's a Fomori demon in disguise.'

'Don't be ridiculous.'

'Are you kidding me? You're the one who's being ridiculous. He wants to *help* you.' He unfolded his arms and gazed at me in frustration. 'He's not perfect but he has your best interests at heart.'

My skin prickled. That sounded ominously like Aifric was planning something else and he'd somehow drawn Byron into his scheme. I knew from the Truth-Seeking Gift that Byron believed every word he was saying. I also knew he was wrong. Heartbreakingly so. 'What do you mean by that?'

His jaw tightened. 'It's a beautiful night. You called me here and I came.' His voice lowered to a husk. 'You want me and maybe I want you too. Let's not spoil things by talking about my father any more.'

That was easy for him to say. He didn't have imminent death hanging over his head. I made a show of acquiescing for now though. 'Come on,' I said. 'The last part of the Adair grove is just up here.' I stalked up the hill, leaving him to follow me while I mulled over the possibilities. Obviously I wasn't going to beat information about his father out of him. I had to trick him into blurting out the truth somehow. Damn it. The trouble with that was Byron was already on his guard and was far too clever. My breath clouded in the cool night air. There was always a way.

Even with the little bud on the far branch, the single tree was stark against the barren landscape. As soon as we reached it, Byron stretched out his palm and placed it against the bark. 'This is definitely it,' he said, as much to himself as to me. 'It's a miracle there's anything here at all. It means that Clan Adair isn't dead, not by a long shot.'

As if in response, the little fireball suddenly flared up, ballooning in size and distracting us both. Byron snapped his head round. 'Did you do that?'

'No. I can't do pyrokinesis.'

Despite softening towards me, he obviously didn't believe that I'd not stolen his other Gift from him while he wasn't paying attention. The little fireball continued to grow and, when the silvered glow of the Foinse appeared from the other side of the hill, rising up behind Byron's head, I suddenly knew why. The Foinse was magnifying Byron's magic. Shite. I couldn't allow him to see that it was here.

Desperate to distract him, I lunged towards him and grabbed his collar. Startled green eyes looked into mine as I pulled him towards me and pressed my lips against his, kissing him as passionately as I could. At the same time, I waved a desperate hand at the Foinse to make it leave.

Byron stood stock still, not responding but not pulling away either. The Foinse bobbed around behind him as if it was having incredible fun. I gestured frantically at it to shoo it away; it responded by executing a perfect somersault. I thanked the heavens that it wasn't making that strange humming noise any more but I really wished it would take the hint. I couldn't afford Aifric finding out it was here.

A deep noise sounded somewhere inside Byron's throat then his arms went round me. He opened his mouth, his teeth nipping at my bottom lip, just as the Foinse finally seemed to get the message and flew off in the opposite direction.

I yanked myself back, panting. 'Sorry,' I muttered. I stepped back, my instincts telling me to be ready to flee. My heart was fluttering almost painfully against my ribcage. Shite.

A slow smile crossed his lips. 'See? You do want me. You lust after me.' He took a step forward. 'Am I in your dreams, Integrity? Are you going crazy imagining all the things I could do to you?' His eyes were fixed on mine with unwavering intensity. 'Is your imagination as vivid as mine?'

For once I was lost for words. I stared at him, my mouth dry. He reached out and pulled me towards him.

'I saw the heat in your eyes. Do you think I'm going to let you pull a move like that and then just waltz back off to your friends?' He lifted his hand and brushed my cheek. I shivered. 'I was right about those feelings you have for me.'

'I made a mistake.'

His heart was thudding against mine. 'A mistake?'

I could feel my cheeks going red. 'Let me go, Byron.'

'This is why we're not friends, Integrity,' he growled. 'This is why we can never be friends.' And then he curved one hand round the back of my head and kissed me again.

I should have stopped things right there. Our situation was too complicated. This wouldn't solve any problems; all it would do was make things worse. The heady scent of his masculinity made it difficult for me to think though. And when his lips left mine and began trailing down my neck, I forgot all about resisting. Fire seared through me.

Byron spun me round, pushing me backwards until my spine pressed against the bare trunk of the tree. This is probably wrong, a little voice said deep in my mind; this was supposed to be a sacred grove, not the back of the bike shed. His hands cupped my breasts and I gasped.

'What is it about you?' he muttered, his breath hot against my skin. 'You fling around accusations about my father, you steal my magic, you dance on the wrong side of the law, you run around cities half naked and you can't even tell a decent joke.'

I would have murmured a protest but his fingers brushed against my nipples, then circled round them, making coherent thought flee my brain.

'All that,' he continued, 'and yet every time I see you, all I want to do is rip your clothes off and chain you to my bed.'

'I might have known you were nothing more than a caveman at heart,' I whispered.

'You have no idea,' he returned. He pulled away slightly, his hands leaving my body and moving up to cup my face. He stared into my eyes, holding my gaze, then he stepped back.

The rush of cold air which replaced the heat of Byron's body was like a bucket of icy water. Why had he stopped? I flicked an unspoken question at him but he shook his head slightly. 'Stay where you are.'

His eyes roved slowly down my body. He paused at my breasts, a tiny smile flickering at the corner of his mouth, then his gaze dropped further. I squirmed. He was taking his time and the fire that was flaring in his expression as he watched me was turning this into one of the strangest – and most erotic – moments of my life. I bit my bottom lip so hard I almost drew blood. There was an ache in my groin that was painful.

'Do you want me to beg?' I asked.

'Stop talking.'

Or what? I swallowed hard. My breath was growing more rapid and, even though I curled my nails deep into the soft flesh of my palms, I struggled to control myself. Fine: two could play this staring game.

I let my eyes travel up and down the length of Byron's body with the same unerring, aching slowness that he'd achieved. For someone who enjoyed a position of privilege, everything about him suggested hard work. I'd once thought that his taut muscles and golden glow were the product of hours in the gym and the tanning salon. Now that I knew his body better, it was clear that his physique was less to do with protein shakes and dumb bells than a simple by-product of his day-to-day life.

I lingered on the obvious bulge of his erection, enjoying his sharp intake of breath. He got his revenge, though, staring at me in return with such sultry, smoky promise that my head swam. We were both fighting for dominance – and he was winning.

'I told you once,' he said silkily, 'that I could make you scream. I think now's the time to prove it.'

Pushing myself away from the tree, I wasted no further time. I pulled my jumper over my head and threw it to the side then I did the same to my bra. This was no sexy striptease; the hungry expression on Byron's face told me I didn't need to do that. When I undid the button on my jeans, rolled them down and kicked them away, he actually groaned aloud. I allowed myself a tiny smile and then removed my panties. 'Do you have a condom?' I asked, ignoring his previous command to stay quiet.

He smirked and pulled one out of his pocket. Had he been expecting this to happen? A delicious shiver of anticipation ran down my spine.

I should have felt cold and vulnerable. I'll admit to the cold part but, even with Byron still fully dressed, I felt an odd sense of power running through me. Maybe he did think I was crazy, maybe his father would be successful sooner or later and would manage to kill me, but right now, all I needed was Byron's hot gaze and I could conquer the world. I crooked my little finger and beckoned him over. He stayed where he was, crossing his arms.

'Admit it,' he said. 'Admit that you need me.'

I narrowed my gaze at him. 'I need you.'

Triumph flared in his eyes. 'How badly?'

I abruptly realised that he needed me to submit. I'd hurt his ego when I'd stolen his Gift from him and told him the truth about his father. Perhaps that was another reason as to why he'd given me the prize he'd won from the Games. He wanted to prove he had sway over me. Byron was used to women fawning over him. Even though I wanted him, I'd not acted like that and he didn't like it. Strangely, the knowledge empowered me, rather than annoyed me.

'I'll beg if you need me to,' I said softly. I dropped to my knees and eyed the bulge at this crotch. Now it was Byron's turn to freeze. From the expression on his face he was struggling to maintain control. Rather than smirk, I shuffled over and stretched my fingers over to his belt, unbuckling it with one swift movement. I was rewarded with a sharp intake of breath. The condom fell from his hand onto the ground with a soft thud.

Ever so slowly, I undid his zip. Mmm. Tighty whities. I eased his trousers down until I had full access then, with his erection inches from my face, licked my lips. 'Please, Byron,' I whispered. 'I'll do whatever you want.' Using the tip of my index finger I ran it down his length. He shuddered. 'Be good to me. Give me what I want. I'll do anything.'

'Anything?' he growled.

I tugged on a stray hair curling up towards his flat, tanned stomach. 'Just give the order.' Although I hoped he'd do it quickly. Despite the lusty fire raging inside me, I was starting to get bloody cold.

He placed his hands on my arms and gently pulled me upwards. 'Like you'd ever follow my orders.'

I smiled. 'Try me.'

Raising his eyebrows, he pointed to a spot on his cheek. I leaned up, wetting my lips and then licking it. Mirroring my movement, he did the same to me, his stubble scratching my skin. Then he undid the buttons on his shirt, revealing the full expanse of his chest and touched his nipple. I ducked my head down and took it in my mouth, nibbling and teasing it with my tongue. Despite the freezing air, I could taste the salt of his sweat.

Breathing hard, he gripped my shoulders and pushed me back. Without touching any other part of my body, his own mouth fixed on my breast, his tongue circling the nipple. Unable to help myself, I moaned. He took it gently in between his teeth and nipped. My moan turned into a cry.

'Integrity,' he said.

I could only mumble incoherently back.

'It's fucking freezing.'

A stifled giggle escaped me. Fighting for control, I found some words. 'Then let's stop playing.'

He growled in agreement and spun me round, pulling me back against him. I could feel him hot and hard against my body, his skin burning mine where we touched. He nudged my legs apart with his knee while his hands left my waist and moved my hair aside as he traced down my spine.

'So beautiful.'

I gasped, my eyes opening wide. Then I wished I hadn't. For the briefest second my gaze focused. The sole tree of the Adair Clan grove was standing there, utterly silent. Judging me. It felt like I'd just been doused in icy water.

Oblivious, Byron ducked down, reaching for the fallen condom before returning back up. And then, as his fingers reached the spot between my shoulder blades at virtually the same point where the cold steel of his father's sword had slid into my father's body, I jerked away.

I spun round, panting. The heat in his expression had been replaced by confusion and wariness. 'What is it?'

My jaw worked helplessly. I stared into his eyes and tried desperately to get him to understand. 'We can't do this. Not here.'

His face shuttered off immediately. His arms dropped by his side while his body shook for control.

'This was – is - my Clan grove,' I said, doing what I could to explain. My back tingled almost painfully. None of this was Byron's fault. 'I want this.' I swallowed. 'I want you. But not here. Not like this.' I congratulated myself for once managing to keep Aifric's name away from my lips. Thoughts about suggesting returning to the mansion before continuing what we'd started flitted through my mind but not only had the moment gone, where would we go? Into a dead room filled with ghosts and the memory of a massacre? Or the lumpy backseat of a smelly car like a pair of teenagers? No.

Byron scanned my expression. At first I thought he was angry but even though his features remained taut, he seemed to understand some of what I was feeling. Some. He nodded slowly, his own inner turmoil reflecting mine. His fist curled round the still wrapped condom. 'Okay,' he said. His mouth tightened. He stepped towards me once more. 'This isn't the most romantic setting.'

I didn't think romance was what either of us had been looking for a few moments ago but I just bobbed my head in mute response.

'Understand this though, Integrity,' he continued in a low voice. 'I will have you. Whether it's on a four poster bed covered in rose petals and with chilled champagne or on a frozen hill, I *will* possess you. I *will* make you scream.'

The magic in my veins buzzed. Byron was telling the truth and both of us knew it.

Chapter Eight

True to form, the next morning I woke early, just as the first signs of light were showing. The darkness of the night was giving way to a dusky pink and I lay there, tracking the shifting colours, my mind empty for a blessed few minutes. I couldn't stay like that forever though. Eventually I pushed myself up and stretched, doing what I could to ignore the pleasant aches from last night mixed with both regret and relief that things hadn't gone further. It was time to get down to business, not dwell on what might have been.

Nobody else was stirring. Brochan and Speck were merely lumps on the ground, their sleeping bags pulled up over their heads to guard against the cold. Only Brochan's size and Speck's rumbling snores distinguished them.

There was silence from Byron's car. Its windows were tinted and I resisted the temptation to sidle up and peer in to see whether Tipsania and Byron were coiled together in slumber. Instead, I jogged down to the border to check on Sorley.

If I'd thought for one moment that the gruff troll would be asleep, I was mistaken. He was sitting on a long wooden pole with his chin cupped in his hairy hands. When I approached, he jumped up and nodded gravely. 'Chieftain.'

'You don't have to call me that,' I told him softly.

'I know.' He paused. 'Chieftain.'

I swallowed. To break the awkwardness of the moment, I pointed at the pole. 'Where did that come from?'

'Lyle and Kirk retrieved it last night.'

'They're the other trolls?' Sorley nodded. I glanced around. 'Where are they now?'

He jerked his head to the right. 'Sleeping over there. All I need from you is some Adair tartan and we can sort out the border.'

Fortunately Lexie had made sure we had plenty of tartan material for the Games last month so getting a swatch wouldn't be difficult. I was sure there would be some lurking around in her bags.

Worrying as the Adair border was, it wasn't my immediate concern. 'Sorley,' I said, seriously, 'you said you could feel the Foinse. Does that mean that they can as well? Lyle and...'

'Kirk,' he supplied helpfully. 'Yes, of course.'

I nibbled at my bottom lip. 'The thing is...'

'They won't tell anyone.'

'Are you sure? Because they're working for the Moncrieffes and if they say a word, we could all be screwed.'

He remained expressionless. 'They won't say anything. Trust me.'

I didn't really have much choice. For the first time, however, I wondered whether I could even trust Sorley himself. It wouldn't be beyond credibility that he was still in MacBain's employ. I pushed the unpleasant thought away and decided to hope for the best. 'Do you happen to know where the Foinse is right now?' I asked.

His deep brow furrowed. 'No. Sorry.'

Shite. 'That's alright.' I gave him a tight smile. 'I'll make sure you get that tartan.'

Sorley bowed and I turned away, walking away from both the border and the mansion. I pulled out Bob's scimitar and rubbed it absently against my leg. He appeared in a flash of light, hovering in the air next to my face.

'Were you just rubbing me against your soft thigh, Uh Integrity?' he asked, arching an eyebrow. 'Is that because Byron Moncrieffe didn't do it for you last night and now you're looking for a real man?' He puffed out his tiny chest.

'Let's get one thing clear, Bob,' I said, jabbing my finger in his direction. 'My sex life is off limits, alright?'

'Oooh! Touchy much!'

I rolled my eyes. 'This is neither the time nor the place, Bob. There are far more important things to worry about.'

'No.' He shook his head solemnly. 'I don't think there are.'

I sighed and rubbed my eyes. 'I need you to tell me where the Foinse is.'

He cocked his head and said in a loud conspiratorial whisper, 'I think you pissed it off last night by shooing it away.'

I put my hands on my hips. 'How do you know about that?'

'I am a magnificent being who—'

'Bob,' I said flatly, 'were you spying on us?'

'There's nothing wrong with a little voyeurism.'

I felt ill. 'Bob...'

'Don't worry. Honestly, Uh Integrity, you are very easy to wind up. I saw what was going down and I left you to it. Alright?' I glared at him suspiciously but he just grinned. 'I think the source of magic is a mile or so that way,' he said.

I strode off in the direction he was pointing at. 'You're welcome!' he yelled after me.

I padded along, the frost making the ground crunchy underfoot. From here it was clear where the border had once lain. On one side were varying shades of green, even at this time of year, but on the other it was a different story. Aifric had really gone out of his way to make this place uninhabitable.

I shoved my hands in my pockets. Why had he done it? To have proof from Bob's wish that Aifric was responsible was one thing, but I couldn't fathom out his motives. Jealousy? Of what? Malice? It seemed rather extreme, even considering what I knew of the Steward. Had my father been blackmailing him? Perhaps it wasn't surprising that Byron refused to believe a word I said; even I couldn't begin to imagine why Aifric had done all this.

I was so lost in my thoughts that I almost missed the Foinse. It was nestled in a tumbled stone cairn and only the dim sunlight reflecting off its edges made me notice it. I paused. Was it sleeping? Is that what magical orbs did from time to time?

I cleared my throat, trying to be quiet but alert the Foinse to my presence at the same time. It jerked as if in surprise, rising half a foot into the air. It remained there, hovering, and I couldn't escape the feeling that it was staring into my very soul. My skin prickled uncomfortably.

'Hello.'

It hummed gently in what I presumed was a response.

I scratched my head. 'Um, I'm sorry if I came off as a bit rude last night. But, well, I think it's probably best if you don't let anyone see you. There might be ... trouble.'

This time the Foinse did nothing. I wondered if I was being completely daft trying to communicate with it. Then, without really thinking, I stretched out my hand, my palm flat. Slowly, the Foinse approached until it was barely an inch away. It hummed again and flopped down. I drew in a sharp intake of breath. It was still incredibly warm to the touch.

'Please?' I asked. 'Please keep yourself hidden. They put you in a box in the heart of a mountain before. I don't know what they'll do this time.'

It felt as if the Foinse was getting warmer. It twitched and started rolling up my arm, coming to rest against my neck and pressing itself against me as if for reassurance. I couldn't stop myself smiling. It felt like its glow was somehow leeching into me through the pores of my skin. I wouldn't say I felt more powerful or more magically imbued, just ... more at peace.

It didn't last. I was closing my eyes as warmth spread through me when suddenly the Foinse yanked itself away with a high-pitched buzz. My eyes flew open in time to see it bury itself back in the cairn as if it was trying to conceal itself. From far behind me there was an angry yell. Something was wrong.

'Stay there!' I yelled, hoping the Foinse understood me. I spun round and sprinted back in the direction I'd come.

All three trolls were on their feet. Sorley had his spear in hand and was holding it against his body as if trying to defend himself. The other two were dancing from foot to foot, jumping backwards and then forwards and then backwards again. I wasn't the only one alerted by the noise; from the top of the drive I saw Byron, Tipsania, Taylor and Brochan jogging down. The trolls' movements grew even more frantic and jerky.

'What's wrong?' I called out.

'Bleeding haggis!' Sorley snarled. 'Get it away from me. Get it away!'

My gaze dropped and I finally spotted the little fur ball. It was in as much of a state as the trolls were. It flung itself at each one in turn, spluttering and squeaking like it was choking on something.

Sorley jabbed his spear at it just as I reached down and scooped it up. The haggis wasn't interested in my protection, however; it shook violently in my hands and tried to squirm away. Notwithstanding the creature's apparent affection for Sorley, it seemed to be acting out of character. 'Something's wrong.' I looked around.

'What's the problem?' Byron said as he reached us. His jaw was set and, rather than glancing at me, he kept his attention on the quivering haggis. There was no doubt that it was severely rattled.

'It's upset,' I told him. 'But I have no idea why.'

Tipsania goggled at it. 'Is that...?'

I couldn't be arsed with her questions. 'A haggis,' I said tersely. 'Yes.'

'Which direction did it come from?' Byron asked.

We turned to Sorley. He recoiled from the still-squeaking haggis with a comical look of disgust on his face and pointed past the border. I couldn't see anything. 'We're very close to the Veil here,' I said, dread fingering its way along my spine. 'And there was a Fomori demon in Perth just a few days ago...'

The three trolls immediately braced themselves, their heads swinging in unison as they scanned the landscape. 'If a demon comes here, we'll take care of it,' Sorley said. His spear shook.

'And what if there's more than one?' I murmured, as much to myself as anyone else.

'Tipsy.' There was an edge of warning to Byron's tone.

She nodded. Her perfect Sidhe skin was even paler than normal; her eyes took on an unfocused look and I tensed as I felt the vague buzz of magic. I stared at her. I'd never stuck around long enough when we were kids to find out what Sidhe Gift she'd been bestowed with. Now curiosity warred with trepidation. Just what was she doing?

A half beat later, it was clear: right before my eyes, she was turning transparent. I turned to Taylor to check that he was seeing the same thing – but he was staring at me. I glanced down at my body and realised that I was doing the same as Tipsania. In fact, we all were.

'Invisibility,' I breathed. Desire collided with fear and I started to run. I had to get as far away from Tipsania as possible. The traitorous part of my subconscious that I couldn't control wanted to rip every last shred of that Gift from her and keep it for myself.

I'd barely gone twenty metres when I realised my feet had vanished completely. My heart was slamming against my ribcage and blood was thrumming in my ears so loudly that I could only just make out Sorley's panicked yelling. I lifted the hands I could no longer see and pressed hard against my temples.

'No, no, no, no,' I moaned. Dizziness swam through me and I felt the now-familiar nausea as I fell to my knees. Bitch or not, she was here as my guest and I'd reached inside her soul and ripped away her magic.

Sorley shouted again. 'Chieftain! Where are you?'

'Tipsania,' I croaked.

I turned my head to look back but there was nothing to see other than the pile of earth beside Sorley's hole. Through dint of her Gift, she'd made us all invisible. I forced myself to my feet. I had to go back and make sure she was alright. If she'd collapsed and no one could see her... Except that was the moment when I saw them.

There were at least twenty of them. They were far enough away that they probably hadn't heard the commotion but now that they'd rounded the curving road, the valley sides would make sound travel more easily.

I ran back up to the others. 'Sorley!' I hissed. 'Be quiet!'

'Chieftain! Where are you? Are you—?'

'Shhh!'

There was a tiny squeak from somewhere to the right of my feet. I bent down, my fingers searching for the haggis. As soon as I felt fur, I grabbed it and held on tightly, bringing up to my chest.

'Fomori,' Sorley whispered.

I thrust the haggis towards the sound of his voice. 'Take this. Get back to the others at the mansion and tell them to stay out of sight.'

'As you command, Chieftain.'

'Tipsania?' I asked shakily. 'Are you there?'

'No,' she said, her voice dripping with sarcasm. 'I'm back at home in front of a roaring fire, completely safe. Of course I'm still here.'

I closed my eyes momentarily in relief. 'You need to get back to the mansion too. Everyone needs to get back.'

'Tegs,' Taylor whispered. I swung my head, trying to work out where he was. 'We're invisible. They can't see us.'

I thought of the way the Fomori demon in Perth had seemed to scent the air. 'There are five senses,' I said in a low tone. 'As you very well know.'

Taylor sucked in an audible breath. 'Okay.'

'Stay quiet as you go,' I warned them all. 'They're getting closer.'

I heard them move away - most of them, anyway. 'You have to go as well, Byron,' I said. 'The Steward won't look kindly on me if you end up with your limbs torn off.'

'I don't see you leaving,' came his hushed response.

'Tracks,' I said tersely. I ducked down and began smoothing the ground. There was nothing I could do about the hole; it was too late to fill it in and, even if I did it in time, it would obviously be fresh. Maybe the demons would put it down to random trophy hunters passing by.

'I'll get the ones higher up,' Byron said, almost in my ear.

I half jumped, keeping one eye on the ground underneath and one eye on the approaching horde. The nausea still wouldn't go away but now it was more to do with the sensation of being off balance because I couldn't see myself rather than because I'd stolen Tipsania's Gift.

When I'd cleared as many of our tracks as I could and I stood up again, I got a head rush that even the most violent of vertigo sufferers had probably never received.

The footsteps I made as I ran away from Tipsania still remained. There was little I could do about them now because the demons were already far too close. At least those tracks headed away from the Adair Lands, rather than towards them because, with the Fomori as close as they were, the only thing I had left now was hope.

These demons were smarter than their counterpart who'd ended up barbecued in Perth. As they drew nearer, and their faces grew more distinct, I saw that they were wearing darkened goggles to shield their weak eyes from the sun. Strangely, it made them look like a contingent of Hell's Angels. It didn't help that they'd smeared their bodies with some kind of gunk to prevent the sun from searing their skin. Of course, they could have avoided all the dangerous UV rays and simply stayed on their side of the bloody Veil. Why were they here? Why now? And why wasn't the Veil keeping them back? Even I found it hard to believe that Aifric could be responsible for all this.

Something poked my waist: Byron. 'That better be your finger,' I hissed.

He didn't rise to the bait. 'We need to get back.'

I shook my head then remembered he couldn't see me. 'Okay,' I whispered. I tiptoed three steps backwards and stayed put. Run and hide? No chance. I had to use this opportunity to find out why the demons were here.

'Integrity,' Byron said through gritted teeth.

'Quiet.' Then, 'You can still go.'

I could picture his eyes flashing in frustration but he didn't leave. We stood together side by side as the Fomori demons approached. The wind blew their foul stench towards us but, as long as it didn't change direction and send our scent back to them, I could stand the reek. If I could stand Taylor and Sorley's bout of wind last night, I could stand almost any smell.

It occurred to me that the Fomori demons' behaviour was markedly different to what I'd observed in the Lowlands. There had seemed to be no order or discipline to the demons when I was in Glasgow. It had been the exact opposite – total, uncontrolled chaos. This lot, however, were marching in time in straight lines, arms swinging by their sides. That was far, far scarier.

The demon on the far right barked a harsh, guttural command and they halted. I held my breath. He stepped out in front of them, flashing some kind of sigil on his arm as he turned our way. He jerked a long gnarled hand down at one of my footsteps and another demon stepped out and crouched down to examine it. Could he tell how fresh it was? His expression remained blank. Then the first demon, presumably the leader, gestured at two others. They peeled away from the group and edged forward.

If their movements had been decisive and militaristic before, they were like nervy cats now, inching forward bit by bit. At first I didn't understand what the problem was but then I realised: they thought the magical border was back in place. Except Sorley was waiting to remove the bones and re-bury them before kick-starting that magic again.

I'd been in plenty of tense situations before but I didn't think I'd ever felt the silent screaming of fear that I did right now. I didn't know whether it was because of our proximity to this group with their militaristic attitude, my concern for my nearby surrogate family or simply that this was happening on my ancestral lands, but I was terrified. Even when Byron reached out, fumbling to find my hand and grip it, my tension didn't lessen.

The two demons came to a halt less than a foot from the hole and their gaunt faces peered at it. The one on the left gave a guttural laugh and threw an indecipherable comment at the leader. Then he stretched out one hand.

Nothing happened. He wiggled his fingers, reached an inch further then shuffled forward a few inches. It seemed as if all of us were holding our breath – Byron, me and all the demons included. The leader shouted another command and the other demon slowly nodded before raising his own hand. A streak of what looked like lightning zapped across, flickering several feet through the air and missing Byron and me by centimetres.

Mutterings rose from the assembled Fomori demons. The one Gifted with lightning lifted a leg, paused as if he couldn't decide whether to move or not, then straightened his shoulders and strode forward abruptly, past where the border should have been. I didn't mistake the look of relief that crossed his expression. He turned round and gave a wide-mouthed, toothy grin that would send anyone scurrying underneath their bed in fear. The monsters were real.

The leader marched up and joined him. He also smiled, although he conveyed more grim satisfaction than his minion. He bent down by the hole where the Adair flagpole had once stood and rummaged around, pulling out a misshapen, cracked and dirty troll skull. He threw back his head and laughed, a cackling sound which made Byron's hand tighten round mine. The demon hawked and spat and a greenish ball of phlegm landing on top of the other bones. A dribble of spittle remained on his lips before slowly making its way down his narrow chin. He threw the skull to one side as if it was nothing more than a piece of rubbish.

'Ach mag ne tre!'

The other demons visibly relaxed. The one crouching down by my tracks stood up and used his index finger to slice a line across his throat. 'Adair!'

I stiffened. The demons, however, found this hilarious and laughed uproariously. A particularly ugly one with limp straggly hair hanging down from one side of his head, pointed towards the mansion. 'Vas?'

The leader spat again and shook his head. He straightened his shoulders and looked in the direction of the Veil. 'Hame.'

The Fomori demons bellowed and thumped their chests. They returned to their formation, wheeled round and marched back off again. They were leaving. Praise be.

I unclenched my jaw, realising how tight it was. My shoulders dropped and I remembered to breathe. Now that the demons were striding away, the air was sweet and fresh again.

'Aifric is working with them,' I half-whispered to myself. 'But he couldn't have sent them here. They're leaving because they think all the Adairs are dead and the land here is still abandoned and empty.'

Byron dropped my hand like it burned him. 'It's obvious, isn't it? My father is not working with them at all. It's yet more proof that everything you believe about him is nothing more than a figment of your imagination.'

I moved away. 'The first time I used an elevator,' I said softly, 'it was really uplifting but in the end it just let me down. When you find out the truth about him, Byron, I really hope you're not too disappointed. He's no hero.'

I watched the Fomori demons disappear round the bend in the road and turned to go back and find the others. I couldn't cope with another with Byron on the subject of his father. Not now.

Chapter Nine

Despite my fervent hope that the demons had only been checking out the Adair Lands and were unlikely to return, our group's mood remained sombre. Even Bob seemed to have developed a nervous tic; his left eyebrow jerked to a fearful rhythm for what seemed like hours. Sorley was tense, barking orders and commands at everyone as he worked to bring the border back to life. When it crackled into action so many years after it had been extinguished, he still didn't relax. He directed Taylor, Speck, Brochan and Lexie to remain on guard as the sun began to dip. Not one of them pulled a face or argued.

Sorley, Lyle and Kirk marched slowly up from the border with the bones of the long-dead trolls placed carefully on an old wagon which Brochan had unearthed. Their ceremonial solemnity would have been comical if the situation were not so tragic. I went on the hunt for Tipsania. I could have asked Byron for help; he didn't seem to be doing anything more than standing by the old tree where we'd almost shagged each other's brains out and glowering. It was testament to how awkward I felt around him that I preferred to speak to bloody Tipsania rather than to him.

I found her in the old kitchen, an expression of disgust pasted on her face. 'This place is filthy.'

'What do you expect?' I asked mildly. 'It's not been cleaned for a generation.'

She flung up her arms as if to convey how ridiculous she thought my comment was. It was difficult not to smirk when her fingers inadvertently caught in a long cobweb hanging from the ceiling and she let out a tiny screech of repulsion.

'I have a question,' I interjected quickly, hoping to forestall any further histrionics.

'What?' she snapped, wiping her hands vigorously on her dress. I decided against pointing out that now she had a snail-trail of cobweb dangling down her thigh.

'The trolls are bringing up the bodies of the guards who were killed here back when—'

'When your father murdered everyone?'

I kept my tone as even as possible. 'He didn't. He was framed.'

'Right,' she scoffed.

I drew in a deep breath. 'Anyway, I'm going to bury them up where the Adair grove used to be. I don't know much about the customs of those places though, or what's expected when the ceremony takes place. I thought you might be able to tell me.'

She lifted her eyes to me slowly. 'You're going to do what?' Her voice rose into a high-pitched tone of disbelief.

'I'm going to bury the remains of the trolls in the grove,' I repeated, reminding myself that patience was a virtue.

'I thought that was what you said,' she muttered. 'I just didn't believe it.' She shook her head. 'Are you out of your mind?'

I crossed my arms and stared at her. She threw her arms up, again catching them on the cobwebs. This time, however, she didn't react to their touch. 'Clan groves are for the Sidhe. They are sacred places which cannot be defiled.'

Defiled? Good grief. Had she even looked around this place? 'I don't see how burying people who belonged to the Clan in the Clan ground can be an issue,' I said stiffly.

'They're not Sidhe!'

I shook my head. 'So?'

'Nobody does that! Nobody allows non-Sidhe bodies to be buried in their groves! Not even the MacQuarries are that insane.'

My eyes narrowed. 'Leave off the MacQuarries. And the trolls will be buried there, no matter what you say.'

'You can't do it.'

I gave her an icy glare. 'I can and I will. You are forgetting yourself.' I drew myself up. 'I am the Adair Chieftain and you are a guest on *my* Lands. I didn't invite you, but here you are. I suggest you keep a civil tongue.' I was starting to sound like I'd been educated at Eton; Tipsania was rubbing off on me – and not in a good way. It seemed to do the trick, though. She paled slightly and dropped her gaze.

'I apologise.'

I blinked in astonishment. I'd never heard Tipsania apologise for anything. 'Well, then.' I scratched my neck. 'Okay.'

She sighed. 'It's not a good idea. Regardless of what these Lands are like, the grove is still a sacred place. To place the remains of someone who's not Sidhe there could cause all manner of problems. The magic—'

'Screw the magic.' I had utter respect for the Foinse but she was talking about the same magic that had allowed me to steal her own essence. Besides, I was going to do this; I'd promised.

She sucked in a breath but she didn't protest any further. That was something. I shrugged. I'd never understand these Sidhe, no matter how hard I tried. I would do this without any help. I'd just make it up as I went along. How hard could a little re-burial be?

By the time I ventured back outside, Sorley and his little cortège had arrived. I fell in behind the wagon and dropped my head. As the sky continued to darken, we made our way slowly towards the solitary tree.

There was probably a particular spot that was designated for burials but, with almost the entire grove destroyed, I couldn't imagine where that would be. I pointedly ignored Byron's curious gaze and took the rusting shovel which Sorley was holding out. He couldn't look me in the eye and I suddenly understood that he was expecting me to change my mind and tell him that his kin couldn't be buried here after all. I gave him a reassuring pat, noting the wide-eyed stares from Lyle and Kirk, and eyed the ground. In front of the tree seemed as good a spot as any.

I walked over and started to dig. Unfortunately, the ground up here was so cold and hard that it took some time before I made any headway. My hands were clumsy and the watching audience of the three trolls and Byron did nothing to ease my embarrassment. After I'd made several attempts, which succeeded in making little more than a dent, Byron stepped forward but I threw him such an angry glare that he backed down. His expression was astonished at my actions but I registered a glimmer of approval as well. I told myself firmly that I didn't care and continued to dig. The only saving grace was that once I got through the top soil, it seemed to get easier. It was bloody back-breaking work, though, and my hair was soon plastered to my forehead with sweat despite the freezing air.

Once the hole was big enough, I turned to Sorley and raised my eyebrows. He nodded and walked to the wagon, carefully lifting the first few bones before passing them to me. I struggled not to recoil at their coldness. My fingers already felt stiff and frozen from gripping the shovel and I willed them not to fumble as I placed the bones gently into the ground. Lyle – or maybe it was Kirk - gasped audibly before mumbling 'sorry' for breaking the silence. One by one, I took the shattered remains of those brave trolls who'd stood at my Clan's defence and added them to the others. Once they were all there, I faced Sorley.

'As Chieftain of the Adair Clan,' I intoned, feeling horribly like a fraud, 'I commit these souls to the ground. There is no doubt that they died as heroes and the memory of their sacrifice shall not be forgotten. They were as much a part of Clan Adair as my father was.' I bit my lip. What had happened to his body and my mother's was a complete mystery. Still, I couldn't explain how I knew it but I was sure that he would approve of this action. 'Ashes to ashes,' I continued. 'Dust to dust.' Was there supposed to be something else? Shite. I was awful at this.

I pressed my lips together, guilt rippling through me because I was doing the trolls a great disservice by not being more eloquent. But it was the sight of the tears brimming at the edge of Sorley's eyes that almost proved my undoing. I cleared my throat awkwardly, hastily picked up the shovel again and filled in the hole.

'When spring comes,' I said, 'we'll plant a tree here. You are welcome to visit any time, as are all of your kin.'

The three trolls nodded solemnly, exchanged glances and turned abruptly, marching back towards the mansion as slowly as they'd come. The soft murmur of their voices reached my ears.

'That was unorthodox,' Byron commented.

I tossed back my hair. 'I suppose you're like Tipsania and you think it was sacrilege to bury them here.'

His expression didn't flicker. 'Actually, no,' he answered quietly. 'That was a good thing you did.' He gazed after the trolls thoughtfully and rubbed his chin. Then his eyes dropped to the spot where we'd been the night before, heat rising up in their emerald depths. I swallowed.

For the sake of something to do rather than think about Byron, I moved over to check on the tree. Where there had once only been a bud, now the entire branch was coming to life. Tiny leaves were sprouting; they were still tightly furled but they gave a hint of what was to come. I smiled then twisted on my heel and left, hugging myself to guard against the encroaching cold. Byron remained where he was, although I could feel his eyes boring into my back. I injected just the tiniest extra swing to my hips, damning myself for it at the same time as I hoped he noticed. I was a lost cause.

It didn't take me long to catch up with Sorley, Lyle and Kirk. They were clearly on a mission to go straight back to the border, but they didn't appear displeased to see me.

'The others will hold the fort for a while yet,' I told them. 'Why don't we get that fire started again and I'll make you a cup of tea? The ceremony can't have been easy on you and you deserve a bit of a breather.'

'It's our job to guard the border,' Sorley demurred. I frowned at his use of the pronoun. Our? He glanced over his shoulder. 'Besides, we have more important matters to discuss.'

His tone was brusque and business-like but something about it set me on edge. 'What?' I asked, warily.

Lyle coughed. 'We will spread the word about what you have done for us, Chieftain. Every troll in the Highlands will know.'

'Uh ... thanks, Lyle. I didn't do much, though.'

'It's Kirk.'

I flinched. 'Sorry.'

'It doesn't matter,' he said earnestly, blinking up at me from beneath his heavy forehead. 'No other Sidhe would have done that for us. You care. You treated the dead as if they were your own family and we will never forget that.' The emphasis he placed on the word 'we' sent shivers down my spine; he seemed to speaking for far more than the three trolls next to me.

Sorley looked over his shoulder again. He was definitely skittish about Byron but I wasn't sure why - unless he knew something about what Aifric was planning. 'Sorley,' I began, testing the waters.

'He's going to poison you!' he burst out.

My stomach dropped. 'Pardon?'

'It's true,' Kirk said. 'We know what he's carrying.'

I could feel my pulse speeding up. 'We're talking about Byron here? Not Aifric?' I searched Sorley's face, attempting to quell my sudden anxiety.

Sorley stiffened dramatically, whipping his head from side to side. 'Aifric Moncrieffe is here? Where? I'll lance his head like a boil! I'll cut off his cock and—'

I held up a palm. 'Unless you know something I don't, our murderous Steward is back at the Cruaich.' Now it was my turn to glance behind. There was no sign of Byron. I couldn't believe that he would try to hurt me, not after everything that had happened between us, but regardless of logic my heart was still hammering against my ribcage. 'Let's slow down and take things from the beginning.'

Kirk swallowed. 'Byron Moncrieffe is going to give you a sleeping draught. It'll knock you out for a day. Lyle is supposed to watch over you while Byron and I travel through the Veil to retrieve the body of Matthew MacBain.'

The worry I felt hardened into instant, vicious anger. That wanker. That total wanker. He really did want to play the damned hero after all. I shook my head in disgust. Screw pacifism. I'd rip his sodding head off. Aifric was one thing but Byron and I had been starting to reach the point of no return in our relationship. We didn't trust each other but we weren't enemies. Far from it. The thought that he would do this stabbed into me. No doubt this was what his enigmatic comment about his father's supposed good intentions had been referring to. I struggled for control. He'd said I was manipulative but his father was a goddamned genius at it. And now he was too. How could he do this to me? How could...? My mind swirled. I struggled to reach for the shreds of my own rationality. It didn't make sense. I reminded myself to breathe. No. He wouldn't do this. He wasn't a bastard.

'Wait,' I said slowly. 'Byron's never struck me as a glory hunter and he's going beyond the Veil anyway, so he can play the hero whether I'm there or not. I suppose the Moncrieffes could be trying to ingratiate themselves with the MacBain Clan but they're already on good terms. So why would he do that to me?'

'The Lowlands are dangerous. He wants to keep you safe.'

I tried to ignore the sudden warmth in my chest. 'That's silly. I've been there before, I know what to expect and where Matthew

MacBain is. I'm not some delicate maiden and he knows that. He also doesn't have a clue about where Matthew MacBain's remains are.' I mulled it all over. 'Aifric gave him the draught, right?'

Lyle and Kirk nodded.

'Did he say anything about it to you? Or did all your orders come from the Steward?'

Kirk picked at a wart on his cheek. 'We picked up the Scrymgeour woman just after we left the Cruaich. He wouldn't say anything in front of her.'

Absence of evidence wasn't evidence itself. All the same... I forced myself to calm down. 'Well, we can pretty much guarantee that it's going to do more damage than send me into dream land. Poison is Aifric's weapon of choice.'

Even surrounded by darkness as we were, I could still see Sorley growing redder and redder. 'We force it down Byron's throat instead. Then he'll get what's coming to him.'

'I doubt he even knows.' I swallowed. 'I hope he doesn't know.' I glanced at Kirk and Lyle. 'You work for the Moncrieffes. Why are you telling me this?'

They exchanged looks, turned to face me and got down on their knees. I took a step backward. 'Wait,' I said. I'd been in this situation before; I didn't need more people on my conscience. It was just more to worry about.

Kirk was not going to stop. 'Chieftain Adair, we pledge fealty to you and your Clan. The honour you have shown us this night proves that you are more than worthy.'

Sorley got to his knees and joined them, clasping his squat fingers together and staring at me beseechingly. I addressed him. 'You said the trolls didn't swear fealty to anyone.'

'We didn't,' he answered simply. 'Now we do. We are yours, if you'll have us.'

'I don't know what I'm doing. I'm making all this up as I go along.'

Sorley smiled faintly, causing huge wrinkled lines to form across his cheeks. 'Chieftain Adair, will you have us?'

'Get up, you gobshite.' I sighed. 'Yes, I'll have you. This is going to be the strangest Clan that Scotland has ever seen. A Sidhe, a merman, a pixie, a warlock, a human and three trolls. Good grief.'

Kirk and Lyle both started but Sorley shook his head at them.

'What?' I asked.

'Nothing,' he said innocently. 'Now, what are we going to do about Byron Moncrieffe?'

***

Two hours later the fire was going and, much to Tipsania's disgust, Taylor had managed to produce some more tins of beans. Sorley, Lyle and Kirk had wanted to stick around but I persuaded them to stay down by the border. Despite their oaths, I wasn't sure I could trust them to not bop Byron on the head and slice off his ears. With everyone clued up, there were more than enough eyes to make sure that Byron didn't spike my food or drink while I wasn't looking. All the same, I was wary of his telekinesis Gift. He'd managed to switch drinks on me once before, so I still had to be careful. For his part, he didn't act any differently to usual. Neither did Tipsania.

'There is a huge dining room in there,' she said, jerking her head towards the mansion. 'Why aren't we eating inside?'

I smirked. 'There are cobwebs.' I gestured to the door. 'You're welcome to go in if you wish.'

It was obviously a struggle for her not to snark out a reply. She managed it though. Barely.

Bob yawned loudly. 'It's so boring here. There are no nightclubs. There are no pubs.' He pouted. 'I need some excitement in my life.'

Brochan sneezed three times in quick succession. 'Go back to your letter opener then. We don't need you.' He wiped his nose. 'In fact, we'll be better off if you keep away.'

'Brochy baby, don't be like that. Besides, you know very well it's a scimitar, not a letter opener. And I can't go back there yet. Daniel Jackson just died in *Stargate*. It's too emotional for me to return to the scene of the crime.'

'It's a television show! There is no scene of the crime!'

Bob shook his head sadly. 'You don't get it. You have no soul, Brochy. I can help you with that. Get Uh Integrity to wish you one.'

'Let me strangle him, Tegs,' Brochan appealed. 'Or at the very least tie him up.'

Bob instantly brightened. 'Now that sounds fun! A bit of BDSM is right up my alley.'

'You're disgusting.'

The genie tutted. 'It's perfectly normal.' He snapped his fingers and produced a length of rope. I was pleased to note that it was dyed hot pink. Atta boy. 'Uh Integrity, you'd like to be tied up, wouldn't you?'

I rolled my eyes. 'Bob, once upon a time, I was a master thief. I can pick locks, break into vaults and I can certainly get myself out of any knot that you could tie.'

He puffed out his chest. 'That sounds like a challenge.'

Tipsania was goggling at us like we were a bunch of maniacs. Byron, however, regarded me with interest and I raised an eyebrow in his direction. Did that kind of sex game float his boat? 'Okay then, Bob. Give it a try.' I held out my hands. 'Tie me up and I promise you that I will free myself in three minutes.'

'Done!' he yelled. 'But I'll have you know that I used to grant wishes for Houdini.' He crossed his fingers and held them up. 'We were like this.'

'Didn't he die in a failed escape attempt?' I enquired. 'Was that because of one of your wishes?'

Bob looked affronted. 'No, he died because of peritonitis. He'd wished to feel no pain, so he didn't feel it when his appendix ruptured and didn't seek help in time.'

Speck edged away from him and collided with Lexie. 'Sorry,' he mumbled.

'I like it when you get close, Specky,' she purred. He turned bright red.

'Come on then, Bob,' I said, drawing away attention from the embarrassed warlock. 'Get on with it.'

Bob flitted over and winked, then made an elaborate show of looping the rope and circling it round his head. He flung it towards me, whistling to himself as he knotted it this way and that, tugging at various points and frowning. He seemed to take an age.

'You know,' I said drily, 'if it takes longer to tie the damn thing than it does for me to get out of it, I'm not sure that it's entirely fair.'

'I'm done. Sheesh! Hold your horses, girl!' He flew backwards and admired his handiwork before holding up his hand for a high-five. Unfortunately no one obliged.

Taylor leaned across the fire. 'Byron, twenty quid says she gets out within sixty seconds.'

'No! Don't you dare!'

'Oh come on, Tegs. It's not a serious bet. It's just for fun.'

'I mean it, Taylor.' I glared at Byron to make sure he understood how much trouble he'd be in if he took the bet.

'Hey! I've not said a word? Why am I the bad guy?' he protested.

Why indeed, I thought sardonically. 'Just a warning,' I said aloud.

Bob sniffed. 'You do realise, you've already had forty seconds?'

'What? That's not fair! Come on, Bob, I've not started yet!'

He shrugged. Exasperated, I turned away and began to extricate myself. It didn't take long. In barely three breaths I faced them, dangling the length of rope in my hand. 'Piece. Of. Cake.'

Bob stared at me. 'You cheated.'

'Nope.'

'You did! You cheated. Was it one of those Gifts of yours?'

'No magic involved.' The corner of my mouth curled up. 'Frankly, your rope work is so poor that I imagine even a toddler could break free within seconds.'

'I want a re-match!' Bob demanded.

'I've already won.'

'Best of three?'

'No. Give it up, Bob. You're a sore loser.'

His bottom lip jutted out. 'I'm very good at rope work, it's just that you're either incredibly lucky or some kind of prodigy. Speck! Let me try it on you! I bet you won't be able to get free so easily.'

Speck pushed his glasses up his nose. 'No, thank you. Hemp brings me out in hives.'

Bob turned to Brochan. 'No,' said the merman. 'Don't even think about it.'

'You guys are shite,' the genie whined. 'You're dull and boring and—'

'Shite?'

'Yes!'

Byron stood up. 'I feel sorry for the wee man. Go on. You can try it on me, Bob. Tie me up.'

I felt a flurry of excitement. 'You don't have to do this.'

He shrugged. 'Where's the harm?'

'At least someone around here is vaguely interesting,' Bob said, zapping over to Byron before he could change his mind. He grinned as he looped round his hands and between his wrists, taking the rope with him. 'Is that too tight for you?'

Byron wiggled his fingers. 'Nope.'

'Damn.' The genie seemed disappointed. 'Do you mind if I tie your ankles too? I did such a bad job with Uh Integrity that I need to save face.'

For a moment, I thought Byron would refuse. Apparently Bob did too, because he didn't wait for a response but flew down to the ground, magicked up another rope and started tying Byron's feet. 'Okay!' he sang out. 'Your time starts now.'

I scowled. 'Why does he get a warning about the start time and I don't?'

'Quit complaining, sweet cheeks.'

We fell silent and watched Byron as he twisted one way and writhed another, straining against Bob's bonds. His face was taut with exertion but it wasn't long before it was clear that he couldn't free himself. He yanked at his hands and tried to wriggle out of the knots at his feet. When that didn't work he paused, and I could sense him trying to use his telekinesis Gift. Frustration clouded his eyes before he eventually shrugged and winked, as if to show he was a good sport. 'I guess I'm just not as skilled as Integrity,' he said. 'I give in. You win, Bob.'

Bob eyed him suspiciously. 'You're not just trying to be nice to me, are you? Pretending that you can't free yourself to massage my ego? Because I have other body parts that you can massage instead—'

'No,' Byron interrupted. 'You've got me. I'm well and truly stuck.'

I raised my eyebrows at Taylor. He nodded and loped over, checked the knots and gave me a thumbs up. I smiled. Lexie reached over and tossed my Byron's bag. I glanced inside, rummaging around while his expression grew darker and darker.

'Undo the ropes, Bob,' Byron said.

'Can't do that, golden boy.'

Byron look from the genie to the others and then to me. Lexie couldn't keep the smirk off her face. Tipsania got to her feet. 'I'll do it.' She turned to Byron and began to fumble. For a moment I felt worried but Bob grinned and gave me a minute shake of his head.

'They won't budge,' she said through gritted teeth. 'You used magic.'

Bob bowed dramatically. 'I'm a genie. Magic is my raisin debtor.'

'Your what?'

'Raisin debtor,' he repeated patiently.

'Bob,' I said, 'it's *raison d'être*. It's French.'

He stared at me for a second. 'I know that! I'm a magnificent being!' He turned and glared at Taylor and I instantly understood what had happened. No doubt my old mentor had been playing around with Bob and telling him porkies. I sighed inwardly. There had probably been money involved.

Bob sniffed. 'I was just testing you. Although,' he mumbled, 'I did wonder what raisins had to do with it.'

My fingers curled round an object at the bottom of the bag and sickness lurched through me. I didn't think the trolls had been lying but physical confirmation of the 'sleeping draught' was not what I'd wanted to find. I pulled it out – a tiny silver vial with veins of red running through it - and held it up towards Byron.

'Do you want to explain what this is?' I asked softly.

Byron glared at me. 'I'm certain you already know.'

I nodded to myself and dug out my phone, searching through the photos. When I found what I was looking for, I got to my feet and walked over, holding it up to his face. 'Remember this?' I asked. 'This was the group shot of us before we found the Foinse. Can you see what your father is holding there?'

Byron's eyes continued to flash cold rage.

'Come on, *babe*,' I urged. 'Surely, you can see it's your wonderful daddy holding a little vial identical to this one. Not long after this shot was taken, Lily MacQuarrie dropped dead from poisoned water. Poisoned water intended for me.'

'The photo doesn't mean anything because that is not poison,' he said angrily. 'The trolls. Lyle and Kirk. They gave me up?'

'They did.'

He tried to get to his feet and failed. Muttering a curse, he exhaled instead. 'Are we really going to do this here? In front of an audience?'

I didn't answer.

Byron rolled his eyes as if he were the wronged one. I struggled to keep hold of my temper, counting to ten as he continued to stare at me. 'I wasn't trying to hurt you, Integrity. It would just have put you to sleep for a while.' He was telling the truth. I closed my eyes for a beat. That was something. 'And,' he added, 'I wasn't even going to use it.'

Another truth. Feeling the others watching me, I gave them a stiff nod. Lexie and Speck relaxed slightly but I could still feel the animosity rolling off Brochan and Taylor. Bob, however, had magicked up a large popcorn and was watching us with a massive, cheesy grin and a pair of nonsensical 3D glasses.

'Why bother bringing it at all then?' I asked softly.

He shrugged with feigned nonchalance. 'Going across the Veil is dangerous. It didn't seem right putting you in that position. After all, if something goes wrong, there are lots of Moncrieffes. My Clan would survive. But there's only one of you. In the end, I figured that you can make that decision for yourself though. I didn't have much time once I received your summons and I was rash when I packed. It's not the end of the world.' He raised a pointed eyebrow. 'I've not actually tried to spike your drink.'

'You have before,' I snapped, referring to when we first met. 'Was all this your idea? To send me to sleep and go find MacBain's body on your own?'

'Yes.'

I gave him a sad smile. Couldn't he see how his strings were still being pulled even though his father was hundreds of miles away? 'You forget that I've got Kirsty Kincaid's Gift.'

'What the hell?' Tipsania exclaimed. 'You have her Gift? Truth Telling? The one she lost at the Games? And what exactly is going on here anyway? Byron—'

'Shut up, Tipsy,' he said tiredly. She flinched but he kept his attention trained on me. 'Fine,' he admitted. 'My father suggested it. But it proves that he's not out to get you because he wants to keep you safe as much as I do.'

I sighed. 'You really do still believe that.'

'For goodness sake, Integrity!' he exploded. 'If he wanted you dead, wouldn't letting you cross the Veil be a good way for that to happen? There are still thousands of Fomori demons over there. It's incredibly risky. Why would he want to stop you if not to protect you?'

'Why indeed?' I murmured. 'Why indeed?' I shrugged. 'That's a question for another time.'

A muscle ticked in his cheek. 'I can see how this looks.' He gestured with his bound hands at the little vial. 'I'll prove it to you. I'll drink it and then you'll see.'

I glanced down at the innocuous looking thing. 'Except,' I told him, 'then you'll be dead and I won't be able to tell you I told you so.' I checked my watch. 'I have to go or I'll be late.' I turned on my heel and began striding off.

'You can't do this on your own!' he shouted after me. 'Untie me and I'll come with you. No more sleeping draughts!'

'You had your chance,' I heard Brochan rumble. 'Now you're staying with us.'

'Tipsania...' Byron appealed.

'What?' she snapped. 'You've made your bed. You lie in it.'

I grinned humourlessly to myself. Clearly, she didn't like being told to keep quiet, even by Byron Moncrieffe.

'It's not fucking poison!' he yelled. 'Integrity, you can't do this on your own.'

I spun round. 'Because it's too dangerous?'

'Yes! And because you know Chieftain MacBain won't accept you doing this on your own. She doesn't trust you.'

'I don't think I'm the untrustworthy one here,' I snarled. 'You're not turning out to be much of a hero.'

Byron struggled to compose himself. 'Fine. Give the vial back to me. You know from your Truth-Seeking that I won't use it against you. And I'll prove to you once and for all that my father means you no harm because I'll take it to a lab and get it independently tested. Then we'll both know the truth.'

Now *that* was a damned good idea. Taylor, sensing my shift in thought, gave me a warning glance. 'Tegs...'

Byron softened his features. 'You don't trust me. Fine. But I don't trust you either, remember? You stole from me while I haven't actually done anything yet. Let me come with you.'

'Why do you even want to come?' I demanded. 'And remember I will know if you're lying.'

Two high spots of colour lit his cheeks. I blinked. Byron was embarrassed. He heaved in a breath. He seemed to be struggling with the answer. 'Fine,' he said eventually. 'I want to come because I want to be with you. I want to make sure you're safe. I want to help you out. I couldn't give a toss about Matthew MacBain. He's been dead for a generation. But I care about you.'

Nobody said anything. Lexie did clasp her hand over her mouth, however, and look rather delighted.

I bit my lip hard. Then I gestured towards Bob. He jerked up. 'Really?' I nodded. He shrugged to himself. 'It's your funeral.'

The tiny genie flapped his way over to Byron at the exact same time as Brochan stood up and wandered over. He flashed an uncharacteristically warm smile and then, without warning, drew back his fist and slammed it into Byron's jaw with a sweeping undercut. Byron's head snapped back and he collapsed with a heavy thud.

'What the...?' I sprang over.

'He's out cold,' Bob pronounced solemnly.

I wheeled round to face Brochan. The large merman was rubbing his fist but he looked incredibly self-satisfied. 'What did you do that for?'

'You're letting your emotions get in the way, Tegs,' he said with an unrepentant shrug. 'You can't trust him.'

'He was telling the truth! He wasn't going to use the poison!'

'But,' Taylor interjected, 'you don't know that he wouldn't do something later on when you least expect it.'

'You too, Taylor? You condone this?'

'Stop thinking with your heart, Integrity,' he said sternly. 'You know better than that. We win by logic not by heat.'

It had been such a long time since Taylor had acted like my mentor and told me what to do that I was momentarily bereft for words. I stared at Byron's prone form. 'We don't do violence,' I said finally. Tipsania snorted loudly but when I glanced at her she shrank back in what could only be a frisson of fear. Anger surged through me. This was why we didn't hurt people. Ever.

'He's not dead,' Brochan pointed out. 'He's just unconscious. You were already prepared to go without him anyway. Stick to the plan. It means you don't have to watch your back.'

I hissed in frustration. This wasn't the way we did things.

'They're right,' Speck said, pushing up his glasses. 'Bringing him along is too dangerous. You're better without him.' Lexie hit him in the arm but he ignored her in favour of blinking owlishly at me.

'But...'

'Do you trust him?'

My shoulders sank. 'No. I can't. Not with Aifric controlling his every move. Not with a price on my head.'

Taylor sucked air in through his teeth. 'There you go then.' He checked his watch. 'You'd better leave now if you're going to make the Veil by midnight.'

I glared at him then at Brochan. 'You still shouldn't done that.'

The merman's expression didn't change. 'Stay safe, Tegs.' He reached down and picked up my bag and handed it to me. 'We'll look after the princeling.'

'You...' I sighed and shook my head. I didn't know whether I was supposed to be angry or relieved. 'We'll talk about this when I get back.'

'I'm sure we will.' He gave me a tiny shove. 'Now go.'

I hefted the bag onto my shoulder and gave Byron another look. What a freaking mess. I sighed, turned on my heel and left him where he was.

Chapter Ten

There was a solitary figure waiting for me just beyond the Adair border. On my side of it, Sorley was gripping his spear with both hands. Judging by the way his shoulders were hunched and his head was thrust forward, he was glaring at the visitor.

'It worked?' he grumbled without taking his eyes off him.

'Yep.' In a manner of speaking anyway.

'You should have let me kill him. It would have been cleaner.'

I patted him weakly on the shoulder. 'I don't do things that way.'

Sorley jabbed his spear, pointing it across the border. 'Can you trust *him*?'

I pushed away thoughts of Byron and managed a grin at Angus MacQuarrie. He waved and dipped into a bow. 'He's sworn fealty, just like you.'

The troll's suspicion lessened only by a fraction. 'He has untrustworthy hair.'

I blinked. 'Eh?'

'It's the way it's styled,' he hissed. 'It's ... untrustworthy.'

Nonplussed, I stepped back. 'He's Sidhe. They all look over-styled, even the good ones.'

Angus ran his hands several times through his hair, messing it up. Now he looked like some kind of boy-band reject. 'Is this better?' he asked.

Sorley huffed.

'He's one of us,' I said. 'Now remember, I'll be back within forty-eight hours. Seventy-two at the latest. Taylor's in charge while I'm gone. If I don't come back...'

Sorley's hand trembled ever so slightly. 'We will come in after you.'

'No.' My voice hardened. 'You won't. You'll be free to stay here or to leave. But you will not come after me.' He mumbled something under his breath. 'I need you to promise me, Sorley.'

He jutted out his bottom lip stubbornly. I wasn't going to yield, however, and he knew it. 'I promise,' he said finally.

'Thank you.' I grinned. 'I really will be back very soon.'

I walked through the border, feeling the magic crackle around me. Angus bowed again. 'Don't do that!' I protested.

He shrugged. 'Would you prefer a handshake?'

I grimaced. 'A hug would be nice.' More than nice. I needed one.

He stretched out his arms and drew me in tightly. 'I'm a champion hugger,' he whispered.

'Thank you,' I said into his chest. 'Not just for the hug but for coming. You didn't have to. You can still change your mind.'

He pulled back and beamed. 'Are you kidding me? I've always wanted to travel beyond the Veil. I'm excited.' He leaned his head towards me. 'And terrified. But mostly excited. I'm not sure why you asked me, though. I reckon you can take care of yourself.'

'I can,' I said absently, moving away, adjusting my jacket and pulling out the headpiece. 'But Chieftain MacBain wanted a representative from one of the big three Clans to come along too.'

Angus squinted. 'I hate to break it to you, but that's not the MacQuarries. We're at the bottom of the heap.'

'You're at the top of *my* heap. But I know what you mean. Recent revelations mean I'm not going to follow her instructions and she won't trust me on my own.' My voice wavered slightly. Damn Byron. And damn Brochan too. 'You're the compromise,' I said to Angus and tossed him the Go Pro.

'What's this?'

'Strap it round your head. As long as you stay behind me, it'll record everything I do. We always have one on hand because it can be handy to look back on our, um, ...'

'Break-ins?'

I bit my lip. 'Yeah. It's fully charged so it should be good enough to satisfy Chieftain MacBain that I'm not looting her beloved uncle's resting place.'

'Nice.' Angus looped it round his head, making sure it was secure. 'Are we ready?'

I nodded decisively. 'We are.'

***

The MacQuarries might be the bottom of the heap as far as the other Clans were concerned but Angus owned the nicest car I'd travelled in for a long time. It certainly beat the rust buckets I'd been in lately. I did my best to put my woes with Byron behind me. He'd feel sore and angry when he came round but I supposed at least he'd be safe. Plus, I knew now that he really did care for me. It was time to start feeling cheerier.

'This thing is huge!' I said, stretching out my legs. 'You could fit the whole of Scotland in the back seat.' I grinned. 'It's an in-car-nation.'

Angus groaned. 'That might be the worst joke I've ever heard.'

'Give me time. I can do worse.'

'That's what I'm afraid of.'

'Hey, if it takes your mind off the hordes of Fomori demons waiting for us on the other side of the Veil, it's worth it.'

He winced. 'That demon you saw in Perth wasn't the only one that ventured through, you know. I've been hearing other reports.'

I sucked in a breath. That wasn't good. 'Just the Highlands? There's been no problem in England?'

He shook his head. 'I checked. Hadrian's Wall is still holding firm on the other side. I don't think the Fomori have tried to breach it.'

I thought of the group that had appeared at the Adair border. 'They're after something.'

Angus tightened his grip on the steering wheel. 'Or someone.'

'Aifric Moncrieffe,' I whispered.

'You think?'

I nodded grimly. 'I do. I found something in his rooms at the Cruaich that ties him to the demons but I have no idea how or why.'

Angus whistled. 'It would explain a lot.'

'Yeah. It doesn't bode well, though.' That was the understatement of the year.

He pulled the car to a halt less than fifty metres from the dark, cloudy expanse of the Veil. For a long moment he didn't say anything but simply stared at it.

'I don't want to take the car across,' I said softly. 'It'll draw unwanted attention. Matthew MacBain's body isn't very far from here. All the same...'

'You're the boss. Better safe than sorry.' Angus's voice was low and nervous. 'I've never been this close to the Veil before.'

'Most people haven't. I think we'd all prefer to pretend it doesn't exist. Let's face it, the Clan-less have got other things to worry about and the Clans don't need reminding of their greatest failure.'

He sighed. 'It does make you wonder, doesn't it? What might have been if it weren't for the demons?'

I thought about that. 'Nah,' I said finally. 'I don't believe in what ifs. We need to live with the hand we've been dealt. There might be an alternate universe somewhere where all this doesn't exist. But if that's the case, there's an alternate universe where Scotland doesn't exist in any form any longer either.'

'I didn't realise you were a student of Plato.'

'I'm not – but I do like *Doctor Who*.' I grinned. 'Let's do this.' We got out of the car. 'This is going to feel strange,' I warned.

A jagged bolt of lightning lit up the section of the Veil in front of us. Angus jumped. 'No shit.'

'Just stay right behind me. You'll be fine.' Without further ado, I ducked my head and plunged inside the Veil once more.

In theory, it should have been easier this time - after all, I knew what to expect and I knew I would come out the other side. Like last time, I held my breath. The smoky clouds which swirled round me still made my eyes sting and the myriad of lightning pinches felt more painful than I remembered. I started to run, willing myself to move as quickly as possible. All I could hear was the hiss and crackle of the Veil itself. I could no longer tell whether Angus was behind me.

I burst through the other side, choking and spluttering. Managing to stagger away a few feet, I spun round and tensed. Ten heartbeats went by, then twenty. Where was Angus? He should have made it by now. I was wiping my eyes and heaving a breath of the foul Lowland air into my lungs, ready to go back to retrieve him if I had to, when he fell through several metres to the left. He must have been confused and moved diagonally rather than taking a direct route.

As he fell to his knees, I jogged over, yanked a bottle of water from my backpack and handed it to him.

'Gah!' he spat. 'That was about the worst thing I've ever experienced.' I grimaced in sympathy as he chugged down half the bottle then squinted at me. 'What? No cheesy joke to mark the moment?'

I was too relieved that he was here and had made it through. 'No.'

Angus pulled himself to his feet. 'Then the situation must be worse than I thought.'

I managed a smile. 'Things seem as quiet as they were last time I crossed the Veil. We need to be careful though, especially with all the recent sightings in the Highlands. I wouldn't be surprised if we pass a cohort of Fomori demons heading this way. If it's easy as that for us to cross over, it's probably just as easy for them. There might be many more attempting it.'

He ran a hand through his hair. 'You call that easy?'

'We made it one piece,' I said softly. 'And as long as we keep our wits about us, we can make it out in one piece too.'

'Amen to that.' Angus wiped his forehead and looked around. 'It's not the most welcoming of places, is it?'

He was right. The landscape was exactly the same as the last time I'd been here – dark, gloomy and devoid of any plant or animal life. The ground was rock hard and almost black in colour. There might have been softly undulating hills in the background and the remnants of what had once been two cities in the distance ahead of us, but the Lowlands were far removed from the Highlands. Even on the dankest, wettest day in Aberdeen, the Granite City - famed for its greyness - there was an explosion of colour in comparison. And it felt a damn sight hotter here as well. My white hair, which was normally flyaway under the best of circumstances, hung limply around my face and shoulders.

'I'd like to tell you things will get better,' I said, 'but I'd be lying.'

'Maybe dawn will brighten things up.'

'I don't think dawn exists here.'

He glanced up at the dark sky. 'It's always like this?'

'Yeah.' I sighed. 'I don't know how or why, but the Lowlands seem to be in permanent darkness.'

Angus shuddered. 'Then let's get going. I don't want to spend any more time here than we have to.'

I nodded in agreement and we set off.

We kept up a good pace. Despite the desolation and lack of life, I didn't want to rush and end up tripping over any demons wandering up to the Veil. Neither did I wish to dally, however. Having Angus at my back was more reassuring than I'd predicted but I still kept scanning the horizon for signs of danger. There was nothing; the only sounds were our footsteps and our breathing. And Angus constantly fidgeting. He was more nervous about this little expedition than he'd let on.

'Tell me what you know about the Lowlands,' I said quietly.

He laughed sharply. The sound was strange and hollow, as if such sentiments could never be welcome here. 'I think you probably know more than I do. You've been here before.'

'Indulge me.' Anything to keep him talking and his mind off our task.

Angus sighed, although I knew without turning around that it was more because he was wondering where to start than with exasperation. 'We don't know where the demons came from,' he began eventually. 'But come they did. There are reports of sightings as far back as the mid-seventeenth century. Back then, Scotland was a very different place. Edinburgh was the seat of power and the Clans were too numerous to mention. There was trade and affiliation between different Clans but no single Scottish group was in control. There was no government.

'There were skirmishes,' Angus continued. 'They grew in size and violence, culminating in a vast, bloody battle near Stirling. The casualties on both sides were horrific. The way the history books tell it, the Fomori demons were growing in such numbers that they were impossible to beat. There are stories about some of the atrocities they committed.' He fell silent.

I kept striding ahead. 'Go on.'

He muttered something under his breath. 'Rape, torture, cannibalism. Do you really want me to go into detail?'

He had a point. 'Okay,' I agreed, 'skip that part.'

'Eventually,' he said, 'four Clans, whose numbers and strength remained the greatest, banded together: Darroch, Kincaid, Moncrieffe and...'

I tucked a curl behind my ear. 'Adair.'

'Yes.' His voice was grim. 'They pushed the demons back in one massive surge but it was only temporary. They knew it wouldn't be long before the demons retaliated.'

'So they had no choice but to create the Fissure and break the country apart.'

'Exactly. Using their combined Gifts, the Clans set up the Veil, forcing the Fomori to stay back. They took as many refugees from the Lowlands as they could before it happened, but we're talking a few thousand instead of hundreds of thousands. The English already had Hadrian's Wall in place. The magic there is ancient enough to keep out just about anyone.' He paused.

'Giving up half the country must have been a hell of a thing.'

'Yeah.'

I scratched my head. 'We can pass through the Veil and we've learnt that now the Fomori can too. Why didn't the demons push on regardless? If they were so strong, the Veil wouldn't have stopped them.'

I pictured Angus shrugging behind my back. 'My old teacher said it was because the Fomori already had everything they wanted. They had our Lands and they had us quaking in our kilts at the very thought of them. Why waste more lives unnecessarily?'

I pondered this then opened my mouth to ask a question. Before I could, however, something flickered at the corner of my eye. Shite. 'Something's coming. We need to take cover.'

'A fine notion,' Angus muttered. 'Take cover where?'

He was right. We'd not yet penetrated far enough to be near any buildings where we could shelter. There weren't any trees and the nearest hills looked miles away. I did have one trick up my sleeve, though. 'Hang on.'

I drew down deep inside myself, searching for the threads of Tipsania's Gift which I'd unwillingly stolen from her. I could feel her magic inside me. I closed my eyes and yanked on it, encouraging it to swirl up to the surface and envelop both Angus and myself.

'What the...?' he exclaimed.

'Shh!' I concentrated harder, I couldn't afford to get this wrong. I drew out more and more until I was absolutely sure. Then I opened my eyes and stared down at my hands. They were no longer there; we were invisible. If only I could mask our scent as easily.

From a distance, there was a harsh shout. Three figures came into view, apparently travelling from Glasgow to goodness knows where. My hand fumbled for Angus. When I found him, I gripped his arm tightly. We stood, unmoving, as the figures approached.

They were preternaturally fast. It was just as well I'd spotted them when I did because if I'd wasted any further time, they would have been on us before we could have done a thing. Yet again, I was struck by how the demons truly were the stuff of vicious, soul-sucking nightmares.

None of them was wearing a stitch of clothing. Skin stretched across their features, making them gaunt and almost skeletal, with sunken eyes and dry, parched lips. They loped towards us, their hairless bodies hunched and warped. I felt Angus tremble beneath my touch and I shared his fear. My heart thrummed like a caged bird making a desperate and futile bid for freedom. All we could do was to stay silent and hope they had stuffed-up noses and couldn't smell our presence. I had a vision of the demons sharing Vick's Vapo-rub and using delicately embroidered handkerchiefs to blow their bony noses. The image was so acute that hysteria threatened to overwhelm me. It was only Angus's presence next to me that kept me in check. I was responsible for his safety; I couldn't lose my head now.

The vile trio drew level and, without faltering, passed right by us. They continued their strange gallop as I breathed out in relief. I was too quick to relax, however; they'd barely gone twenty metres when the nearest one stopped in his tracks. The other two came to a stand-still and looked at him curiously.

'Vas?'

'File en chan,' the first one grunted and walked back in our direction.

I dropped my hold on Angus and clamped a hand over my mouth, terrified that my breathing would give me away. A waft of bitter sweat from the Fomori demon tickled my nostrils as he inched closer.

He stopped less than a metre away from our frozen bodies. He tilted back his head and sniffed loudly. It didn't sound like he had a blocked nose. I could see his chest expand, his ribcage standing out in stark relief.

I thought quickly. He could smell us but he couldn't see us and we had to use that to our advantage. Of course, I had no idea what Gift he possessed but if he used it, perhaps I could encourage my sub-conscious to steal it from him. If Angus stayed here and I...

The demon stumbled backwards and a strange expression crossed his face. His two companions, alarmed by his actions, sprang towards him. He spoke harshly and they both drew themselves up, their scrawny heads swinging from side to side as they searched for us.

'Vitarnic.'

All three nodded then sprang forward without warning. For a horrifying moment I thought they knew exactly where we were and were preparing their attack but instead they whipped past us, sprint-ing hard in the direction they'd come from. I didn't move or speak until they'd completely disappeared.

'That's not good,' I whispered to Angus. 'I think they know we're here. What do you bet they've gone for back-up?'

I felt him jerk beside me. 'That's what it looked like.'

'We should leave, go back home and re-group. It's too dangerous.'

'How far is it to MacBain's body?'

'Maybe ten minutes, I think. If we sprint.'

He drew in a deep breath. 'Then let's keep going. We just need to be fast.'

'Angus...'

'Integrity.' He cleared his throat. 'Chieftain. We are here for a reason. Let's complete our mission.'

'Matthew MacBain is already dead. We're not, not yet anyway. And what if it's mission impossible?' I asked.

'You're Integrity Adair. Nothing's impossible.'

Indecision warred inside me. We were so close now – and I'd given Chieftain MacBain my word. Besides, I was here for more than a collection of old bones. 'We'd better get a move on then. That demon, he had the oddest look on his face when he scented us.'

Angus remained silent for a few seconds. 'Fear,' he said finally. 'The expression on his face was fear.'

Chapter Eleven

Still invisible, we ran. My eyes darted all over the place, terrified that at any moment a vast army would appear, on its way to kill both Angus and me in the most brutal and painful manner possible. It didn't help that I wasn't sure which ramshackle little house Matthew MacBain's remains were in. When I was here last time, I'd been focused on other things.

At least with my worry about what might appear on the horizon, I wasn't looking at my feet as I ran and therefore avoided the strange nausea I'd experienced when Tipsania turned us all invisible. It wasn't much to be grateful for but I'd take whatever I could to keep my spirits up.

The small stone houses began to appear, lining the road. They were in an even greater state of disrepair than I remembered, with cracks and holes in the stonework. From time to time, I double-checked the roofs; that had been where the demons had sprung from – literally – when I was in Glasgow retrieving Dagda's harp. Fortunately, these outer reaches seemed to be as silent and dead as they looked.

With relief, I spotted the building where Matthew MacBain lay. I hissed a warning to Angus. 'On the left! The third one along with the broken door.'

'Gotcha.'

I sprinted forward, taking one last look ahead. There was still nothing. Darting inside, I came to a skidding halt in the gloomy interior, right next to poor Matthew's body.

Angus's voice drifted over. 'Wow. When you said there was nothing more than bones, you weren't kidding.'

'Yeah. He must have been lying here undisturbed here for years. With the rate of decomposition, there must be insect life around here. He's all but picked clean.'

I dropped my backpack and rummaged through it. It was as invisible as I was, making my attempts to find the body bag Brochan had fashioned almost impossible. I cursed loudly. 'This invisible-man malarkey would be a hell of a lot easier if I could turn it off and on when I wanted.'

'Yeah, about that...'

'I'll explain later.' My tone brooked no argument. Considering Angus was under fealty to me, he wasn't likely to argue. It was an odd piece of knowledge to have. 'Here, help me get him in the bag. We need to move quickly before more demons show up.'

I obviously hadn't thought this through carefully enough. Although both Angus and I took great care lifting MacBain's body and manoeuvring him into the bag without losing so much as a skeletal finger or toe, his bones weren't under the same invisibility spell as the bag was. When I zipped it up and hefted it over my shoulder, Angus squeaked, 'It's like a weird floating skeleton.'

'*Evil Dead* eat your heart out.' I paused. Half a dozen skeleton jokes zipped through my brain but I managed to ignore them. This really wasn't the time.

'This isn't going to endear Chieftain MacBain to your Go-Pro plan. She won't be able to see you.'

Shite. 'Look at me. Or at the body.' I stretched out my fingers until I could feel his face then made sure I was pointing in his direction. 'Chieftain MacBain, we have been forced to use a Gift to conceal ourselves but you can see that I am carrying Matthew MacBain.' I turned. 'Angus, move your head round slowly. Let the good Chieftain see that there's nothing else here.'

'Doing it now,' he informed me. There was a moment of silence before he spoke again. 'Hang on. There's something written on that wall.'

'It's not relevant. MacBain is only concerned that I might steal her family heirlooms.'

'But—'

'Leave it, Angus. Let's get out of here.' I edged back to the door and peered out. No demons in sight. 'The coast is clear. Let's vamoose.'

With Angus's footsteps right behind me, I ran as hard as my burden would let me. The bones clanked together sickeningly but I couldn't afford to be squeamish. I had to get Angus and Matthew MacBain back to the border.

Angus matched me step for step. Our invisible feet pounded the hard ground as we ploughed back towards the Veil. There were still no marauding demons behind us; maybe we'd been very, very lucky.

'I can see the Veil!' Angus called out. 'We're almost there.'

Praise be. I ran the last half mile, coming to a halt on the edge of the mass of the lightning-sparked cloud. 'Angus! Take my hand!' I jerked it out in front of me, searching frantically for his body.

'Here.' He lunged and grabbed my wrist.

'Don't let go,' I warned him. 'I can't risk you veering off again.'

'Believe me, I'm not letting go.'

I tugged and he followed. We plunged back through the Veil and I concentrated on staying in a straight line. One foot then the next; one foot then the next. Less than twenty steps later, we were out in the Highlands. The first streaks of dawn were appearing, lighting up the sky with pinks and blues and purples.

'Red sky in morning,' Angus muttered. 'Shepherd's warning.'

'Minced lamb and potatoes,' I returned. 'Shepherd's pie.'

There was a high-pitched scream. 'It's the walking dead! The zombies are after me. I knew it would come to this. I just knew it!' Something flew at my face, whacking into my nose.

'Ouch!' I shrieked. 'Bob, you bloody idiot.'

'Uh Integrity? Is that you? Run for your life! Run! The dead have arisen.' His voice dropped into an impressive Vincent Price impression. 'When darkness falls across the land—'

'It's morning. It's already light.' I took a deep breath and straightened up, rubbing my nose and wincing. 'And the dead have not arisen. This is Matthew MacBain. I'm invisible, you dolt.'

There was a pause. 'Oh.' He flapped round and peered at a spot several feet to my left. 'Are you alright? Did you manage to lose that MacQuarrie kid?'

'I'm right here,' Angus said drily.

'Oh. Better luck next time.' Bob raised his eyebrows. 'Is it a good idea to be invisible right now?' he enquired. 'I'm not sure this is the best time for hide and seek.'

I rolled my eyes. It was a shame he couldn't see me do it. 'I'm not sure how to remove the magic and I don't want to lose it just yet.'

'You think the demons are still after us?' Angus sounded nervous.

Bob pulled back his shoulders. 'Demons?' he squeaked. 'Fomori demons?'

'I think we're in the clear,' I told him.

'You *think*? Think is not good enough, darling. I need to *know*.'

'You're a magnificent being, you work it out. What are you doing here anyway?'

Bob's eyes widened as he tried to appear innocent and guileless. 'I thought I'd come and welcome you home.'

'Bob...'

'Alright.' His shoulders sagged. 'There's a problem – but it's only a teeny problem. In fact, I don't even think you should let it worry you.' He fluttered his eyelashes and clasped his hands together.

Worry squirmed through me. 'What is it?'

'I can't have this conversation with you when I can't see you. It's like talking to Skeletor.'

I gritted my teeth. 'Bob, I swear to God if you don't tell me I'm going to pick you up by the scruff of the neck and fling you into the Veil as hard as I can.'

'Jeez!' he whistled. 'Testy, much? I told you it's not that big a deal. It's just that Byron woke up…'

'That's good.'

'Mmm. Then he got himself free…'

'What?' I shrieked.

'And he came here after you…'

My voice got even higher. 'What?'

'And he went through the Veil.'

I almost dropped Matthew MacBain's body. *What?*

Bob winced. 'You don't have to screech like a banshee. It's just Byron Moncrieffe. I know you fancy the pants off him and he's your love bug and dreamy and sexy and—'

'When was this?' I demanded. 'Why didn't you stop him? How on earth did he escape? Those were supposed to be magic ropes.'

Bob heaved a dramatic sigh. 'So many questions.' He held up his index finger. 'About an hour ago. He was gone before anyone realised. He used one of the opened tins of beans to saw through the bindings.' He shrugged. 'I only protected them against magic. I wasn't expecting bloodymindedness. Anyway, didn't you see him?'

'Bloody great neep!' I yelled.

'Is that me you're referring to?' Bob asked. 'Or Byron Moncrieffe?'

I pinched the bridge of my nose. Unbelievable. Reaching round, I lifted the body bag and held it out in the vague direction of Angus. 'Here. Take this to Chieftain MacBain and tell her my promise is fulfilled. Then you'd better get yourself home.'

'Whoa. No way. Are you going in after Byron? Integrity … Chieftain … if he was foolish to wander in by himself then it's up to him to get out.'

I nodded. 'Yes, it is. But I was always going back in. Take the bag.'

Angus reached forward, fumbled with it and took its weight. 'You're really going back in? Through the Veil?'

'I have to,' I said simply.

'Don't worry, mate,' Bob chirped. 'We've already told her she's as mad as a MacQuarrie for doing this. She wouldn't listen.'

'I'm coming with you,' Angus said. 'After all, I'm a mad Mac-Quarrie.'

'Oops.' Bob pretended to look apologetic.

'No. You're not coming, Angus. I promised Chieftain MacBain she'd get her uncle's remains back. I need you to do this for me. Please?'

He didn't speak immediately. Not being able to see his expression was making this conversation incredibly difficult. Then he asked, 'Has this got anything to do with the words you wouldn't let me read? The ones written on the wall of that cottage?'

'Yeah.'

He sighed. 'The genie is right. You *are* madder than a MacQuarrie.'

'There's method to my madness.' I bit my lip. 'Thank you for all your help.'

'Hey,' he said, 'any time you need someone to travel through a fifteen-foot cloud of pulsating electricity into a scorched land where it's permanently night so you can play dodge with some ugly naked demons and turn yourself invisible in order to pick up a skeleton, I'm your man.'

I grinned. 'You're a good guy.'

'And you're still nuts.'

I spun round and shook out my hair. Not as nuts as a certain Moncrieffe heir I knew. Byron was an idiot for doing this; he clearly thought he could still play the hero. He'd learn his lesson if he ended up with his entrails hanging out and a demon munching on his brain. He was lucky I'd intended to go back and would be able to save his skin. If he needed saving.

'Uh Integrity?' Bob piped up.

'Yes?'

'I can come with you. You might need to make a wish. In fact, you could just make your last wish and then we can finish all this right here and now.'

'You're staying here. I won't be long.'

'Famous last words,' he said in a loud stage whisper, magicking up a noose and pretending to hang himself from it.

I tutted. And then I passed through the Veil once more.

***

There was no sign of any more demons; unfortunately there was no sign of Byron either. Without knowing where Matthew MacBain's remains were, he could have wandered off in virtually any direction. Yeah. He must have veered off course or Angus and I would have seen him.

I gnawed the inside of my cheek. I wanted to find evidence – or, preferably, a lack of evidence – that the Fomori demons had captives, the captive descendants of all those poor Scots who hadn't made it out of the Lowlands after the Fissure. I didn't know where to look exactly, although Glasgow or Edinburgh seemed likely bets. Along the way, I could search for Byron though I wasn't sure how much time I could devote to him. For all I knew, he'd strolled around for a bit and was now leaving the Veil at a different spot. Clan lordling he might be, but he wasn't completely stupid; he was an idiot but he wasn't a total idiot. Unless he was spotted by any demons, he'd probably extricate himself. Probably. But he wasn't invisible like me.

I took off at a jog. I'd expended a lot of energy in my sprint with Angus and it seemed prudent to recoup some of it by taking my time.

'Did you hear about the best way to confuse an idiot?' I whispered to myself. 'Show him two shovels and tell him to take his pick. Byron Moncrieffe should have brought a damned shovel with him. At least then he'd have something to dig his own grave with.'

I was already talking to myself; I was as crazy as Bob had suggested. I shrugged. If I already knew I was crazy, then I couldn't actually *be* crazy. Or something. I slapped myself round the cheek a few times. That was better.

By the time I reached the MacBain cottage again, I'd stopped mulling over the issue of my own sanity and was focused on my irritation and anger. I should have been glad that no demons had reappeared; instead, I was pissed off at Byron for complicating my life. At least I told myself that I was pissed off. That was better than being petrified.

I had a quick look inside but the building was as empty as it had been when I'd left. Maybe I should have brought Bob along after all. I dampened down that thought quickly. If I wished for Byron to get out of the Lowlands safely, he'd probably be followed by a teeth-gnashing demon who would rip out his throat the moment he exited the Veil. If I wished to be led to Byron, I'd come across his corpse. Wishes were just too damn tricky.

'He'll be fine, Integrity,' I said aloud. 'He's a big boy. He's not your concern.' My stomach still churned with worry.

I was turning to leave when there was a snuffling sound. I froze - I was sure the place had been empty an hour ago. Then I heard it again. I twisted round, scanning the gloomy interior. This was the point in horror movies where the dippy girl went to investigate the strange noise and ended up as victim *numero uno* of the serial killer. Don't do it, Tegs, I warned myself. I rose up on my tiptoes and stepped forward.

It could be Byron, I reasoned. Or it could be a Fomori demon on my trail. If I called out, I'd know for certain but it wouldn't be a wise move. I tiptoed forward until I was against the wall and, as silently as I could, pressed my back against it and hunkered down. The safest thing to do was to wait. The walls were damp and musty with mould.

My low position might mask my scent slightly. Right now, it was the best I could do.

The sound had come from the far corner of the house where there was another room. It was too dark and gloomy to see inside so I closed my eyes and focused on what I could hear. The snuffling sound continued, followed by a harsh, guttural *ack*. Crapadoodle. No Sidhe made that kind of noise. I clenched my fists and waited.

'Ack! Eg. It. Ee.'

Perhaps whichever demon was lurking around inside was trying to learn the alphabet.

It came again. 'Eg. It. Ee.'

Why couldn't they speak English? Captain Kirk never had this problem; every alien he met had no problem communicating. This wasn't even an alien and it sounded like it didn't have a frog in its throat but a warty toad with lung cancer. I hadn't understood the other Fomori demons when they spoke but at least the sounds they made seemed like words. I paused. Hang on.

I opened my eyes and cocked my head. A hand appeared round the edge of the lintel; I could just make out long, cracked fingernails. The hand was followed by a head – a remarkably familiar head, even if it did boast a lack of hair and several old, vicious-looking scars. My eyes travelled down as her body appeared. That looked like a tattoo on her shoulder and she was missing a nipple. I was right: it was May, the demon I'd helped after she'd been maimed by some of her colleagues for attempting to give me up.

My eyes narrowed. Of all the abandoned houses in all the world...? No. This couldn't be a coincidence.

'Eg. It. Ee,' she said again.

Her head turned and there was the faintest glow in her eyes as they swivelled in my direction. I forgot to breathe as she straightened up and her mouth opened, a wide tongue-less chasm.

'Eg. It. Ee!' She clapped her hands and rushed forward.

I held up my hands to ward her off. I might have helped her, and we might have managed to introduce ourselves, but she was still a Fomori demon. She'd also been wounded last time. She didn't attack me, though; instead her hands clutched downwards, digging into my shoulders and dragging me up. She pulled me forward in what I could only describe as a hug. Unfortunately, it was the strangest – and probably most unpleasant – hug of my life. When her cold skin touched mine, I couldn't stop myself shuddering.

Trying to free myself gently from her embrace, I stepped away. 'You can see me?'

'Ack?'

Shite. I took her hands and gently lifted them up to her eyes. 'Can you see me?'

She shook her head vigorously and pointed at her nose instead. 'Ay eh.'

'You can smell?' I sniffed loudly to add emphasis to my words.

May nodded, comprehension gleaming.

'May,' I hedged, knowing it was probably a pointless question, 'why are you here?'

I assumed she wouldn't understand me. We didn't have any words in common and there was no point of reference for us to bounce off. But she was a smart cookie; she jerked her head once and pointed to a scar on her neck which looked fresher than the others. Then she beamed her strange, wide-mouthed smile again. 'Eg. Eh. Ee.'

I swallowed. 'Integrity.'

'Eg. Eh. Ee.'

Close enough, I supposed. 'You wanted to catch up for old times' sake? Say thank you? It was nothing. *De nada.*'

May's eyes widened and she spun round. Alarmed, I followed her into the other room. She knelt down on the floor and started scrabbling around. Her fingers curled over something and she let out a crow of triumph. She hopped to her feet and presented it to me, flat on the palm of her hand.

I peered at it. When I saw what she was holding, my veins ran ice cold. May bounced from toe to toe and thrust the thing out to me once more. Reluctantly, I took it. It was cold, a warped thing made of what appeared to be iron. It was also incredibly grimy – but there was no mistaking what it was. It was a facsimile of the old Adair coat of arms, virtually identical to the one which hung over the ruined fireplace back at the mansion.

I stared at it for a long moment. How had she known? She hadn't given me this by chance. Her smile started to falter and she looked upset, apparently worried that she'd offended me.

'Where did this come from, May?' I asked quietly.

She shuffled her feet and looked down. And that was the exact moment that I heard the shouting.

I spun round, a knee-jerk reaction that propelled me towards the door and the outside world. May also reacted immediately: she lunged towards me, grabbing a fistful of material from the back of my jacket. As she pulled backwards, I pushed forwards. She clacked her teeth and made a low, urgent, hissing sound.

I wrenched to my right. May was still clinging to the invisible piece of material but the action allowed me to catch a glimpse of what was happening outside.

There was a cluster of demons, jabbering to each other and hissing – and encircling someone. I twisted, desperate to see more. There was a loud crack and several of the demons fell backwards, scattering to the ground as if blown back by a massive gust of wind. As they fell, they revealed Byron. His expression was calm but his shirt was ripped and, while he concentrated on calling up a fireball which sparked at his fingertips, he couldn't see what I could. I opened my mouth to yell a warning but May flung herself bodily at me, knocking me to the ground. I raised my head in time to watch one of the

Fomori demons swing a chunk of wood at Byron's head. He crumpled in an instant.

I writhed against May, desperate to get out there and do something to help him. Anything. She clung on to me. 'May, let me go!'

'Ack!'

One of the demons closest to us swung his head in our direction and his eyes glittered in suspicion. At that moment, however, Byron groaned and all attention turned back to him. Another demon clumped him on the head and he went limp.

A demon strode forward, hands on hips and pelvis jutting out. I recognised him instantly: this was the leader of the gang that had approached the Adair Lands. He frowned at Byron's prone figure then bent and grabbed a hank of his hair, lifting up his head to get a better look at his face. For what seemed like the longest moment, he examined Byron's slack features before finally turning and barking an order to someone behind him.

The remaining Fomori parted and, from behind them, came two thin and gangly humans. They weren't as naked as the Fomori – loincloths covered their modesty and one had a scrappy length of scarf wrapped round his neck – but they definitely looked cowed to me.

The leading demon jerked his head imperiously and the pair of them knelt down and hauled Byron up by his armpits, holding him between them. Byron's head hung loosely, his brilliant golden hair dull in this gloomy light. The two human men shuffled round, displaying a criss-crossed network of scars on their backs. They'd been whipped – and more than once.

I struggled against May's hold. 'I have to get out there,' I tried again in an urgent whisper. 'I have to get him before they drag him away.'

She wasn't having any of it and her response was to tighten her grip on me. I reached down inside myself. If I could find the last vestiges of the telekinesis Gift that I'd stolen from Byron, perhaps

I could do something. But there was nothing there; I'd used it up when Chandra and her team set up their ambush.

May's bony arms pinned me down and she hacked out an incomprehensible whisper into my ear. Without understanding the words, I knew what she was saying. There were too many of them and, if I went out there, I'd be captured too. All I could do was watch helplessly while the leader kicked his fallen companions until they struggled to their feet and returned to formation. They wheeled round and marched off, with the two humans and Byron between them. He was lost.

Chapter Twelve

It was some time before May released me. I guessed she was worried I was going to hurl myself upwards and start pelting after Byron and his captors. That moment – if it had ever existed – had gone now. When she finally relaxed her hold and I slowly got to my feet, all I did was stumble to where the scuffle had taken place and stare down at the marks on the ground. There was a strange, heavy emptiness inside me.

'This is my fault,' I whispered. 'The demons wouldn't have come here if Angus and I hadn't been spotted.'

I passed my hand across my eyes and, with detachment, noted that I was becoming visible again. I wasn't solid; I was more like an opaque, ghostly being. I knew it wouldn't be long before the last of Tipsania's Gift slipped away. A rescue mission at this point, and on my own, was futile.

May came and rested her head on my shoulder. I gave her arm a quick squeeze and straightened up. I had to get a move on. There was no telling how much time Byron had left.

I pulled away from May and started running back towards the Veil, calculating the time in my head. An hour to reach the Veil – less if I really pushed myself. Without mechanical transport, another hour or so back to the Adair Lands. I worked through different scenarios. There was a way out of this; I just had to find it.

I was so focused on my thoughts and plans that I'd been running steadily for almost fifteen minutes before I realised that May was behind me, keeping pace. I looked at her curiously over my shoulder. Her eyes were fixed on me and there was a half-hopeful, half-pleading expression in their glowing depths. I nodded once and kept going.

This time I barely even paused at the Veil. All I did was grasp May's hand, shuddering again at her icy touch. The part of me that wasn't consumed with thoughts of Byron wondered whether she was cold-blooded. Before I could think about it too deeply, however, we were inside the Veil and slamming our way through.

I didn't feel the relief I'd previously experienced at emerging in the sunny, colourful Highlands. I didn't have time. Unfortunately, I'd forgotten about the effect of the sun's rays on May's skin and eyes. As I started running again, she screamed and let go of my hand. By the time, I turned round she was curled into herself, a shivering, screaming, foetal shape on the ground.

I yanked off Byron's jacket and covered her shaking body. Her screaming subsided to a loud whimper but my jacket alone wouldn't be enough.

A flash of bright light made May cower even more. Bob, dressed in what could only be described as a superhero costume, replete with billowing cape and underpants on top of his trousers, beamed at me.

'So,' he grinned, 'what do you have this time to scare me with? Have you dressed bootilicious Byron Moncrieffe as a Fomori demon? Because, Uh Integrity, you can't fool me. I'll admit the skeleton had me going but you can't catch me like that again.'

'Byron has been captured by the Fomori,' I said tersely, ignoring his shocked look. 'This is May. I need to cover her properly or she'll burn to a crisp.'

'And May is...?'

I gestured in irritation. 'A Fomori demon, of course.'

Bob folded his arms. 'Yeah, yeah.'

'I am not playing this game,' I snapped. 'Are you going to help or not?'

There was the beep of a horn and I looked up to see Speck careening down towards us in the rusty car. I exhaled in relief as he jumped out. 'I need a blanket! Or your clothes!'

He blinked at me. 'Er...'

'Now, Speck!'

He knew me well enough not to ask questions. He ripped off his coat immediately and luckily it was a long, *Matrix*-esque affair. I grabbed it from him and hastily draped it over May, covering her as best I could and helping her up. I made soothing noises but she wouldn't stop whimpering.

'Open the car door!'

Speck did as he was bade and, with one arm round May's tragic figure, I helped her inside. She got into the back seat and hunkered down in the foot rest.

Bob's mouth was a perfect circle. 'That's a Fomori demon.'

'As I told you. Come on. We need to get home straightaway.'

'But Uh Integrity...'

I wasn't in the mood. I spun round, beckoned Speck to get in and hustled into the back with May. Bob merely gaped.

'Angus came back via us before heading onto the MacBain lands,' Speck threw over his shoulder. 'He said you might need a lift back.' He glanced at May. 'Is that really a Fomori demon?'

'Yes.' I waited for him to do his usual and freak out. Instead, he simply bit his lip and nodded then started the engine. 'Byron?'

'Is not here. That's why we have to hurry.'

The car wheels spun in the dirt as he made a quick U-turn. Bob appeared on the dashboard, staying as far away from May as possible. 'Speck,' he said seriously, 'I know we were joking about Uh Integrity being crazy before but now she really has flipped. She's gone through the Veil one too many times and it's addled her brains. I'm a magnificent being with superior power that you can only dream of and I'm telling you we need to perform an intervention.'

Speck turned the steering wheel sharply and Bob fell off the dashboard. 'Hey!' he yelled. 'Watch it!'

I put a hand on May's back. 'Just get us home, Speck.'

Thankfully, he drove like the demon May was.

***

Sorley held up his hand to stop us in front of the border. 'Chieftain,' he intoned, looking relieved as I rolled down the window. 'I am extraordinarily glad that you have returned. I just need to check the vehicle for any bugs or hidden intruders and then you can be on your way.'

I reminded myself that I'd given the troll *carte blanche* over security. 'Sorley,' I said, 'time is of the essence here. Just let us through.'

'I cannot.' He peered in, turning a shade of white that I would have thought was impossible for a troll. 'Demon!' He grabbed his spear and immediately thrust it into the car. My hand shot out, stopping its progress before it could impale May.

There were several high-pitched squeaks. I frowned and looked around. At least seven or eight little haggis fur balls were jumping around Sorley's feet. How odd.

Bob gazed at me smugly. 'See? You can't bring a demon here.'

I drew in a deep breath. 'I can and I will.' I looked away from the haggis and met Sorley's eyes. 'She's one of us. She needs our help. But right now she's not the only one in trouble. I need to get some things and get to a phone.'

Sorley didn't move a muscle. I thought he was going to refuse but then he stepped back and gestured us ahead.

'You stupid troll!' Bob shrieked. 'That's a Fomori demon! What do you think you're doing? She'll murder us all in our sleep! There's already been one massacre here and now you're going to be responsible for another one!'

I stretched my hand through the gap in the front seats and pinched Bob's foot, holding him upside down in the air. Then I pulled out the water bottle from my backpack, emptied the rest of the contents and rammed him inside it before screwing on the lid. He formed tiny fists with his hands and began to beat against the sides. I ignored him and tossed the bottle away. He'd be able to get out if he really wanted to.

Speck accelerated up the driveway, bringing the car to a screeching halt in front of the main doors. Taylor, Brochan and Lexie were already waiting. I flung open the door. 'Help me!'

They raced over. 'Is it Byron?' Lexie asked. 'Is he alright?'

I tugged at May as gently as I could. Speck got out too. 'It's not him.'

Taylor squeezed round to help me, his fingers brushing against May's skin as he did so. He instantly pulled back. 'What...?'

'Just get her inside.' I squinted at him. He swallowed once and agreed.

It took some doing but between us we got May into the mansion, up the stairs and into one of the few rooms which still possessed functioning curtains. I made sure they were tightly shut. May scuttled into a corner and hid her face in her hands.

Lexie, watching from the doorway, eyed me with trepidation. 'Is that what I think it is?'

'Probably,' I answered.

'Yes,' Speck said.

'Good idea,' Taylor broke in. We all turned and stared at him. He shrugged. 'Interrogation will help. We can find out all there is to know about the Lowlands from our visitor and then Tegs can rescue those forlorn souls trapped there.'

'She's not a prisoner.'

He did a double take. 'Er ... what?'

'You remember I told you about the demon I helped? The one I used the whisky on? Well, that's her.'

Taylor scratched his neck. 'Tegs...'

'No. Absolutely not!' Lexie looked at Speck and Brochan. 'This can't be happening.'

'She's not a bad person,' I began.

'She's not a person! She's a demon!'

I took Lexie's hands and squeezed them. 'If ever you need to trust me, this is the time. May is good.'

'May? As in sunshine and daffodils and dancing round poles?' Lexie flicked her hair. 'And you know I don't mean stripper poles, Speck, before you say anything.'

He muttered something under his breath. She glared. 'Don't worry about it,' I said. 'May's under my protection. She all but saved my life.'

'She's a *demon*, Tegs.'

I pointed to the shivering, huddled heap on the floor. 'Look at her. I mean really look at her.'

They did as I asked. 'She doesn't look dangerous,' Brochan admitted. He shuffled his large, webbed feet and avoided looking at me. Apparently someone was feeling a tad guilty. I pushed away my desire to begin protracted recriminations. What was done was done.

Lexie still wasn't happy. 'Yes, but...'

'Enough.' I didn't shout but the tone in my voice was so strong that the four of them stared at me in astonishment. 'If it makes you feel better, lock her in here. I don't think she's in any fit state to go wandering around anyway. I'll sort her out later and then you'll see what she's really like. There are other matters I need to attend to. Byron's been...'

My voice faltered as Tipsania strolled into the room. Her normally intricately styled hair was tied up in a dirty scarf and she was carrying a mop and bucket. She seemed as surprised to see me as I was to see her.

'Oh. You're back. I didn't realise this room was occupied. I'll come back.'

I shook my head in disbelief. 'Tipsania, what are you doing?'

She gave me a funny look. 'I'm cleaning, of course.'

I couldn't help myself. 'You?'

She sniffed. 'If you think I'm going to stay here while the place in this state, you are crazier than your friends think you are. You lot might be Clan-less idiots prepared to live in a hovel but *I* am not.'

Even Lexie's attention was diverted from May. 'There's no shame in being Clan-less,' she hissed. 'Although we are Adair.'

Tipsania sighed. 'Yes, I suppose you are. You should have stayed Clan-less. It would mean you're free of Byron's slimy prick of a father.' I did a double take. She glanced at me. 'You can't trust him, you know.'

'Tell me something I don't know,' I said, surprised at her words. 'Have you mentioned your feelings to Byron?'

'He won't believe anything bad about his father.' She sniffed as if it was of no importance. 'Most people don't. Anyway, I was going to talk to you about the whole Adair Clan thing. I want to stay. If you'll have me.' She shrugged awkwardly and looked away. 'I'll swear fealty if it's that important to you.'

I almost fell over and we all gaped at Tipsania. Even May seemed to sense the change in atmosphere because she stopped whimpering. 'What?' I managed.

Tipsania raised a hand dismissively. 'I'll become part of the Adair Clan and swear fealty to you.' She paused then dropped both her hand and her voice. 'Please.'

'Why?' I asked in a strangled voice.

She inspected her fingernails. 'My father wants to marry me off to Byron. If that doesn't work, he'll find some other noble sap. I don't want that.'

I noticed that her hands were shaking. She was also telling the truth. Wow. 'What about your responsibility to the Scrymgeours?'

'I have lots of cousins,' she said simply. 'They'll be more than happy to step into any breach my departure might create.'

Tipsania was obviously unaware that I had her father's true name and could make him do whatever I wanted. One word from me and he'd let her marry whoever the hell she wanted. I couldn't cope with this right now, though. I tucked my hair behind my ears and rubbed my face. 'You can stay,' I said. 'We'll talk about the fealty thing later.'

Her expression tightened and I knew she was thinking that I didn't want her in my Clan. Truthfully, I didn't; I wasn't even sure I wanted this damn Clan at all. Every time I turned around, there seemed to be more people clamouring to join.

Tipsania inclined her head stiffly then looked at May. 'Who's that?'

'She's a Fomori demon.'

For a moment Tipsania's jaw worked in shock then she shrugged resignedly. 'I suppose she'll need cleaning too.' She stalked over, knelt down beside May and started talking to her in soft tones. At that point, Elvis Presley and Lord Lucan could have strolled arm in arm into the room and I would no longer have been surprised.

I edged over to Brochan. 'Do you think Tipsania has been possessed?'

'It's possible,' he admitted. 'Listen, Tegs, about Byron...'

I held up my hand. 'I don't agree with what you did and if you ever do anything like it again then you will leave. I don't care who you are, Brochan, or what you mean to me. But,' my voice softened, 'I do understand why you did it.'

Relief flashed across his face. I gave him a tight smile. 'We have another bigger problem.' I tilted my chin and looked at my friends. 'Byron has been taken prisoner.'

Brochan swayed back on his heels, paling, while Taylor inhaled sharply. 'That's not good.'

'No.' I clenched my fists. All I wanted to do was to pelt back through the Veil and rescue him but my logic was beginning to reassert itself. I had to be smart. I had to take my time, think it through and do what was best for him. Blindly sprinting after him wouldn't make for a successful venture. I already knew that I'd have to wait until midnight when the Fomori demons seemed to sleep. I needed every advantage I could find to slip through undetected if I was going to find Byron.

Lexie raised her eyebrows and, her voice dripping with sarcasm, said, 'Let me guess. He's been captured by the Fomori demons? *Her* kinsmen?'

'I told you her name is May.' I sighed. 'But yes. I don't know what they're going to do to him but it's probably not going to be good.'

Taylor straightened. 'We've been in some tight situations in the past. This probably beats them all.'

Lexie snorted. 'I'll say.'

'Stop it.' Speck's voice was quiet. 'Do you think I'm not scared that there's a Fomori demon in the corner? Or that the Steward, who was already gunning for our blood, now has us to blame for his son being a Fomori prisoner? And that's without mentioning the bugs and the bats and the ghosts that this place has to offer. Of course, I'm scared. I'm petrified. But Tegs will find a way out. She'll have a rescue plan. She's our friend.' He paused. 'In fact, she's our family. We trust her so you need to stop complaining. It's really not helpful.'

I wasn't sure I'd ever heard Speck make such a long speech before. I'd certainly never heard him speak to Lexie like that. Apparently neither had she because, after gaping at him for a moment, she wound her arms round his neck and planted a very big, very wet and very long kiss on his lips.

'I'll get everyone to stop moaning if you stop going on about my gambling,' Taylor said in an aside to me.

'Nice try,' I told him. 'No chance.'

'I love you, Speck,' Lexie breathed.

He flushed bright red. Brochan ignored the pair of them and glanced at me with worried eyes. 'Can we get back to the matter in hand? What on earth are we going to do about Byron?'

I breathed in deeply. 'I need to get to a phone line.' I curled my fingernails into the palms of my hands until my flesh stung. 'I'm going to have to talk to Aifric.'

***

In the end, I was forced to take the car and travel more than forty miles north to get a damned phone signal. The thought of speaking to the man who had so cold-bloodedly murdered my father made my skin crawl but I couldn't rescue Byron on my own. I needed his help.

Brochan came with me for moral support. He was obviously keen to make amends. When I finally got bars telling me I had enough signal to make the call, I gestured at him to pull over. He gave me a long look. 'Are you sure about this?'

'It's Byron. I can't just leave him to rot.' An image of him strung up and horribly tortured sprang unbidden into my mind. I quashed it down with difficulty.

'I'm sorry he's been captured.' He heaved in a breath. 'But you still give that boy far too much of your concern,' he chided gently. I shrugged helplessly.

Brochan nodded once and passed me the number. With trembling fingers but a steely heart, I pressed the keys. Unfortunately, when the phone started to ring, my so-called steely heart lurched into imminent vomit.

I raised my eyebrows to Brochan. 'When does a horse answer the phone?' He squeezed my free hand. 'Whinny he wants to!'

He didn't smile. 'You can do this, Tegs. You're already the better person. Better than Aifric, better than Byron.' He paused. 'Better than me.'

I frowned at his last words although it appeared I was even more transparent now than when I was invisible. I took a deep breath and prepared to put on my best phone voice just as the ringing ended.

'Good morning. You have reached the Cruaich.'

'Good morning!' I trilled back. 'This is Integrity...'

'To speak to a member of the administrative team, press one. To find out when you can make an appointment to...'

I cast my eyes upwards. Automated bloody machines. I glanced at Brochan. 'Your call is important to us,' I mimicked.

'Your call is very important to us,' said the disembodied and overly cheerful voice.

I waited, eventually pressing nine to connect to a real person. At least the delay meant that some of my tension dissipated.

'Hello! This is Mhairi. How can I be of service to you today?'

Finally. 'Hello Mhairi. This is Chieftain Adair. I have an urgent phone call for the Steward.'

'Hold the line please.' The sound of some tragic bagpipe dirge filled my ears. Appropriate. I drummed my fingers and waited. 'Hello, Chieftain Adair. I'm afraid that the Steward is unavailable.'

'But...'

'Thank you for your time.' She hung up.

I cursed loudly. 'He's refusing to talk to me. Typical.' I sighed. I needed to try a different tack. I pursed my lips and located the Bull's number; at least after our last phone call, I knew he'd answer. Unfortunately it didn't make him any more polite.

'What?' he snapped down the line.

If he was going to dispense with the niceties then so was I. 'You are going to do me a little favour.'

'I don't have time.'

'I don't care.'

He huffed. 'Listen up, *Chieftain*. You might enjoy playing lady of the manor but the rest of us have real issues to deal with.'

'My heart bleeds.'

'Funny you should say that because I was under the impression that it did bleed for the Clan-less. I guess you're just like the rest of us, after all.'

I sat up straight. 'Explain yourself.'

The Bull couldn't refuse. 'You've heard about those little Fomori incursions, I presume? The one in Perth? The others further north?'

'Yes.'

'Well, it appears they were just the beginning. Last night, there was a full-blown attack.'

My world shrank in on itself. Fear tugged at my soul and I gripped the phone so hard, I heard the casing crack. 'Where?' I whispered.

'Aberdeen.' I didn't think I was imagining his note of smug satisfaction. I'd all but grown up in Aberdeen after I'd abandoned the horror of the Bull's household.

It was a struggle to get the words out. 'What happened?'

'Union Street is burning. Estimates place the casualties at more than two hundred. It's difficult to tell. We're never sure about how many Clan-less vermin there are in one area.'

The Bull was very, very lucky he was on the other end of the phone and not in front of me; at that moment, I would have happily renounced my pacifism. I'd almost felt sorry for him when Tipsania said she wanted to stay with me. I was starting to change my mind. A lot.

'What are you doing about it?' I said through gritted teeth.

'Well, it's the city's main thoroughfare so there are a number of Sidhe businesses. We are trying to put the fires out.'

'I'd hate to see a loss in Sidhe revenue,' I spat.

He didn't seem to realise I was being sarcastic. 'Exactly. The current economic climate is bad enough as it is.'

'Where are the demons now?'

'Apparently they've vanished but I have a feeling they'll be back. I wonder where they'll strike next,' he mused. 'Your lands are very close to the Veil, aren't they?'

What was going on? Why was this happening now? The thought that it was related to my incursions into the Lowlands nibbled at the edges of my heart. I couldn't breathe and there was a roaring sound in my ears. Brochan reached over and punched my arm. 'Ouch!'

'Have you hurt yourself?' the Bull enquired, not in the least bit solicitous.

I glared at Brochan but he merely shrugged. 'Where are you now?' I said into the phone, rubbing my throbbing bicep.

'I'm at the Cruaich, of course. All the Chieftains have been summoned to an emergency council. Well,' he amended, 'almost all of them.'

I didn't pay any attention to the snub. 'Take this phone and hand it to Aifric. Tell him it's a Moncrieffe Sidhe up in Aberdeen who needs to speak to him right away.'

'Lie to the Steward? He already mistrusts me enough as it is. Are you out of your tiny mind?'

Funny, Tipsania had asked me exactly the same question not that long ago. 'Just do it.' My voice hardened. 'Now.'

He huffed and puffed but he had no choice. I waited a moment or two, ignoring Brochan's repeated gestures to tell him what was going on.

'This is Aifric Moncrieffe.'

I breathed out. 'Your son has been captured by the Fomori. He's across the Veil and he needs your help now.'

Cold silence answered me. I wondered whether I'd have to repeat myself and was about to when Aifric finally spoke. 'Chieftain Adair, I presume.'

'You should have spoken to me when I first called,' I told him.

'I am a busy man.'

'Too busy to mount a rescue to save your own son?'

This time, Aifric's voice vibrated with anger. 'Don't you understand what's going on right now? The demons are attacking the country.' He blew out air, making the line crackle and hiss. 'This is all your fault.'

The truth-telling Gift didn't work down the phone but for some reason, I knew he wasn't lying. 'Because I went across the Veil?'

'What else, you brat? You're just as arrogant and narrow-minded as your father.'

His words had the opposite effect to what he intended. The hot tears which had been brimming in my eyes were held at bay and the pain I felt inside coalesced into an icy anger.

'Why did you try to stop me from going? It's a dangerous place. If I had died there, you would be free from blame forever.'

There was a pause. Aifric roared some garbled words which sounded vaguely like 'get the fuck out of here'. I made out some scuffling of feet and slamming of doors, then he came back on the line.

'You just don't get it, do you? This was the deal.'

I held my breath. 'What? What deal?'

When he answered this time, his voice was more even and controlled. Although I instinctively knew that this was it – that I was finally about to get some answers – I was also painfully aware that there was very little Aifric did without reason. Even with his only child in mortal danger, he still knew what he was doing. This was a calculated move. 'The deal to keep the Highlands safe.' He laughed harshly. 'You think all this is about you but you're just a leftover. It's your heritage that counts, not you. You're nothing more than a tiny piece of the puzzle. And an inconsequential piece, at that.'

Somehow I doubted that. He wouldn't keep going to such trouble to do away with me if that were the case. I stayed silent, however. I didn't want to interrupt him now he was on a roll.

'Twenty-five years ago,' Aifric continued, 'when I first became Steward, the demons sent an emissary. They wanted more land. Unless we agreed to move back the Veil, they threatened to come here. To kill babies, Highland babies. *Sidhe* babies. I put my own safety at risk to broker a deal to stop them from taking what they wanted. They agreed to it with a single proviso.' He paused dramatically. Considering I didn't think this phone call could be any more dramatic, it was a wasted effort. 'Destroy the Adair Clan. Wipe out the entire line and erase them from history.'

He was doing it; he was admitting what had happened. 'So,' I said, with a quick look at Brochan, 'you're saying that my father didn't kill anyone. You did.'

'What would you have you done in my place? Would you be brave enough to take one life in order to save a thousand?'

I knew I was brave enough not to; compromise your morals and you compromise the fabric of society. I didn't bother answering his question. 'Why?' I asked. 'What did the Fomori demons have against the Adairs?'

'The prophecy, of course,' he snapped. 'That the one Adair will save Alba.'

I froze. Aifric had used the old Gaelic word for Scotland but there was no denying the direct simplicity of the prophecy I'd heard so much about. I was the one Adair - I had to be because I was the only one left. But how could I save the entire country? My world flipped on its head.

Aifric continued blithely. 'The demons took it to mean that if an Adair lived, they would destroy the Veil and destroy them. They wanted you all dead and gone before that happened. In return, they left us alone. The only reason you weren't killed was because you were an innocent baby. I'm not a complete monster.'

Trying to overcome my shock at the revelation that I was supposed to be some kind of national heroine, I almost laughed. 'That's not true, is it? You wanted leverage against the Fomori in case everything went tits up. Plus, there was the small matter of the Foinse possibly failing. Even then, you probably knew the magic was faltering and you'd need me to help bring it back.'

'You're very cynical for one so young. *I* saved you. Now you need to repay that favour. Your trip across the Veil before the Games must have alerted the Fomori to the fact that the Adairs are not all dead and buried. That's why they've returned. They're searching for you. I could have persuaded them that they were mistaken but you went back to the Lowlands again. You just couldn't help yourself. You are the master of your own destruction – and my son's. The question that remains is how many are you prepared to bring down with you before that happens?' He spat in disgust. 'The only thing that will save Byron – and the rest of the Highlands of Scotland – is if you give yourself up to the demons. Then the Adair Clan will be finished for good and the country can live in peace. You brought this on your own head.' He waited a beat. 'And this is how you fulfil the prophecy.'

I swallowed. 'And what if I say no?' I asked, my mind whirling. 'You'll just leave your own son to be tortured? Enslaved? Murdered?'

There was a moment of silence. 'He's only one person. To send anyone after him would be to send them to their deaths. We can't beat the Fomori, we can only negotiate.'

'And your only negotiating power is me?'

'Your life for his. And Scotland's. Chieftain Adair,' he spoke the name disdainfully with his treacherous tongue, 'the choice is entirely yours.'

And with that, he hung up.

Chapter Thirteen

We sat cross-legged in a circle in the main courtyard. Although Brochan's gills were bristling, the tips of Speck's ears were bright red and Lexie was clutching the fabric of her skirt so tightly that it was a wonder she had any circulation left in her fingers, no one said a word.

Taylor was absent-mindedly rolling the water bottle, with Bob inside it, up and down his thigh. I could only imagine that the genie had elected to stay inside because he was making a point – whatever that may be. The continuous spinning motion seemed to be turning him green. Eventually, as Taylor paused for a moment, Bob rapped sharply against the plastic sides and glared. Realising what he'd been doing, my old mentor placed the bottle upright in the centre of our circle.

'Byron's already been gone for almost four hours,' I said, when it became clear that no one else was going to break the silence. 'We know from my first visit that the demons rouse themselves at midday. If we're going to mount a rescue plan, we have about twelve hours before we can head back into the Lowlands.'

Taylor folded his arms. 'You need to take Byron Moncrieffe out of the equation.'

'I can't.'

'You don't even know whether Aifric was telling the truth.'

I fingered a curl, wrapping it round my pinkie. 'He was telling a version of the truth. There are still a lot of unanswered questions.'

'Such as,' Brochan said, 'whether that damn prophecy is true.'

'And,' Lexie piped up, her eyes now filled with concern rather than censure, 'how the freaking Fomori found out about it.'

I released the curl and flicked it over my shoulder. 'They have Gifts too. There could well have been a Fomori demon with precognition who foretold the same prophecy as the Sidhe.'

'Prophecies are tricky things,' Taylor argued. 'They are only one possible version of the future. Our lives are not set in stone. Even if you sacrifice yourself, it might come to naught.'

I nodded distractedly.

'What about Aberdeen?' Speck asked quietly. 'Should we go up there and try to help?'

'That was my immediate reaction,' I admitted. 'But I get the feeling that whatever has happened up there has been and gone. By the time we reach the city, things will be under control.'

Bob knocked against the side of the bottle and I unscrewed the lid. 'What?'

'You could make a wish! That would solve everything.'

I put the top back on again. 'Aifric said that this all started because the Fomori wanted more land but that doesn't make sense. They have lots of land. As far as I can tell, the demons all live within the city limits. They've got acres and acres of countryside.'

'Tegs, I'm not sure how this started is relevant right now. I know you. You're going to do what Aifric said, aren't you?' Taylor ran a frustrated hand through his white hair and gazed at me. 'You're going to sacrifice yourself.'

I lifted my chin. 'Last time, the entire Clan was massacred. The trolls who worked for the Clan, the pixies, the warlocks and the mermen and whoever else had sworn fealty – they all died.'

Speck blanched. 'When we shared blood, does that mean...?'

'It doesn't matter. If I'm gone, they'll still come after you. Aifric or the demons or whoever. Sacrificing myself means sacrificing all of you too.'

They absorbed this for a moment then Lexie got slowly up to her feet and tossed back her blue hair. 'So be it. If you're going to kill yourself to save Scotland then so we are we.' She fist-pumped the air. 'For the Highlands! At least that demon hanging out upstairs with Tipsania won't be a worry any longer.'

'Martyrdom isn't my idea of a good time,' I said drily. 'I'm not about to throw myself to the demons on Aifric Moncrieffe's say-so. I'm certainly not going to do it to you.'

Her relief was palpable. 'Oh. Good.' She sat down again.

There were some muffled words from inside the water bottle. Once more I unscrewed the lid. 'Say that again, Bob.'

'I said,' he called upwards, 'I've known some great martyrs in my time. It won't be that bad. I'll make sure there's a statue built of you all. Something with a fountain. It'll be pretty. We could even make it pink.'

'Gee, thanks Bob,' Brochan said sarcastically. 'Except you're one of us so you'll need to martyr yourself too and become a piece of pink stone. And get out of that stupid bottle.'

Bob wrinkled his nose. 'Not until Uh Integrity apologises.' He paused. 'Am I really one of you?'

'Yes,' I told him. 'As I keep telling you. But I have nothing to apologise for.'

He got to his feet and began railing. 'You put me in a bottle! I am not the genie in the bottle! I am the genie in the scimitar!'

'Christina Aguilera would like you if you were a genie in a bottle,' Lexie pointed out.

Bob's brow furrowed. 'She is kind of cute.' Then his expression cleared. 'But no. Apologise or I'm staying right here.'

I shrugged. 'Stay there then.'

Before he could launch into yet another tirade, Taylor interrupted. 'So you're telling me that you're going to let Byron be tortured or executed or whatever by the Fomori demons and you're going to let the threat of more attacks hang over everyone's heads?'

'Don't be silly.' I forced a grin. 'I'm going to come up with a fabulous fool-proof plan to save Byron and protect the Highlands.'

'Ah.' He scratched his chin and leaned over to Speck. 'I'll give you good odds that by this time tomorrow we'll all be dead.'

***

I started with Perth because it was the closest city of any reasonable size. If I'd had more time, I'd probably have tried elsewhere but I was painfully aware that, as far as Byron was concerned, time could mean vital organs. And that was before I started worrying about what was happening in the rest of the country.

Speck parked the car as close to the city centre as he could and we all piled out. Lexie threw me a baseball cap. 'To hide your hair,' she explained as I caught it. 'So no one knows it's you.'

I tossed it back to her. 'I think the time for worrying about staying incognito is gone.' I didn't feel good about what I was going to attempt but it was the best I could come up with at short notice. 'It's probably wise to not let anyone see the Foinse though.'

Taylor held up the drawstring bag containing the magical sphere. It thrummed happily and golden light leaked round the edges of the cotton. It didn't look natural; if anyone happened to see it, they'd wonder if we were hoisting around a lump of radioactive plutonium. 'Is this going to make a difference?' he asked dubiously.

'I have no idea but having it with us can't do any harm. If we're lucky, it'll help me steal just that little bit more without damaging anyone too much in the process.'

'They're only Sidhe,' Speck grumbled. 'Steal away.'

I grimaced. My feelings on that matter were complicated. I'd just have to be careful, that was all.

I'd been slightly nervous that, despite the time of day, there wouldn't be any Sidhe around but I shouldn't have worried; apparently the terrible events up in Aberdeen had brought the locals out in force. Unfortunately, far too many of them were using the opportunity to make a big deal out of their status, stopping people in the streets. Both ends of the pedestrianised precincts had been closed off and there were burly Moncrieffe, Polwarth and Calder Sidhe bullying passers-by and interrogating them about their purpose. When one little old lady, who appeared Clan-less, refused to show any identification, one of the Calders conjured up a black cloud that enveloped her entire body. The Clan-less, whether they were little old ladies or not, were made of strong stuff but even so I could hear her screams from inside it and my blood curdled.

'What Gift is that?' Speck asked.

'Buggered if I know. It might come in handy, though.' I concentrated hard, focusing on the Sidhe and telling myself I wanted the Gift because it could help with concealment. I had to fight with my own subconscious; I didn't want to make anyone scream like that. My stomach flipped and I staggered. It had worked. I could already feel the magic flowing through me.

The Calder Sidhe let out a strangled yell and his own cloud dissipated. He clutched at his chest. His companions seemed to think this was the old lady's doing and prepared to advance.

'I've got this,' Brochan said.

He strode forward, reached into the cloud and yanked the woman out. She fell backwards with him. She was scratching all over and her eyes were wild, writhing white in their sockets. Even Brochan seemed to be affected and he started rubbing at his arm where it had connected with the cloud. His movements grew more and vigorous and there was a strange keening moan deep inside his chest. He jerked and twitched, then he began remonstrating loudly. The Polwarth Sidhe seemed to take umbrage at his interference and flicked his fingers. Whatever he'd just done, it wasn't good for us. Brochan's voice faltered and he began to choke.

'Tegs,' Taylor warned.

I grimaced. 'I'm trying.' It wasn't working. No matter how hard I concentrated, I couldn't make myself believe that I wanted any part of that Darth Vader-like Gift. Fortunately, another Moncrieffe Sidhe showed up, placed a hand on the Polwarth's arm and forced him to quit. Brochan gasped, apparently released from the spell.

'I know that guy,' Speck said.

I glanced up. It was Byron's buddy, Jamie. Shite. I didn't want to let him see me - it would just mean conversations and delays. 'Let's try a different street,' I suggested.

We moved away from the main thoroughfare. Brochan rejoined us soon after. 'Are you alright?' I asked.

He grunted in assent. We all pretended not to notice the red marks round his throat.

A female Sidhe, who could have been from the Jardine Clan judging from the colours she was displaying, stepped off the pavement and began to cross the street. 'Lexie,' I said, 'you're up.'

She grinned and nodded, peeling away from our group. As soon as she got close to the Sidhe, she started shouting. 'Are there more demons? Are you going to protect us?'

The Sidhe woman looked horrified. She obviously hadn't expected to be accosted on the street. 'We are doing our best,' she said in clipped tones and tried to move away.

Lexie wasn't about to let her prey go. 'Do you have a Gift? If a Fomori demon showed up right now, could you use it to help us?'

The woman tapped her foot. 'There are no demons in the vicinity.'

'How can you tell?' Lexie clutched at her arm. 'They could be on their way. An entire army. They'll rip out our entrails and use our intestines as washing lines. They'll chop off our fingers and toes and throw them to their children to play with. They'll...'

'My Gift is far-sensing,' the woman snapped. 'I can tell there are no demons anywhere near here because I can sense what's coming from up to two miles away.'

'Have you tried recently? When was the last time you used it? Because two miles isn't far, you know. All they have to do is teleport and...'

'Oh for goodness' sake! Stop babbling. I'll try now.' Her eyes rolled up into her head. I stretched out my senses. This time, I caught a snag of her power in the air. The trail of magic led me right to her Gift and it was a simple matter then to pull at the strands and draw some of it into myself.

The woman gasped.

'What?' Lexie demanded. 'Are they coming?'

She passed a hand across her forehead. 'No. I just felt a bit light-headed.'

'You should see a doctor about that.' Lexie beamed and danced away, leaving the Sidhe woman frowning after her.

'That'll be handy,' Taylor said.

I nodded. 'Definitely. Two miles isn't far but I can make good use of it. Maybe I can use it to locate Byron.'

'We should try down by the river,' Speck threw in. 'We might get a catch there as well.'

'Good idea.' I turned on my heel, forgetting how taxing stealing Gifts was. My head swam and I felt my knees wobble.

Brochan grabbed me. 'Are you alright?'

I squeezed my eyes shut until the moment passed. 'I'm fine.'

He and Taylor exchanged looks. 'You have to be careful, Tegs. You've never stolen more than one Gift at a time.'

'I told you, I'm fine.'

'If you pass out for days as a result of all this, your Byron is going to be pretty much screwed,' Speck said.

I couldn't argue with that. 'Just one more then. Something I can really use.'

A dark shape pushed off from the wall by the far side of the street. 'I can help.'

We all jumped. How on earth had someone managed to follow us and stay hidden? We were normally better than that. I squinted. 'Who are you?'

The figure bowed and swept off his hat. 'You don't remember me?'

'Fergus,' I breathed. 'The Bauchan.'

He smirked. 'At your service. It's good to see you again, Integrity Adair.'

'Yep. I'm kind of busy though. Maybe—'

'I looked you up,' he interrupted. 'After our last encounter. You had me ... intrigued.'

Damn. As much fun as that had been, this wasn't the time for more fake orgasms. If there ever was a time.

'You're an interesting person,' he continued. 'And now I've just seen a little more, I'm even more interested.'

'Mate, you need to back off,' said Speck.

'I told you,' Fergus said casually, 'I can help.' He kept his eyes trained on me. 'You can take their Gifts, can't you? That's what you just did.'

'I have no idea what you mean.'

'Please. You said you were busy. Let's not play games.'

I watched him. He had an easy smile and the manner of a con artist. I liked him. 'Go on then.'

'I make it my business to know the people in my town. Knowledge is power, after all. Tell me what kind of Gift you'd like, and I'll tell you if there's anyone in Perth who has it.'

'Tegs, this isn't a good idea.'

'It's alright,' I murmured to Speck. I raised my voice. 'What would you get out of such an arrangement?'

His eyes gleamed. He knew he had me. 'Bad times are coming,' he drawled. 'It's going to be survival of the fittest.' He winked. 'Or at least the smartest.'

I snorted. 'Or the most underhanded.'

He didn't take offence. 'Call it what you will.' His mouth crooked up. 'I want sanctuary with the Adair Clan. Not right this minute, you understand, but if and when the tide turns and there are more attacks. If there's war, well, you have magical borders. I don't.'

'You're not a very optimistic fellow, are you?' I gestured agreement. 'Fine. Lead me to a Sidhe with the Gift of my choosing and I will grant you sanctuary on my land.'

'Me and my friends.'

'You and your friends.'

'Tegs!' Taylor hissed. 'You don't know how many 'friends' he's talking about.'

I leaned back and lowered my voice. 'Are we really going to deny anyone safety if they need it?'

Speck coughed. 'I don't want to break up the party but I'm not sure the Adair Lands are the safest place.'

I placed my finger on my lips. 'Hush.' I went to Fergus and held out my hand. 'You have my word.'

He grinned and shook to seal the deal. 'What manner of magic would you like?'

I bit my lip. If I were anyone else, I'd ask for something powerful and violent but I was me. I thought of all those visions I kept having of Byron being tortured, not to mention the suffering happening up in Aberdeen. I knew exactly what I wanted. 'Healing,' I said finally. 'Lead me to someone who has the Gift of healing.'

Fergus snapped his fingers. 'I have just the person.'

***

Even though it was broad daylight, I was dubious about where Fergus was taking us. He veered away from the main streets almost immediately and strode down a small cobbled alleyway. At least he was setting a good pace. I couldn't stop repeatedly checking my watch; the more time that passed, the more danger Byron was in.

The alley might have been small and cramped but it was remarkably clean and well-maintained. Here and there, planting boxes hung off the walls. They contained little more than soil – it was far too early in the year for any spring blooms to be emerging – but I spotted some snowdrops stretching up their heads.

'I don't like this,' Taylor muttered. 'We don't know where we're going. We don't know what to expect.'

I understood his worries. Back in my thieving days, we never engaged in a heist without thorough planning and preparation. More and more these days we were flying by the seat of our pants, jumping into precarious situations without looking for an exit route. But then again, we'd never had this level of danger and imminent death to worry about before.

'Chill, old man,' Fergus said. 'She's my ticket out of here. I'm not going to jeopardise it.'

I pondered his words as we twisted right and moved further and further away from the crowds at the town centre. 'What do you know that we don't? Why are you so sure there are going to be more attacks?'

Fergus swung his head towards me, a curious look in his eyes. 'It's obvious, isn't it? They've not bothered us for centuries and now the demons are popping up all over the place. They're planning something. Whatever it is, you can bet it's not going to be good for the people of Scotland.' He sniffed. 'What I *should* say is it's not going to be good for the *Clan-less* people of Scotland. The Sidhe will hide behind their magical borders with their underlings to serve them. They'll be alright. It'll be everyone else who suffers.'

Brochan placed a heavy hand on my shoulder and squeezed. He knew exactly what I was thinking. If Aifric was right and my death would put a stop to the Fomorian attacks, then countless thousands could be saved. The stupid prophecy, which was the new bane of my life, would be fulfilled.

I wasn't particularly afraid of death; after all, I'd been brought up in the knowledge that my entire Clan was made up of corpses. But I wasn't going to run and embrace it until I had all the information. And I wasn't a lone wolf; my pack needed me if they were going to survive.

Fergus stopped in front of a brick wall. He turned and grinned. His expression was open but I felt my stomach tighten; there was no way out of here other than back the way we'd come. If there was going to be an ambush, this was the perfect spot. The others tensed as well but the Bauchan only laughed at our expressions.

'I hope none of you are afraid of heights,' he said. 'Because now we go up.' He pointed at a drainpipe that led up the building on the left-hand side, reaching up to the roof about five storeys above us.

Speck stuck his hand in the air and waved it around. 'Me. I'm afraid of heights.'

Brochan gazed at him askance. 'You'll brave the mad blue-haired pixie's wrath but you're afraid of that? It's not a skyscraper. We've been up far higher.'

Speck bared his teeth. 'When we planned it out and we had appropriate safety equipment.' He paused. 'Fancy a dip in the ocean after this, Bro?'

The merman's eyes narrowed but he refrained from making any further comments.

'Stay here and make sure no one else comes down this way,' I told Speck.

'If they do...?'

'Then yell as loudly as you can.'

He nodded grimly.

Taylor rubbed his hands together. 'It's been a long time since I've done any climbing. Let me go first.' He hoisted himself upwards. The drainpipe creaked and groaned alarmingly but it held his weight. He flashed us a quick smile and scurried up.

'He's pretty spry for an old geezer,' Fergus commented.

Speck, Lexie, Brochan and I glared at him and he held up his hands as if in surrender. 'Whoa. Sorry. It was intended as a compliment.'

'Perhaps,' Lexie said sweetly, 'you should keep your comments to yourself.' She sprang up after Taylor.

Brochan waited until she was pulling herself up over the edge of the roof before he began. I stepped back and frowned. Lexie appeared to be struggling; she was normally much more nimble. Perhaps she was just out of shape. When the top of Brochan's head reached her foot, however, I understood. Her legs flailed around and then her foot landed on his forehead. Her hands let go of the roof's edge and she balanced herself on one tiptoe.

Brochan cursed and snarled. 'What the hell are you doing?'

Lexie bent down, her head swinging towards his. 'You called me mad. Do you want to take that back?'

He scowled up at her. Taking that as a no, she pivoted on his head with all the delicacy of a ballerina and reached for the gills on the side of his neck. She stretched her fingers forward and began to tickle. Brochan's body shuddered. 'Do you want to take it back now?' she enquired.

'Fine! I'm sorry I called you mad!'

Speck applauded. Pleased with herself, Lexie leapt onto the roof, finally leaving Brochan free to continue.

'Crazy bunch of people you work with,' Fergus murmured.

I smiled proudly. 'Yeah.'

'You know, your bag is glowing in the most peculiar manner.'

I twisted away, using my body to shield the drawstring bag containing the Foinse from him. 'What of it?' I gave him a little shove. 'Your turn.'

Looking amused, Fergus shimmied up. As he hauled himself onto the roof, I nodded to Speck and followed. When I got to the top
and looked around, I finally saw where Fergus was taking us.

'That,' he said with a grandiose sweep of his arm, 'is the town res-
idence of Ochterlony Clan.'

We stared at the high walls and impressive façade of a large, ex-
pensive-looking townhouse. Directly below us was a perfectly mani-
cured garden, including a lawn worthy of Wimbledon, and a pretty
fountain.

Fergus jerked his head at the building next to it. 'That place
houses seven families and it's a fifth of the size. And it is used by one
Sidhe Clan family who spend less than two weeks a year here.'

Taylor raised an eyebrow. 'So it's empty and you've brought us
here to point out the inequalities of society?'

Fergus held up an index finger. 'Right now, it's very much occupied. And I suggest we all get down before we're seen.'

Lexie opened her mouth to speak just as the sound of a door
opening reached our ears. In an instant we were flat on our bellies,
peering over the parapet in a bid to keep out of sight but see what
was happening.

A human woman, dressed in a French maid's outfit, stood at the
door as a Sidhe girl with bright red pigtails flew out. She couldn't
have been older than thirteen or fourteen. A small dog barrelled
along at her feet.

'Just five minutes, Nana!' she cried. 'I've been stuck inside all day
and Baxter needs to run around.'

I put my head in my hands. 'Her? Tell me you don't mean her.'

'Got her Gift about two months ago. She's only the fifth person
in the whole of Scotland to be currently bestowed with the power of
healing.'

'How do you know all this?' Brochan asked.

'I told you,' Fergus said, 'I pay attention to the people in my town.' He looked at me pointedly. 'Especially the ones who are ... interesting.'

I drew in a breath. 'I can't steal a child's Gift.'

'She's thirteen years old,' Taylor said. 'Pre-Fissure she'd already have been married off and popping out more little Sidhe-lings.'

'We're probably related. My mother was Ochterlony. And she's just a kid.'

'So were you. You were younger than that when you ran away from them. That dog is being treated better than you were.' There was considerable rancour and bitterness in his voice about what had happened to me before I'd met him.

Below us, the girl threw a ball and the dog bounded after it while she laughed.

'You said she was the fifth,' I appealed to Fergus. 'Where are the others?'

'Two are in Shetland,' he said, referring to northernmost islands which were way out of reach. 'One is over ninety and hasn't left her Clan Lands in more than thirty years. I believe the other is currently hosting an emergency council meeting at the Cruaich.'

I started. 'Aifric Moncrieffe? His Gift is healing?' I couldn't keep the disbelief out of my voice. I knew he possessed telekinesis like his son, but a benevolent Gift like healing seemed beyond the pale.

'One of them. I thought you, of all people, would have known that,' Fergus said easily.

'God,' Lexie whispered. 'He killed all those people.'

Fergus looked interested and I shook my head at her to keep quiet. Fortunately she got the message – but she was right. How could someone who was Gifted with magic that had such potential for good be so damned evil? I watched the girl for a moment longer. If I only I could take Aifric's Gift instead. He wasn't there, though; the young teenager was.

'If you're going to do this,' Fergus said, 'you need to get a move on.'

I could feel everyone watching me. I pinched the bridge of my nose. There was no telling what stealing from someone so young might do; she might recover in an instant or it might be her undoing.

'I've got such little control,' I said. 'I could get this all wrong.'

'Byron might be injured...'

I waved an irritated hand. 'I know, I know.' It just didn't seem right.

Another figure stepped into the garden, a tall man with similar features to the girl. He watched her proudly for a second. 'Frances, it's time to come back in.'

'There's no one here! It's perfectly safe.'

A shadow crossed his eyes. 'We're leaving in ten minutes. You need to make sure you've packed everything.'

'We only just got here,' she complained. 'If the demons come, then we'll fight them.'

The arrogance of youth. No doubt her father was thinking the same thing because he shook his head in dismay. Then, however, his facial muscles twitched ever so slightly.

A tabby kitten appeared at his feet. It batted his shoelace and meowed and the dog instantly jerked up its head. A heartbeat later, it was bounding after the ball of fluff. The kitten tumbled and ran indoors with the dog hot on its heels.

'Did you have to do that?' Frances shouted. Her father frowned and rubbed his head, looking rather woozy.

'Illusion,' Brochan murmured.

I nodded. I could already feel it flowing through my veins and tracing into my soul. It might not help Byron but that didn't mean I couldn't put it to good use.

I scrambled backwards. 'Come on. I've got everything I need. We need to go.'

I felt a tug of regret as Frances sulked her way back inside. I hoped I hadn't condemned Byron to death by not stealing a tiny part of her Gift. Darkness gripped at my heart while the three new strains of magic pumped round my body.

Chapter Fourteen

My plan began to coalesce as we raced back towards the Adair Lands. Despite the severity of the situation, I was imbued with sudden, buoyant hope. There were a few problems but I could iron those out. There was always a way. I lifted my chin. I could do this. As long as Byron was still alive, it would all work out.

'You seem to have recovered your zest,' Lexie commented.

I grinned. 'When life gives you lemons, squeeze them in someone's eye.'

'You know what you're going to do,' Taylor said, glinting approval.

'I do. And when all this is over, it'll work perfectly in our favour.' I outlined my idea.

Speck swallowed. 'Is that really going to work?'

I bobbed my head. 'Yep.'

'If it does, it'll open up lots of possibilities for learning more about what Aifric is really up to,' Brochan said.

My smile grew. 'Yep.'

'It's very dangerous,' Taylor said.

I patted Taylor's arm. 'Life's no fun without some risk.'

'We should come with you across the Veil this time.'

'No. It's vital that you stay behind because you'll need to...' My voice trailed off as I saw what awaited us at the Adair border. 'Crap. A. Doodle.'

There were hundreds of them. Speck rolled the car to a halt and we all gaped.

'It's a sea of trolls,' Lexie breathed.

'More like an ocean,' Taylor said.

Speck shook his head. 'No. It's a bloody tsunami.'

'Stop using sea metaphors!' Brochan roared, loud enough to draw the attention of the nearest trolls. Their squat heads turned towards us. Like a bizarre Mexican wave, the crowd rippled until every single troll was staring right at us. Or rather, right at me.

'Reverse!' Lexie shrieked.

Speck crunched the gears but, in his haste, he couldn't work the gearbox. The wheels spun and the panic inside the car grew.

'There are too many of them!'

'Why are they even here? It must be because of Sorley. Damn that ugly bastard, I'll...' Taylor shouted.

Before he could finish his sentence, the mass of trolls dropped down. Lexie threw me a look. 'Was that you?'

I shook my head slowly. I pushed the handle, ignoring Speck's yelp of warning, opened the door, and stepped out. As soon as I did, the trolls' heads fell. Suddenly everything made sense.

I closed my eyes. I really didn't need this.

'Chieftain!' Sorley's familiar voice shouted.

I searched the crowd. He appeared from towards the back, stumbling to his feet. The trolls, still on their knees, parted awkwardly as he loped towards me.

'What's going on?' I asked faintly.

He wrung his hands. 'I wanted to warn you but you've been to-ing and fro-ing so much that I didn't get the chance. They're all here. *We're* all here.'

I passed a hand across my eyes. 'I can see that. Why, though?'

He straightened his shoulders. 'To serve you, of course.'

I cast my gaze across them. There were so many different colours on display. Many were wearing the livery of whichever Clan they had just come from; I spotted Orrock, Kincaid, Innes, Ochterlony ... in fact, I bet if I looked hard enough I'd see the colours of every damn Clan in the Highlands.

'Sorley, if they're all here, who's guarding all the borders?'

He grinned toothily. 'Who cares? The magic is still in place. None of those stupid Sidhe have the faintest idea how to maintain the boundaries but that's their problem now. They can do their own grunt work for once.'

'So,' I said, struggling to make sure I wasn't being obtuse, 'all the trolls have come here instead. To ... work for me?'

Sorley licked his lips. 'We swore fealty.'

'No,' I said slowly, 'you and Kirk and Lyle swore fealty. I'm pretty certain I'd have noticed if there was an army around at the time.'

'We are one and the same. My word counts for everyone's word.'

I stared at him. 'You're the trolls' Chieftain?'

'We don't have a Chieftain.' His brow furrowed even more. He seemed worried that I was displeased but I was more flabbergasted than anything. 'We speak for each other.'

I took several deep breaths. 'All I did was bury some of your old comrades.'

'No,' he said seriously, 'you treated us as equals. We will serve you and we will serve Clan Adair however you see fit.'

I looked round. Every so often a head bobbed up and beady eyes fixed on me. As soon as our eyes met, the head jerked down again. I felt like I was trapped in some strange Salvador Dali painting or that I'd gone to sleep and woken up as Eva Peron.

I opened my mouth and tried it out. 'Don't cry for me, Scot-laaaaaand,' I sang.

Sorley clamped his hands over his ears. 'What was that? You dunderhead! Is that what passes for music in your world?' He stopped. 'I mean, er ... shite. Sorry, Chieftain.'

'Not to worry. I was just testing a theory.' I bent down to speak in his ear. 'Could you get them to stand up? They're kind of creeping me out like that and it can't be very comfortable for them.'

He nodded vigorously and started waving his hands around. One by one, the trolls began to rise. Some looked embarrassed, others awed. I was pleased to note that one or two seemed sceptical;

at least they hadn't been brainwashed. I dreaded to think what five hundred Manchurian trolls would be like.

'Sorley, you realise we don't have enough food for ourselves? We can't look after this many people.'

'We'll work it out. The old woman said she'd help.'

I frowned. 'Which old woman?'

'Morna Carnegie. I wouldn't let her in without your permission and she said that there were so many of us that she felt claustrophobic. She went off for a walk.'

'Morna Carnegie is here?' Guilt flashed through me. She had caught my attention at the Games with her life-giving performance during the opening ceremony. She also knew exactly what I was capable of doing to Sidhe Gifts. I'd been supposed to go and see her to learn how to control myself but there was never enough time. I didn't have much time now.

Sorley scowled. 'Yes. She brought more haggis with her too.' Then he pursed his lips. 'We could always eat *them*.'

I breathed in. 'Let's wait before we skewer them, shall we?'

He reluctantly acquiesced. 'Fine. And don't worry, Chieftain, we know how to be discreet and unassuming. You'll barely even notice we trolls are here at all.'

Considering how many of them there were, I very much doubted that. 'Tell you what,' I said, 'let everyone through the border for now. We'll worry about later, well, later.'

Sorley beamed. 'Yes, Chieftain.'

I turned and waved to the others in the car to reassure them. Their faces were pressed up against the windows, their eyes wide and their mouths open. Even Brochan looked like a fish. 'Tell that lot to get themselves inside as well.' I checked my watch. 'I don't have long.'

'Yes, Chieftain.'

I began to stride away. 'I'm going to search for Morna,' I shouted. I spotted a haggis a few hundred feet away. It seemed like a good place to pick up the older woman's trail. I hoped she wasn't bringing more problems. If she fell to her knees and swore fealty, I might drop everything and find the nearest boat heading for Timbuktu. Enough really was enough.

***

I found Morna about a mile away. She was bending over, carefully examining a tiny patch of grass on this side of the border. I couldn't see what was so interesting about it but, hey, I wasn't exactly green-fingered like she was.

She didn't bother to look up as I approached. 'So you're finally back.'

'Hello, Morna. It's so lovely to see you again.'

'Why haven't you answered any of my summons?'

I blinked. 'What summons?'

She hissed in frustration. 'I've sent at least twenty! What's wrong with you, girl?'

'I didn't receive anything.' A haggis squeaked at Morna's feet. Suddenly I understood. 'Oh. You mean them. *You* sent them.' No wonder so many of them kept appearing.

'Obviously. I thought you'd understand that you should stop playing house and come and see me. You're not as smart as I gave you credit for.' Despite her words, her tone was mild. She brushed her fingers against the ground. As I watched, a cluster of tiny snowdrops burst up from beneath the soil. Wow.

Morna grunted, wiped her hands and stood up straight. When she looked directly at me, her mouth twitched. 'Ah.'

'Ah what?'

'You've been practising. I can see the magic in you.'

'Really?'

'I've been doing a little practising of my own,' she told me. 'When there's someone running around with powers as dangerous as yours, it seemed appropriate to put my knitting to one side for at least a short spell.'

I couldn't tell whether she was making me a joke or being deadly serious. 'Look,' I said awkwardly, 'it's very kind of you to come. But I can't stick around here. Byron Moncrieffe has been—'

'Taken prisoner by the Fomori.'

I drew back. 'How did you know?'

'I pay attention.'

I watched her for a moment. I should introduce her to Fergus. 'Well,' I said with a shrug, 'I'm going to rescue him. So I really can't hang about.'

'I wouldn't worry about him,' she said dismissively. 'There are plenty of Moncrieffes. Besides, I had the impression that he didn't want anything to do with you.'

'That was last month.'

She rolled her eyes. 'You might be able to draw Gifts inside you more effectively but can you stop yourself from taking them? Do you have the self-control to deny yourself something that you want?'

I thought of Tipsania and the way I'd had to run off to avoid stealing all of her invisibility. 'I'm working on it,' I said stiffly.

'Then you have to realise you're putting others in incredible danger.'

I cocked my head. 'Moi?' I clasped my heart dramatically. 'But I'm supposed to be the saviour of Scotland, not the destroyer.'

Morna sighed. 'So you've finally heard the prophecy.'

'Is it true?'

'How the hell should I know?' she snapped. 'You're the one connected to the magic and with the Foinse strapped to your back. No wonder your border feels so strong. It's not just the trolls bolstering it – you have the source of all magic here with you.'

I'd forgotten about that. I coloured. 'I didn't steal it. It just ... came here of its own accord.'

She regarded me seriously. 'Then I think you already know whether the prophecy will come true or not.'

I shivered involuntarily. 'I didn't ask for this.'

Her expression told me exactly what she thought of that statement. 'Deal with it.'

I unhooked the bag from my shoulders and reached inside. The Foinse buzzed as I drew it out. Bathed in its glow, Morna's expression was one of awe. I took advantage of her distraction. 'Is that why you're here?' I asked. 'You want to help me save the Highlands?'

The Foinse jiggled slightly then zipped up into the air in a giddy spiral. It tumbled across the border and vanished, unimpeded by the magic.

'I'm here to stop you from hurting innocent people by stealing from them,' Morna said when it was clear the Foinse wasn't coming back for more aerial displays.

She was telling the truth. I thought of how closely I'd come to stealing the magical essence of a thirteen year old. Perhaps she had a point.

I ran a hand through my hair, realising just how tangled it was. Using my fingers to work through the knots, I sighed. 'I told you. I'm going through the Veil to rescue Byron Moncrieffe.'

'You don't have time to dilly-dally around with love. What about the rest of the country?'

I gritted my teeth. 'I'm working on it.' Giving up on my hair, I dropped my hand and looked down at the ground. 'Can you make other things grow? Not just plants?'

'Maybe. Why do you ask?'

I tapped the corner of my mouth. 'There's someone I think you should meet.'

***

May was still in the same corner of the same room. The door was unlocked but Bob, who was still inside the empty water bottle, was sitting cross-legged and watching her in case she did anything dangerous like raise her head. I noticed that she had been cleaned up. She was wearing one of my over-sized Hello Kitty T-shirts. I tried not to feel irritated that Tipsania must have rooted through my things and reminded myself that I should be grateful she was making herself useful.

This time, Morna was genuinely surprised. 'That's a Fomori demon.'

I was getting a bit tired of people stating the obvious about May. 'She doesn't have a tongue,' I said briskly. 'Can you make it grow back?'

The Carnegie Sidhe just stared. I snapped my fingers in front of her eyes. 'Hello?'

She shook herself. 'I can try,' she said. She didn't sound very confident.

'We're all about trying around here,' I told her.

'You're certainly very trying,' Bob harrumphed, his voice muffled. I ignored him.

Morna held herself well back. For all her brusque demeanour, she was clearly terrified of May.

I edged forward and knelt down, putting my hand on the demon's shoulder. She jumped about half a foot in the air. 'Sorry,' I said.

'Ha!' There was a flash of light from behind. May squeaked in terror and buried her head in her arms again.

'Bob, you idiot!' I complained.

He flapped up to my face. 'You apologised. I knew you'd apologise sooner or later. You realised you were in the wrong and you're making amends.' His smile stretched from tiny ear to tiny ear. 'You are permitted to grovel now.'

I stared at him. 'I was apologising to May.'

'No, you weren't.'

'Yes, I was.'

'No, you—'

I held up my hand. 'Enough.' I turned my attention to the demon. 'May,' I said softly. 'This is Morna. She's going to help you.'

'I cannot promise anything,' Morna said.

I took May's hands. Her skin felt less cold this time. As gently as I could, I drew her up to her feet and she stood there, cowering. The hot pink T-shirt reached to her knees and looked ridiculous against her scarred, grey body. She looked like an embalmed corpse dressed for a children's party.

'Can you open your mouth?' I asked.

'Eg. It. Ee.' May whispered.

I nodded. 'Yes. Integrity.' I motioned to Bob. 'Bob. Morna.'

May looked at them both for a second and then flinched. I placed my index finger under her chin and tilted it up then I opened my own mouth and pointed, before gesturing to May to do the same. She started to shake.

'I'm so sorry, May. Please?'

She stared at me pleadingly, as if desperate for me to let her escape. The empathy I felt for her almost overwhelmed me but this was important. It would help both of us. I gestured again.

Still shivering uncontrollably, May did as I asked. Very, very slowly, she let her mouth to fall open. As soon as she did, both Morna and Bob gasped.

'Did we know that Fomori demons don't have tongues?' Bob asked.

I kept my voice even. 'May's was cut out.'

Morna moved beside me and took May's right hand. Obviously her own sympathy for the demon was overtaking her fear and she smiled reassuringly. 'May I?' She lifted her free hand to May's mouth.

May submitted like a whipped dog as Morna brushed feather-light fingers across the demon's scarred lips. There was the faintest change in the atmosphere and a look of intense concentration on Morna's face. Sweat broke out on her brow. May whimpered. I didn't think she was in pain or uncomfortable but she was still terrified.

After several long moments, Morna pulled back. 'I can't,' she said finally. 'I'm not Gifted in healing, I'm Gifted in growth. This wound is too old and the nerve endings are completely sealed over. There's nothing for me to work with.'

I forced a smile; it had always been a long shot. 'Thank you for trying.' I thought about Frances. 'Maybe one day we'll be able to persuade a Sidhe Gifted in healing to help her. I hoped May could tell me where to find Byron. I managed to steal some far-sensing, though. That'll probably be enough.' I hoped. A two-mile radius in an area the size of Luxembourg wouldn't be easy.

'You've already gotten into Byron's pants. Leave him with the demons. It'll do him some good,' Bob said. I threw him an irritated look and he grinned. 'True love. Honestly, it's much more trouble than it's worth. You're lucky you have a magnificent being with powers you could only dream of on your side.' He spun across to May. 'Var heptylon?'

I blinked. 'Bob? You speak Fomori?'

May stared at him. 'Ep?'

Bob turned and pointed at me. 'Byron a Uh Integrity.' He wrapped his arms round himself and pretended to be in mid-snog. To my amazement, May giggled. Bob smiled and snapped his fingers, changing his clothes into a kilt and a white shirt open to his navel. He puffed out his chest and swaggered. 'Gan ep var?'

May looked from Bob to me and back again. There was a sudden light in her eyes that I'd not seen since we passed through the Veil. She gave a little hop and began babbling. 'Ar. It. Ah.'

'Paper,' Bob said. 'And a pencil.' I was still gaping at him. He tutted loudly. 'Honestly, Uh Integrity. Jump to it! Paper, pencil. Now.'

I ran off, returning a few minutes later. Silently I handed the paper and pencil to Bob. He stared at the hot pink fluffy ball on the end of the writing implement and rolled his eyes then he gave them to May. She hunkered down on the floor and immediately started drawing, all the while jabbering to Bob. He nodded knowingly.

Morna tilted her head towards me. 'I've never heard of a genie helping someone out willingly without a wish before.' She looked at me appraisingly. 'Then again, I've never heard of trolls swearing fealty before either.'

'We're all about firsts in the Adair Clan,' I replied.

May leaned back, satisfied, and handed the paper to Bob. He squinted at it and shrugged. 'Well,' he said, 'it's no Ordnance Survey map but I think it's clear enough.' He thrust it at me.

I had no bloody idea what I was looking at; it was nothing more than a scribble. It was like looking at a foetal scan. But May was so proud of herself and I was ridiculously happy that she was no longer cowering in the corner.

'You really were absent the day that brain cells were handed out, weren't you?' Bob pointed. 'The castle.' He moved his finger along. 'The Royal Mile. A bunch of other streets.'

My expression cleared. 'This is Edinburgh.'

Bob looked at me. 'Hang on,' he said. He flew down, grabbed one of the spare sheets of paper, wrote a massive D on it and curled it into a cone. Then he deposited it on top of my head. 'That's better.' He glanced at Morna. 'Don't you think?'

I pulled off the dunce's cap. 'Let's focus on the matter in hand, shall we?' I jabbed at the X. 'I guess this is where the prisoners are taken.' I frowned. 'But that's not the castle.'

'No. And that would be the logical place to keep enemies of the state.' Bob frowned. 'It proves we can't trust your pet demon.'

I ignored him. 'If not's Edinburgh Castle, what is it?'

Morna looked over my shoulder. 'Arthur's Seat. It's the hill that overlooks the city.'

'You've been there?' I asked in astonishment. All I knew about Edinburgh was that there was a castle and... Nope: all I knew was that there was a castle. That's what happened when demons overran a place and stopped anyone from visiting it.

Morna tsked. 'Don't be ridiculous.'

I dismissed her comment. 'Well,' I said, 'I've got the power and I've got the destination. I'll memorise the route. Now all I need is the prince.'

'If she kisses him, he turns into a frog,' Bob said. 'Ribbit.'

May giggled and I grinned at her. 'Thank you, May. You might just have saved our lives.' She didn't understand what I was saying but I was sure she looked pleased.

'Hey! Don't I get a thank you?'

I blew Bob a kiss. His apple cheeks went bright red and he ducked his head.

Morna raised her eyebrows. 'Good luck,' she muttered. 'You're going to need it.'

Chapter Fifteen

Jamie showed up five minutes before midnight. We were all hovering around the border, stamping our feet and shoving our arms into our armpits to stave off the cold.

'You know,' I said conversationally, 'it's actually pretty hot on the other side.' They looked at me. 'What?' I asked. 'It just is.'

'I was expecting the lead-in to another joke,' Brochan said.

'Me too,' Lexie agreed.

'I can do that if you want.'

'No.'

'What do you call a Fomori demon crossed with a—'

'Tegs?'

'Yes?'

'Shut up.'

'One day,' I promised, 'I'm going to tell the funniest joke you've ever heard. You'll be laughing for days. Weeks, even.'

'I'll wait with bated breath.' Speck narrowed his eyes. 'And that is not a cue.'

'You just don't know genius when you see it.'

'I keep telling you all that,' Bob interjected. He raised his hand and I gave him a teeny high-five.

Tipsania, who for some reason had managed to invite herself along, tittered and we all looked at her. She tossed back her hair and grabbed my arm, leading me away from the others. 'Go on then,' she said, when we were out of earshot.

I stared at her. 'You want a joke?'

'No, you white-haired cretin.' Her lip curled in disgust. Anyone would think I'd just offered her a plate of mouldy Brussel sprouts instead of some fabulous humour. She sighed. 'Take my Gift.'

'Eh?'

'That's what you do, isn't it?'

I stepped back warily. 'Byron told you that?'

'You're like everyone else, you think I'm stupid because I happen to be beautiful.'

The words were out of my mouth before I could stop myself. 'You're beautiful?'

Something flashed in her eyes, reminding me of the Tipsy I used to know, but she didn't stamp her feet and walk off or slap me around then kick me when I was down.

'Do you ever take anything seriously?' she enquired icily. 'You're about to pass through the Veil and risk your life. If you die, who the hell knows what'll happen to all your little Clan-less friends? Byron might already be dead. Or worse.'

'This is how I cope,' I said. 'You act like a bitch to hide your vulnerable, soft-as-marshmallow centre. I act like a fool.' What I didn't add was that the fear I'd initially felt at Byron's capture was growing inside me like a malignant tumour. If I didn't stay focused, there was every chance it would overwhelm me.

'You got that right,' she said. 'The fool part, I mean. I'm not vulnerable.' She took a deep breath and in a great rush, spat out a trail of words. 'I-am-a-bitch-though-and-I'm-sorry-I-shouldn't-have-treated-you-like-that-I-have-no-excuse.'

I blinked. 'Excuse me?'

Tipsania composed herself and tried again. 'You are right. I am a bitch. I am sorry for what I did to you. There's no excuse.' She opened her arms wide. 'You took Kirsty Kincaid's Gift. I don't know how, and frankly I don't want to know, but take mine too. You've already had part of it anyway and invisibility could mean the difference between life and death. Take all my Gift and then we're even.'

Tipsania was right on one point – she was smarter than I'd given her credit for. I couldn't believe she was being entirely altruistic but it was a hell of thing to offer. As tempting as it was to take her up on it, I couldn't be sure what my limits were. I'd already drawn in three different kinds of magic. Any more and I might keel over. 'Thanks,' I said gruffly. 'It's probably not a good idea though.'

Her pale face tightened. 'Why not? It's not defective. *I'm* not defective.'

'I don't know what my limit is,' I tried to explain. 'I've already stol— I mean, taken – Gifts from three others. If I had more time to experiment then I would, but I can't risk taking too much and collapsing. Byron's already been in there for almost twenty-four hours. We can't leave him for much longer.'

She stared at me for a long time before speaking. 'There's nothing going on between us,' she said finally. 'Between me and Byron, I mean. I know it might look that way but,' she heaved in a breath, 'there's someone else.'

'I got that impression when you said you'd rather swear fealty to me than return home to marry Byron,' I said drily. I didn't mention that I already knew about Candy the Wildman. Tipsania was being more honest and open with me than I ever could have imagined; telling her that I was aware of her deepest, darkest secret probably wouldn't endear me to her.

'I could come with you,' she said. 'Help you out.' She didn't want to, that much was obvious, but the fact that she was offering made me realise that I had underestimated her. Not for the first time, I wondered just how much damage our forebears did in setting us against each other. Maybe she wasn't all bad.

'I'll be fine,' I reassured her. The headlights of Jamie's car appeared in the distance and I jerked my chin in their direction. 'I even have a plan.'

Tipsania kept her eyes on me. 'I really am sorry.'

The truth of her words sang inside me. An apology didn't make up for years of hurt and she still possessed a mean, bitchy streak. There was still that hint in her posture that showed that she believed she was better than everyone else. But we all had our faults and I knew deep down that her desperate words weren't just so she could absolve herself of guilt. Whatever her relationship with Candy was doing for her, it was making her a better person. I knew what it took for Tipsania to admit culpability and I admired her for it.

'I accept your apology,' I told her. To prove it, I bit back the terrible pun that was on my lips. If she could admit her past failings, I could show restraint.

She relaxed slightly. 'You know,' she said, 'for someone whose father was a genocidal maniac, you're not that bad.'

I stared at her. 'Gee. Thanks.' I paused. 'As I've already said, he wasn't a genocidal maniac.'

She simply gave me a pretty smile in return. We watched Jamie approach. When he pulled up and got out, it was clear that he'd rather be anywhere else in the world. 'Hey,' he said weakly.

I threw him an enthusiastic wave. There was no point in being anything other than zippily optimistic. He needed to see that I could do this – so did everyone else, for that matter. The glum expressions on their faces when they thought I wasn't looking were getting to me.

'Thanks for coming!' I trilled.

'Byron's my best friend,' Jamie answered. Despite his show of bravery, he had to shove his hands in his pockets to stop them shaking.

I walked over to him. 'Relax. I just need you to stay here. I asked you because I trust you. Byron trusts you. When I return with him,' my voice wobbled slightly, 'he might need medical attention.' I thought of Frances, away in the Ochterlony Lands. 'You'll be better placed than me to help him if he needs it.' Jamie looked beyond relieved then beyond guilty for feeling relieved. I patted him on the shoulder. 'The others will stay here until Angus arrives. He'll keep you company.'

'MacQuarrie?'

I nodded. It was all part of the master plan.

'And what are they going to do then?' Jamie asked.

'Oh,' I said airily, 'they're going to make sure Chieftain MacBain keeps her promise. She's sending a contingent to help clean up my Lands.'

Jamie looked at me oddly. 'While you're risking life and limb, they're going to be cleaning?'

I grinned. 'Yeah. I got the better part of the deal, didn't I?'

He didn't smile. 'Why did you steal the trolls? We need them now more than ever. Without their expertise, our borders are weakened.'

'I didn't steal them, Jamie. They're not objects.'

'Yes, but...'

'They chose to come to me.' I sighed. It wasn't Jamie's fault that he'd spent his life believing that everyone who wasn't Sidhe was at his beck and call. I softened my tone. 'Frankly, there are far too many of them. I can't feed them and I don't want them. If you want to persuade them to go back, then be my guest.'

'If the Fomori demons attack again...'

I chose not to mention that the people who'd suffered the most from the last attack had been Clan-less. The Fomori had stayed well away from any Clan Lands. Apart from mine, anyway. 'We'll worry about that later,' I said. 'Let's focus on Byron for now.' I reached into my pocket and threw him the brooch which May had given me. 'Here. Keep yourself busy while I'm gone. Use your psychometry Gift to find out what you can about that.'

He stiffened as if even touching it gave him the heebie-jeebies. He did, however, give me a tiny bow. 'I'll do what I can.'

'Thank you.' I met his eyes. I should have felt guilty about all of this but I couldn't muster up enough sorrow for it to make a difference. This was the way it had to be – for all our sakes.

I returned to my friends and hugged them tightly. Taylor, in particular, clutched at me as if he was afraid that if he let go I'd dissipate into a puff of air. 'I'll be fine,' I told him. 'I can do this.'

'The odds of this working...'

I drew back for a moment and frowned. 'Have you made a bet?'

He shook his head. 'Not this time. Not when you might not return.' He swallowed.

I enjoyed the safety of his arms for one more moment. 'I'll return,' I whispered. 'I keep telling you that I'm a bad penny. You can't get rid of me.'

His arms tightened. 'I'd better not.'

I stretched up on my tiptoes so that my lips were by his ear. 'Tell Tipsania the truth about what we're planning.'

He was so surprised that he jerked his head back. That would have been fine except Speck was standing right behind him and he received an inadvertent head butt as a result. The warlock let out a sharp howl and glared.

'Are you sure?' Taylor asked me.

I glanced at her. Tipsania's fingers were twitching, plucking anxiously at the folds of her skirt. There was a lot at stake for her as well. I could ask her to swear fealty – she had already offered to do so after all – but somehow I knew it was better not to go down that road.

'Yeah.' It felt right.

'You're the boss.'

'You're not going to try and tell me I'm wrong?'

Taylor smiled. 'You're not a little girl, Tegs, you're my Chieftain. Brochan and I shouldn't have argued with you about Byron. Go bring your boy home.'

My bottom lip trembled. I stepped away and looked at the others. Lexie had a curious sheen to her eyes that probably mirrored my own. Speck's glasses had fogged up and Brochan wouldn't look at me.

I raised my hand. 'I'll be back before you know it.' And then, before I had to look at their forced smiles, I spun round and plunged back through the Veil. Third time lucky.

**

Secrecy was far more important than speed. I had to keep my presence hidden; it was the only way I had a chance of rescuing Byron. Rather than rushing, I took my time. I had to be absolutely sure that there were no demons around. I was even wearing the Hello Kitty t-shirt which I'd taken from a reluctant May. It reeked to high heaven but, if it helped to disguise my scent, it was worth it.

I skirted away from the route I'd taken on my two previous visits. I was heading in a different direction and I needed to change others' expectations. If I were a balding, ugly demon with murder in my heart, I'd expect the object of my desire - me - to take the same path she'd taken before. Of course, if I *were* that demon and I possessed any iota of sense, I'd also keep an eye out everywhere else too. But I reasoned that the demons couldn't be everywhere at once.

There was a considerable expanse of land between here and the old capital. Aifric had said that the Fomori had wanted more land but that didn't make sense; they really did have all the space they could possibly want or need. With the sky obscured as it was, they didn't grow anything; not even weeds could live in this barren landscape. I couldn't see the Fomori as farmers; whatever they ate – and I was trying not to think about that part too much – the need for more land was the one point I was sure Aifric was lying about. The other thing I couldn't reconcile was that he was prepared to lose his son because of whatever was going on with the demons. That was a level of unfeeling callousness that, even knowing what I already did about him, was impossible to fathom.

Although I was travelling in a different direction, the Lowlands were still depressing in their uniformity. The atmosphere was sticky and unpleasantly humid; the ground was hard and dark. Everything was still shrouded in an unshakeable evil. The idea that Byron might spend his last hours on earth here was untenable. I set my jaw. His father might not care enough about him to mount a rescue but I was damned if I was going to abandon him – no matter how little he trusted me.

I was just getting used to the silence when there was a low whistle. Managing not to shriek out loud, I lunged for the tiny figure that appeared from nowhere. I'd left Bob's scimitar back at the Adair mansion so he must have hitched a ride without me noticing.

'What the hell are you doing here?' I hissed. 'You know I can't risk this getting screwed up!'

'It *is* pretty grim, Uh Integrity,' he said. 'Let me take you somewhere nicer. The Caribbean is looking particularly good at the moment.'

'Bob, so help me God...'

He sighed dramatically. 'I thought you might need some help. And if not help, then some company. It's not my fault that you can't control yourself when I'm around. You only have one wish left anyway. How much damage can one teeny little request do?'

I glared at him but his face was the picture of innocence. He knew damned well just how much damage could be wrought. If I found Byron and he was in a bad way, there was no telling what I'd wish for. Bob could harp on about self-control all he wanted, but if temptation was there I'd reach for it if I couldn't see any other way. And the consequences could be catastrophic.

'Get yourself back home,' I told him. 'Now.'

'You're not my boss.' He paused. 'Well, you are, sort of. But I'm tied to you. I can't risk you dying before I get what I'm owed.'

'I'm not going to die. Besides, if I die you'll just find a new owner who'll probably be more than happy to make lots of wishes.'

Bob scowled. 'The merman said that if you die, he'll bury my scimitar in the ground.'

'I doubt he meant it.'

'He did.' Bob flounced. 'I know he did.' He leaned into my ear. 'I don't think he likes me. It hurts my feelings. I'm a congenial genie.' He flashed a grin. 'Congenial genie. Cool, huh?'

I rolled my eyes. 'Do you see what I'm doing now? Where we are? I do not have time for your petty bullshit.'

'Just because you don't care what others think doesn't mean the rest of us can be so blasé.' He stuck out his tongue. 'Just for that, I won't tell you about the twenty demons that are about to show up.'

I froze. Shite. Bob beamed and burrowed his way back into my bag while I swung my eyes from left to right. I couldn't see anything but I knew that the Fomori could move at ridiculous speeds. They could be on me at any moment. I twisted round, checking my back. Nothing there. The Veil was already out of sight. Where...?

'Made you look,' Bob trilled.

I counted to ten very slowly; when that didn't work, I lunged for Bob's squirming figure. 'Hey!' he cried. 'You make jokes all the time. Obviously you don't like it when you're on the receiving end.'

'Why the hell doesn't Kirsty Kincaid's truth-telling Gift work with you? Nothing told me that was a lie.'

He tossed his head. 'Duh. I wasn't lying, I was telling a joke.' He waved his tiny hand in the air. 'It's all about intentions, darling.'

My eyes narrowed. That was an interesting – and sobering - difference. 'It wasn't a joke because it wasn't funny.'

'Then how do you get away with being unfunny all the time?' he enquired. 'Besides, it was a little bit funny. The way you panicked...' He halted mid-speech and his eyes widened. 'There are demons heading right this way.'

'I'm not going to fall for that again, Bob.'

'I'm being serious this time! Uh Integrity, hide!'

Even Bob couldn't fake that note of terror. I flung myself on the ground and flattened my body as much as I could. My heartbeat was so loud that I was certain any creature within a ten-mile radius could hear it. I did what I could to regulate my breathing.

The only saving grace was that the demons, who numbered at least thirty, were taking some pre-designated route which didn't involve coming this way. I watched them; it was difficult to tell from this distance but there seemed to be a tension about them that I'd not seen in our previous encounters.

I thought about what Angus had said about the look of fear on the other demon's face. I considered what I knew of the prophecy. Were they more afraid of me than I was of them? The thought wasn't comforting. Fear made all living creatures act rashly; in terms of fight or flight, it didn't take a genius to work out which option the demons would take.

I was worried that the troop was heading to the Veil to attempt another attack on the Highlands but they veered away from the border. They were searching for something. Or someone. I nibbled on the inside of my cheek. Hm.

'Uh Integrity,' Bob whispered, once they were out of sight, 'I have a bad feeling about this.'

I swallowed. 'Me too.'

'Is he really worth it?'

There was no point asking who Bob was referring to. 'It's not just Byron,' I said. 'The Fomori have enslaved others. They need my help too.'

'You don't know that. They might be perfectly happy working for the demons.'

I didn't bother to answer. Bob sighed. 'You don't know how many are enslaved. You wouldn't come to their rescue without knowing as much as you could about them first. Don't kid yourself. No matter what is going on in this godforsaken land, you're here for Byron Moncrieffe. There's no shame in it but you're risking your life for someone who doesn't believe a word that comes out of your mouth.' There was no censure in his tone; there wasn't even any amusement. He was merely stating a fact.

I inhaled deeply. 'I've accused his father of genocide, of trying to kill me. Why would he believe me? It's his *father*.'

'He didn't choose Aifric Moncrieffe as his father. He chose you, though.'

I shook my head sadly. 'I don't think it's possible to choose who you fall in love with. If it was, the world would be a far happier place.'

'You think he's in love with you?'

I shrugged awkwardly and stood up. 'I don't know, Bob. I think he feels a hell of a lot of lust for me, whether he wants to or not.'

'Are you in love with him?'

I thought about the way I couldn't get him out of my head. The way his golden hair flopped across his forehead. How his green eyes flashed when he was angry. The tone of his voice when he spoke to me and only me. The stiffness with which he'd held himself when he'd given me the prize for the Games, even though he'd won. 'I'm here, aren't I?' I said eventually.

Bob cocked his head for a moment before flying up to my cheek and leaning against it as if in sympathy.

'Thank you, Bob.'

He didn't reply. We remained there like that for a moment longer. 'You know,' he said eventually, 'we could call you Byntegrity. A romance for the ages.' He frowned. 'No. The other way around. Integron.'

I grunted. 'Sounds like a Transformer.'

'Yeah, you're right. You should call this whole thing off. It's not going to work after all.'

'No,' I said. 'It's probably not.' I tucked my hair behind my ear. 'You need to go, Bob. It's too dangerous.'

'I don't want to leave you here on your own.' His voice was small.

'I appreciate the thought, I really do, but I can't risk having you here. Go enjoy yourself in the Caribbean. Have a cocktail for me.'

Bob nuzzled against me. 'I'll go. But don't get hurt, Uh Integrity.' He paused. 'You're the only friend I've got.'

And then, before I could say anything else, he'd gone.

Chapter Sixteen

There was part of me that regretted sending Bob away. Annoying as he could be, and as much as we sniped at each other, I enjoyed his company. It was oddly reassuring having him by my side and I was pretty certain he felt the same way. He was my friend, as Speck or Lexie or Brochan or Taylor were. I couldn't imagine asking the little genie for my last wish but, if I did, I worried about what would happen to him afterwards. I sighed. It seemed like all I did was worry these days. I pushed him out of my head. At least he was safe for now. For my part, the solitude and silence were clawing at me and there was a tightness around my shoulders that belied my own tension. I had to get on and find Byron. There was simply no other choice.

Wary after seeing the troop of demons pass by, I moved in a more easterly direction than I'd planned, curving round the valleys and hills until Edinburgh grew close, looming up out of the darkness.

If I'd expected a city like Glasgow, I was mistaken. Glasgow was all low-lying buildings and cracked stone; Edinburgh, even from a distance, was completely different. The castle rose above the city, watching over everything and giving the place an air of drama and mystery. Given its history, that was hardly surprising. Even with my limited education, I knew what role the city had played in Scotland's past, but I hadn't imagined that it would appear so majestic. I'd seen a couple of ancient oil paintings - I was pretty certain I might even have stolen one once from a merchant's Aberdeen townhouse - but seeing the castle was entirely different. It was also comforting to know that the demons hadn't destroyed it. It had stood for eleven hundred years; maybe it would stand for eleven hundred more. One could only hope.

As I got closer, it was clear that the castle was in need of some repair. A tower on the eastern side was little more than rubble. That wasn't surprising; apparently this was one of the last strongholds to maintain a presence against the demons after their invasion. The people inside – both Sidhe and otherwise - had fought hard. No one knew what had happened to them. It was believed that they'd all died when the castle had fallen. Considering what I now knew, the truth was probably worse.

In any event, it wasn't Edinburgh castle that I was aiming for. I tore my eyes away from it and focused on the buildings and the roads which surrounded me. They seemed as empty and lifeless as the ones in Glasgow but this time I knew better than to take things at first glance. I peered into dark interiors and kept a close eye on the rooftops. Getting here had taken ages and I was nervous about time slipping away. I knew the demons roused themselves at midday so I'd have to find cover before then. I didn't know how long they stayed up for, however, or what they did during those hours of wakefulness. I guessed I'd soon find out.

I kept on a straight path, heading for Arthur's Seat. From time to time, I twisted away as odd noises travelled over the rooftops. They were never anything definite, just muffled thuds breaking the eerie silence, punctuated by the occasional swishing sound. There were no voices or snarls or screams but each time my hackles rose and I adapted my course to keep well away.

The only thing I was thankful for was that I didn't have to cross any rivers. The memory of the stinking, viscous Clyde was more than enough to live with. I'd jumped in there when I was avoiding the demons in Glasgow. The waters had concealed me then, but I didn't feel the need to go for a dip in another Fomori river again.

As I wended my way forward, I reminded myself that the Gifts I'd stolen were finite; I had to resist the temptation to use them because I was feeling nervous.

To keep my spirits up I sang in my head, where I was pitch perfect and no one could complain that their ears were bleeding. As I arrived at a crossroads and prepared to turn left, I launched into a rendition of 'I'm Too Sexy'. I hadn't even finished the first line when I spotted a flurry of movement down one of the streets. I flung myself backwards, using the corner of the nearest building to shield my body. Then I peeked round.

Whoever they were, they weren't Fomori. For one thing, they were too tall and I caught a glimpse of a flap of fabric and a flip of long hair. I had yet to see a single demon which wasn't naked or virtually bald. Curiosity got the better of me and I looked again.

There were a lot of them; I counted at least thirteen heads crossing the cobbled street before they were swallowed up by the darkness. They appeared to be carrying objects from one broken-down old house to another.

I didn't know what to do. I wanted to know who they were and what they were doing. The demons slept on the rooftops, not inside, and I'd seen no evidence that they entered any of the buildings. Perhaps the houses were kept purely for their slaves, those poor souls descended from the people trapped here when the demons annexed the Lowlands. It was also almost ten o'clock at night which didn't tally with the other information about the demons either.

I could edge my way forward and see whether any of them spoke English. If they spoke Gaelic, I could probably use my own meagre smattering to have a quick conversation - but there was no way of telling whether they'd want to talk to me or not. Whoever they were, they knew no other life than this. They might be terrified and immediately raise an alarm. They might adore their demon overlords and run to tell them that the scary Adair was here.

I told myself firmly not to get side-tracked. Byron needed me. These others might need me too but right now I couldn't be sure. Until Golden Boy was safe and sound, I had to deal in absolutes.

I waited until the last of them disappeared and sped across the road. It looked like there was another street veering left a couple of hundred feet away. It wasn't too much of an adjustment to my course.

I stayed close to the walls of the empty buildings, maintaining a good pace but staying vigilant. The desolation of the old city was starting to get to me. From time to time I spotted objects lying forlornly on the ground: bits of broken wood that looked like they might once have made up the parts of a children's toy; a glass bottle or two; some china plates lying intact, as if they'd been used for a game of Frisbee before being abandoned abruptly. There was even a mottled cannon ball that had gouged a hole in the cobbles. I shivered. I could only wonder at their providence.

There was another turning ahead. I could choose to go straight on or turn right. I knew from May's crudely drawn map – and Bob's explanation – that going straight was the most direct route but that didn't necessarily make it the best one. It was important that I stayed away from main thoroughfares in case some of the Fomori got up early, looked over their parapets and saw me. And there was the tiny matter of those patrols.

I glanced in both directions. On the right-hand side, about halfway towards the next crossroads, the road seemed to be blocked. Timber, chairs, tables and beds, which had probably once adorned the house of some rich, dead dude, were piled up to create a barrier that would be awkward, although not impossible, to get over. The road straight ahead was completely clear.

Rather than immediately taking the easy path, I pursed my lips and leaned back against the wall. The troop of demons which Bob had forewarned me about had led me to enter the city limits at a different angle to the one I'd planned. The non-demon workers had made me change course again, if only slightly. There were distant noises which had spooked me enough to make me keep away. Now there was a very obvious barrier so I was forced to go ahead rather than right.

'I don't believe in coincidences,' I whispered. Considering where I was, I didn't think I was being paranoid. I thought I was moving towards Arthur's Seat through dint of my own free will but what if they knew I was coming? What if I was being herded?

I squashed the sudden, sharp stab of terror and shuffled further back into the shadows. It made sense. If the Fomori knew about the prophecy and believed in it – and were scared of what I might do as a result – then they'd want to be careful. Maybe Aifric had told them I was on the way. That scenario was the most optimistic: he'd have bargained Byron for me. I hoped that the Fomori wouldn't want to hurt the Steward's son too badly – but I couldn't bank on that.

Regardless of how they knew I was coming, they'd take their time approaching me. If I were them, I'd wait until I had the perfect spot for an ambush before setting my trap. I'd want the odds to be in my favour.

I was canny enough to avoid falling into that kind of trap. The issue was that if the Fomori already knew I was coming, they'd know where I was heading too. They'd use Byron as bait to lure me. On the one hand, that was good; it meant that, they'd keep him alive. On the other hand, it made my task harder.

I wanted to reserve my stolen magical Gifts until I really needed them. I was sure that the Foinse had helped me to draw in more magic without harming the original owners too much, but they were still finite resources. All the same, there was no point in keeping the Gifts back if it meant risking capture. I closed my eyes and concentrated. I wasn't going to be particularly good at this part because I'd had no practice. I had to be sure, though.

It was the oddest sensation. I pulled on the threads of the Jardine Sidhe's far-sensing and sent them out in all directions. I didn't want to expend all the energy at once so I was very, very careful. A vague awareness tickled at the back of my mind. I couldn't explain how it worked but it was like when your subconscious felt someone looking at you from behind and you turned without even realising it. Unfortunately for me, it wasn't just what was behind me that was the problem.

I was completely encircled by a mass of demons, too many of them to count. It was a net of Fomori which would tighten and tighten until I had no way out. Even if I had the wherewithal to fight, I'd never manage it. There were simply far too many of them.

For now, they were keeping their distance; there was a radius of about a mile before I could sense a single Fomori soul. That left a considerable margin of error on their part. It only made sense if they had someone doing the same thing as me – far-sensing. I was looking at them but they were also looking at me. Crapadoodle.

I didn't want to reveal that I knew they were surrounding me so, after massaging my joints for a few minutes, I took off again. I did as the demons wanted and ignored the barricaded street. I might have managed to continue moving as if nothing had changed, but my mind was flying through the potential outcomes. Things were not looking good.

My best bet was to take out whoever was doing the far-sensing, otherwise I'd be tracked to hell and beyond. Sticking to the shadows like before, I focused on drawing out a single thread. This time I wasn't searching randomly, I was looking for a specific demon. I trained my mind on that thought: find the far-senser.

I felt the magic strain away from me as if it was being drawn by a magnet. It wasn't hampered by buildings or stone or makeshift barricades; instead it stretched out and made a beeline for the east. A face flashed in my head: a male demon with sunken eyes and a dreamy expression which contradicted the frozen snarl on his lips. His mouth was pulled back to reveal sharp, yellowing teeth.

I sucked in a breath. He was directly in front of me, surrounded by a cluster of other Fomori. As the Gift slowly drained out from me, I memorised his face. The magic tugged at me, leading me towards him and I cursed under my breath as I fought to think of a way out. Then I lost control. The Gift surged and I tripped.

Whether it was a result of my stumble, or because it was hard to manage the three Gifts I held within my body, I wasn't sure. Perhaps it was a combination of the two. Either way, as the ground rushed up towards me, I lost my hold on the magic.

There was a hiss and I was abruptly enveloped in a dark, choking cloud. I couldn't breathe. It filled my lungs and stung my eyes and, as the cloud smothered me, everything around me evaporated. My fingers clawed at the air as panic set in and I hit the ground with a thump. My legs kicked and writhed. Burning. It was burning everything.

It was only the tiny insistent voice inside my head which brought me back. You, it said, you are the one doing this. I forced my hands to still, curling them into tight fists. I rolled clear of the cloud, even as it started to dissipate. I lay on my back, panting, while the atmosphere cleared.

There wasn't much point in being afraid of the demons surrounding me if I was going to lose control and do their job for them. That had been worse than the damned Veil, worse than ducking my head in the Clyde, worse than just about anything. My head spun but I struggled to my feet.

For the first time, I was fully cognisant of how dangerous the ability to steal and hold others' Gifts could be. The black, choking cloud was my own creation and yet, when it swirled around me, I couldn't think of anything else. It wiped away almost all coherent thought. The Lowlands, the danger Byron was in, the demon watching my progress ... they all slipped away as I panicked.

I paused. That was it; that was what I had to do. If I could send that cloud to cover the far-sensing bastard, I could momentarily mask my presence and use it to slip clear. Could I make myself to do such a thing to another living being? Even though I was in mortal danger, I wasn't sure.

I checked my watch. Midday was approaching and time was not on my side. Finding cover for up to twelve hours seemed pointless when the entire horde was apparently already awake. I pulled up a mental image of May's map. There was an open area facing the castle which would be the logical place for the demons' ambush. In theory I should avoid it at all costs. The space was less than two miles from here and there had been no flicker of Byron's presence when I'd far-sensed, so I had to work on the premise that he was still being held up on Arthur's Seat. I didn't have to go through the centre of the city to reach the small mountain.

The Fomori didn't know that I had May or that I knew they didn't keep their captives at the castle. Logically, the castle was where I would start searching for him. That was one of the reasons they were directing me to that spot; they expected me to try the castle first and they didn't want to alert me to their ambush just outside it. I'd do what they wanted for now. In a manner of speaking.

I grinned. 'Arthur any demons going to stop me?' I said aloud. My voice echoed round the empty streets. No one answered. I took that as a no. I was going to do this.

I started by changing tactics. Instead of taking the route I'd originally intended, I veered off, not enough that the demons would notice but enough to get me where I needed to be more quickly. After about ten minutes, I flipped on my internal far-sensing switch once more. This time I was very careful not to lose control. I just needed the right moment.

The Fomori demon's face flickered into my head. He had the same intense expression as before. Speck had said that the average person could only concentrate on one thing fully for twenty minutes; I hoped that held true for demons. My watcher must have been focused on me for far longer than that. All it would take was a short distraction and I'd have the advantage I needed.

It took longer than I hoped. The Gift inside me was unravelling and slipping away. My nerves began to fray. This would be much harder if I lost it before the demon broke. I estimated that I only had a few minutes left when he finally blinked. He pinched the bridge of his nose with dark, claw-like fingers and shook his head. A hand holding a cup of something dark and unpleasant appeared in front of him. As he reached for it, I spun round and ran. Usain Bolt had nothing on me. I sprinted like the hounds of hell were after me – which they pretty much were.

It was a full twenty seconds before the demon turned his attention back to me. As soon as he realised I was off course, he opened his mouth in a silent scream. Then he disappeared from my head as the last vestiges of the Jardine's Gift left my system. It didn't matter now.

My heart raced and my feet clattered, thumping on the ancient cobbles. I wasn't going to lose the demons so I needed to throw them off their game and encourage them to lose some of their poise and balance. The only thing that would help me win the day now was if I did the unexpected.

The alarm was raised quickly and I heard hoots and calls around me as the demons reacted. They dropped all pretence of concealment and I knew that they were moving in for the kill. I kept the castle in my sights. It was vital they thought I was heading for it. My sprint for escape meant they'd catch me before I got to their planned ambush spot. All to the good.

They began to crowd in from the sides and a thunderous roar headed in my direction. Plenty of the Fomori demons had wings and I knew they'd be on me within seconds. I had to lock eyes with the far-senser first though.

I ignored the keening cries and wheeled round a corner as something swooped. I ducked and threw myself out of the way just in time. There was a screech of anger. I lifted my head, ready to sprint again, but I was faced by a wall of demons. They bristled, some spat at me and one or two ventured forward a step. They were all as ugly as each other and they all had murder in their eyes. I was going to be ripped apart. I swung my head across, searching for weak points but there were none. This time they were using their own bodies as a barrier.

Playing along, I pivoted on my heel. Demons were advancing from behind. I looked left and right and saw that I was hemmed in on all sides, plus there were hundreds of flying Fomori above my head. It seemed as if all of us were holding our breath.

I slowly turned to the front again and started to lift my hands as if in surrender. Once more my gaze swooped across the wall of demons and this time I found my target: the far-senser was there. I was pretty sure that he was now giving a snarl of triumph rather than one of concentration.

Angling my body towards his I inhaled, drawing in as much of the reeking air into my lungs as I possibly could. Then I straightened my shoulders. I'd give them something to be afraid of. Instead of continuing to raise my hands, I flung them outwards, away from my body. I was rewarded with a collective flinch from the demons. I gave a massive war cry and then I let the black cloud of the Calder Sidhe's Gift envelop me once more. I'd let this damned Gift attack me again rather than the Fomori. All they had to do was get out of the way.

This time I felt less panic because I had consciously instigated the cloud of doom rather than triggering it by accident. All the same, its suffocating madness clawed at my skin. I barrelled forward towards the far-senser. Dimly, I heard the demons shriek. I didn't know whether they'd tried to enter the cloud surrounding me or not but no claws ripped into my skin. If any demons broached the darkness, they didn't get very far.

I yanked on every part of the Gift, doing whatever I could to let the damn thing grow. At the same time I kept moving ahead, taking the cloud with me. The demonic shrieks ebbed and rose and time itself seemed to stand still. It was just me and the encroaching darkness. It was seeping into me, I was absorbing it through the pores of my skin. I'd turn mad ... or worse. It was only when I was sure that what I felt was my very brain cells withering and dying that I broke loose. I just had to pray that I'd already done enough.

I doubled over and ran, pushing my way through the choking miasma and leaving it behind me as a pulsating mass of fear. As soon as I crossed through, returning to the usual humidity of the Lowlands, it no longer felt as if I were surrounded by foul air. For once, the atmosphere seemed sweet and clear. Frankly, the aftermath of a nuclear explosion would seem sweet and clear after being inside that cloud.

All around me was utter bedlam. Demons were scattering in every direction. I couldn't see the far-senser; with any luck, he was panicking and fleeing like everyone else. Chaotic screeching filled the air and I was jostled and shoved. I saw white eyes writhing in terror but none of the demons seemed to recognise me; they were all too concerned with the desperate need to get away. All the same, I stayed low. I had to get as far away from here as possible. The cloud would only remain where it was for a short while before it vanished into the ether. I could already feel the magic leaving my body as I slammed through. Then I ran and ran and ran.

Chapter Seventeen

I slowed down eventually, not because I was certain I'd escaped but because I didn't have enough energy to continue running at full pelt. So far nothing had stopped me. No claws had raked into my back. There were no angry shrieks at my departure. In fact, although I estimated I was only a mile away from my doom cloud, it was so silent that I could have been on the other side of the world.

I began taking stock. My heart was still battering my ribcage and my skin felt as if it was coated in that damned darkness but my legs were still working. So were my arms. Unless I was hugely mistaken, I was alive and well.

I kept jogging, glancing over my shoulder as I went. Nothing followed me. I'd have felt a lot better if I could have tried far-sensing again to be sure but there was none of that magic left inside me. All I had left was Truth Telling, which was apparently now permanent, and Illusion. And I needed to keep the Illusion part until later.

Still, if I'd played my cards right, the demons would re-group and assume that I'd ventured up to the castle to look for Byron or that I'd skedaddled back towards the Veil with my tail between my legs. Fortunately the castle was large, so it would take them some time to realise that I wasn't there. Nevertheless, I still had to be pretty damned quick. They'd probably send an extra contingent up towards Arthur's Seat just to be sure I wasn't there. I was praying to Lady Luck that there wouldn't be so many of them that I couldn't slip past.

Although I'd been prepared to see the people enslaved by the Fomori, I was still shocked when I approached the small mountain. Hundreds of wooden poles, thousands probably, stretched from the foot of the mountain as far as my eye could see. At the base of each one there were heavy-looking chains; some were attached to huddled figures and some appeared empty. As far as I could see there were no guards but I was well aware how quickly the Fomori could be upon us.

With my heart in my throat, I stepped up to the nearest pole. Whoever was chained to it was in a sorry state, with matted dark hair, ragged clothes and their head buried in their arms. I bit my lip hard. Maybe I could rescue at least one of them.

I knelt down, searching for the lock. I was a thief and there were few locks that I couldn't unpick. It didn't take me long to realise that there was no lock. This poor soul wasn't actually chained to the pole; if they wanted to get up and walk away, they could.

Puzzled and desperately worried, I reached over to shake the prisoner's shoulder. Before my fingers touched them, there was a shout from several feet away. 'Blas ack na var!'

My blood froze. It was only when I slowly rose and my gaze pierced the darkness that I realised the words hadn't come from a demon. Unless I was seeing things, the person standing up and gesturing at me was Sidhe.

I licked my lips nervously and edged towards him. He wasn't yelling for help or running for back-up, so I guessed I was relatively safe for now. As I got closer and noted his hair colour, fine features and pointed ears, I knew my initial reaction was correct. What I hadn't spotted until I was less than a few feet away was how scared he was.

'I don't speak Fomori,' I said softly.

His eyes widened and he stared.

I tried to smile. 'Er ... Chan eil Fomori agam,' I tried, using my rudimentary Gaelic.

The Sidhe looked at me as if I'd just swallowed a frog. I scratched my neck. Shite.

None of the misshapen bundles around us looked our way, although I did see one or two twitch nervously. I guessed they were hoping to deny seeing anything when the Fomori came and asked questions.

The Sidhe lifted his shoulders in a nonchalant shrug. 'She is tired. She needs to sleep.'

For a moment, I didn't have the faintest idea what he was talking about, then there was a grunt and I realised he meant the huddled shape I'd approached. 'Okay,' I said. His eyes narrowed as if he didn't understand me. 'So you speak English?'

'Yes.'

I breathed out in relief. 'Cool.'

He frowned again. 'Cool?' He glanced around. 'It seems temperate to me.' He understood English but he wasn't *au fait* with contemporary slang. I nodded to myself. That figured; he'd been stuck here without any contact with the outside world - why would he speak a modern dialect?

I smiled at him. 'My name is Integrity.'

He blinked. 'Oh.'

I waited but he didn't say anything else. 'What's your name?' I asked eventually.

'I don't have one.' He spoke like I was a stupid child. 'Only the Fomori have names.' He appraised me. 'But you are not Fomori.'

I bit back a sarcastic remark and focused on what was important. 'You really don't have a name?'

'No.'

That wasn't so strange to me. I hadn't had a name until I was eleven years old and I'd run away from the Bull and into Taylor's beat-up car. Keeping people nameless was a great way to stop your minions getting uppity and thinking for themselves. It was ironic that the Fomori were doing to the Sidhe what the Sidhe had done to me.

'Why aren't you chained up? Why isn't she chained up?'

Again, he looked confused. 'We have done nothing wrong.'

'But,' I paused, 'if you're not a prisoner why don't you escape?'

He stared blankly. 'Escape? From what? To where?'

I sucked in a breath. Okey-dokey. Tempting as it was to bring up Pavlov's dog, I didn't have time to argue the merits or otherwise of conditioning. I glanced over my shoulder to double-check I was still in the clear, then squinted further up the slope.

'Are there any Fomori here?'

'They are at the top, guarding the villain.'

Villain? 'Does this villain have blond hair? Green eyes? Strange clothes?'

'You know him?'

My heart leapt with hope. 'Yes. He's not a villain though, he's a good guy.'

'Guy?'

I tutted. 'Man. I mean, man. How many demons are there?'

'Five. Six. I do not know.'

I bit my lip. Five or six was a pitiful amount and that didn't make sense. If Byron was the bait to lure me in, did that mean there were other demons hiding elsewhere?

Somehow I didn't think my new nameless friend could help; I already knew he was telling the truth. I threw out a quick thanks and began jogging. As pitiful as this man's situation was, Byron was my priority.

I'd only gone about twenty feet when something occurred to me. I half turned. The Sidhe was still standing beside his pole. 'What's your Gift?' I asked.

He seemed puzzled. 'I do not know what you mean.'

'Magic. What magic do you have?'

'Only the demons possess magic.'

I tightened my jaw. Well, that answered a whole bunch of questions. I thanked him once more. The Fomori plot was definitely thickening. Concentrate on Byron, I told myself. Worry about everything else later.

Time was not on my side. I was still expecting masses of demons to start flinging themselves my way. They'd drawn me towards the castle but they'd catch on sooner or later that I was on my way here to Arthur's Seat. I pelted up the hill, scree flying in all directions. Some of the figures got to their feet and watched my ascent but others didn't raise their heads. The eeriness of the whole set-up was starting to get to me.

Not every 'prisoner', if I could call them that, was Sidhe. I spotted pixies, Bauchans, humans, trolls ... virtually every race was represented in some way. There was no doubting who was in charge; the Fomori's grip was iron-clad. The demons had a hell of a lot to answer for – and maybe we did too for letting this continue for so long. The thought spurred me to move faster.

It was hard going. I was used to mountainous terrain from my short stint with mountain rescue and this was more like a big hill than a mountain, so it should have been easy for me to climb. Adrenaline was still pulsing through my veins, which helped considerably, but the knowledge of the demons both behind and ahead of me, and my worry about Byron's state, made climbing difficult.

I was sweating, my clothes sticking to my skin and my hair plastered to my forehead. Whatever scent I'd got from wearing May's discarded T-shirt was no doubt gone. Eau de sweaty Integrity was all that remained. The gnawing feeling that I'd have to fight if I wanted to rescue Byron wouldn't leave me. It's inevitable, an irksome little voice whispered; your true name means warrior. It's time to go to war.

I was getting used to the silent, huddled shapes around me. They were a sorry, downtrodden lot – so when a hand stretched out and grabbed my ankle, it was so unexpected that I went flying.

I twisted, kicked away and scrambled backwards, my breath coming in short, heavy gasps. I blew back the damp hair that had fallen into my eyes and peered at whoever had made me fall. My hands were already up to ward off the next attack.

It was a pixie but not a cheeky, dimpled pixie like Lexie. This version was covered in a layer of grime so thick I could probably grow daisies on her skin. Unlike almost all the other people here, she was chained up. She raised manacled wrists and pressed a finger to her lips, warning me to be quiet. I gaped at her.

'You have white hair. Purple eyes.' She stared at me in wonder. 'You are the one they fear,' she whispered. 'I've heard about you.'

I scrambled forward. 'What? What have you heard?'

'They say that there's a prophecy, that you will kill them all.' Her eyes gleamed through the darkness. 'Do not hesitate. You must do it.'

'I...' I shook my head. 'I cannot. The prophecy is wrong.'

She leaned towards me. 'If it was wrong, the demons would not be so terrified.'

'They're mistaken.'

She bared her teeth into the semblance of a smile. 'They are not. We need you.' She clanked her chains as she jerked her hand and pointed. 'You are here for him.'

'The Sidhe man?' I asked urgently.

She laughed softly. 'The well-fed one? Yes. They thought you would go to the castle and take the dreeocht. You will need to do that but now is not the time.'

'Take the what?'

'Dreeocht,' she repeated.

I couldn't work out what she meant. 'Dree...' My voice faltered. She was using the Gaelic word. Draoidheachd.

'Magic,' I whispered.

She smiled again and nodded. 'You will return. And you will take it.' She lunged forward and I thought for a moment she was going to attack me. The intensity in her expression was painful to look at. 'You will save us.'

'I'm not the one you want,' I said. Putting hope in me would only lead to desperate disappointment.

The pixie didn't argue. 'Go now. I will help you.'

I opened my mouth to ask her another question but it was too late. She flipped back her head and began to shout at the top of her voice. Her words were nonsensical to me but, whatever she was saying, it was loud enough to wake the dead. Or the Fomori.

I hurtled away in a bid to put as much distance as possible between me and the pixie. It was just as well I reacted so quickly because, within a few breaths, several Fomori demons came clumping along, hissing and spitting in her direction.

She yelled and shrieked. They were so focused on the screaming pixie that they didn't notice me barely a few metres away.

And then I finally saw him.

He was set apart from others and tethered to a pole with a chain which was wrapped cruelly round his torso. His trousers were ripped and he was shirtless. Several cuts were visible across his chest but there didn't appear to be any fresh blood seeping from them. His head had fallen forward so I couldn't see his face. If it wasn't for the slight rise and fall as he breathed, I'd have wondered whether he was dead.

There were no other demons in sight. The pixie continued to screech. There were harsh words from the demons, followed by a loud crack. I shuddered. A whip.

I wasted no more time. I still expected to be waylaid by hordes of the ugly, naked bastards but, as I darted towards the pole, nothing happened.

'Byron!' I hissed.

He groaned and I gritted my teeth. Still no more demons came. Were they waiting until I released him? Maybe they wanted me to think I'd won and then they'd snatch away my victory.

I fumbled with the rusting padlock that held the chains in place. It was solid and looked impenetrable but it was old and the lock mechanism was simple. It took very little effort to wield my lock pick and force the padlock open.

I pulled at the chains as quietly as I could. Byron lifted his head, his pain-glazed eyes taking me in. 'Hallucinating,' he muttered.

'You're not bloody hallucinating!' I hissed. I unwound the last of the chains and carefully lowered them to the ground whilst attempting to support Byron's body. He fell heavily against me.

'You smell awful,' he said. He frowned. 'You're really here.'

'That's how you know I'm real? Because I smell bad?' I put my arm round his waist and tried to get him to move.

'Normally,' he murmured, in a voice so shaky and weak it was barely audible, 'you smell like strawberries. If this was a dream, then that's what I would smell.' His head dropped onto my neck. 'You smell like shit.'

Unbelievable. All this way to rescue his sorry arse and all he could say when I showed up was that I was stinky. 'Shut up,' I whispered tersely. 'Conserve your strength. We need to get the hell out of here.'

There was a loud crack and the pixie abruptly fell silent. My stomach tensed. What had they done to her? 'We need to go, Byron, otherwise we're both dead meat.'

We stumbled away, slipping and sliding in our bid to get down Arthur's Seat and as far away from here as possible. I spun round once we were almost out of sight. I could already see the stretching shadows of the returning demons. I squeezed my eyes shut and prayed this would work. Illusion was a difficult Gift to master – or so

I'd heard. I only had it in limited quantities and there was very little time. I had to concentrate or all was lost.

Heady power swirled through my veins. I felt Byron tense and my shoulders tightened. Come on. Come on. Then I opened my eyes. 'It worked,' I gasped.

There, bent against the pole, was a near-perfect illusion of Byron. It was like he'd never left it. A shiver rippled through him. 'You stole Illusion,' he whispered.

'Let's not get into an argument about the rights and wrongs of thievery till later.' I twisted round once more. Byron fell against me but I managed to catch him. Once again we began half stumbling, half running down the hill.

'Integrity,' he said, his voice barely audible, 'the illusion won't last long. We've got minutes at best.'

I grimaced. 'Then we need to damned well hurry.'

Chapter Eighteen

Rather than re-trace my steps through the silent – and potentially deadly – city streets, Byron and I went in the opposite direction. We could skirt round most of the buildings. It meant we'd be exposed but we'd have more warning if thousands of Fomori demons came after us. What was left unsaid was that, no matter what we did, if we found ourselves in that situation we were not going to make it.

Byron was in a bad way. He put up a good show of not being in pain but the white lines around his mouth and the frequently glazed look in his eyes gave him away. The demons hadn't treated him kindly; I guessed the Geneva Convention didn't apply to them. When he started shivering, I hastily peeled his jacket off my shoulders and draped it round him.

We were still stumbling along old cobbled streets when his legs gave out completely and he collapsed into a heap. 'Integrity,' he gasped. 'You...'

I knew exactly what he was about to say but I wasn't going to give him the chance. I put my finger to his lips then took a bottle of water from my bag and discarded everything else. If we were further away, I'd let him rest but we had to get away from the city limits first.

Without saying a word, I put his arms round my neck. He instantly understood but tried to resist. Fortunately for both of us, he was as weak as a kitten and I was stronger than I looked. I took his legs and staggered up so he was hanging over me piggy-back style. He groaned, whether in pain, embarrassment or relief I had no idea. I shifted his weight and we continued, albeit far more slowly. Now I wished he didn't have all those heavy, sexy muscles. Why couldn't he be a skinny runt instead?

'When we get back home,' I huffed, 'I'm going to have you arrested for those guns.'

He didn't answer. Panicking, I paused in mid-step but I could feel his hot breath on my neck. He was still with me. Barely.

I struggled on. The buildings began to thin out and become even more derelict. I had to put as much distance between us and the city centre as possible because I was still wary of the far-senser. The Gift I'd stolen only had a radius of two miles but his might be very different although I had to assume, given that I'd made it this far, that he couldn't stretch it indefinitely. But I was getting weaker and my knees were starting to buckle under Byron's weight. It didn't help that I had to clutch at him to prevent him from sliding off my back.

When I was certain I could go no further, I left the road and headed for the nearest building. To be honest, building was probably a generous description - it was only two walls and half a roof - but it would do for now. I needed a break to regain some strength.

I meant to let Byron down gently but unfortunately he landed with a heavy thump, cracking his head on the dirty flagstones. I winced and hunkered down to check him over. His pulse was weak but steady. Hopefully I'd not done his skull any permanent damage.

I unscrewed the lid on the water bottle and tipped a small amount of liquid into his mouth. His swallow reflex kicked in so I gave him a bit more before taking a tiny swig myself. Then I leaned back against the nearest wall, closing my eyes. Ten minutes. All I needed was ten minutes' rest.

It felt like about ten seconds. My entire body ached but as much as I wanted to curl up and get a proper sleep, I couldn't afford to. I glanced down and realised that Byron's emerald-green eyes were fixed on me.

'Hey.'

His tongue darted out, wetting his lips. 'You shouldn't have come for me,' he said huskily.

I shrugged, ignoring the shooting pain the movement sent down my spine. 'I was at a loose end.'

He forced himself up to a sitting position. 'I mean it, Integrity. Leave me here. You need to get back to the Highlands. The demons...' He shuddered. 'The demons are after you.'

'Tell me something I don't know.' I smiled. 'It's fine. We're less than two hours away from the Veil. We'll make it.'

He shook his head. 'They kept saying your name.'

'Well,' I replied, 'it is a pretty cool name.'

'Your Clan name,' he said. 'They said it over and over again. Adair. Adair.' He pushed back a lock of golden hair. 'Every time a new demon appeared, they got into my face and said it again. Adair.'

'Did they say anything else?'

'That was all I understood.'

I rubbed the back of my neck. 'They're scared of me. It's something to do with that stupid prophecy. They think I'm going to save Scotland by killing them all.' I hadn't thought he could get any paler but he did.

I laughed without humour. 'What no one seems to realise is that I've already saved Scotland. I freed the Foinse. By saving the magic, I saved the country. All this demon stuff is nonsense.' I tried not to think about the magic the chained-up pixie had mentioned.

'I don't think they got that memo.'

'No.' I dropped my eyes. I didn't want to do this but, considering what was coming next, I had to try. I had to give Byron one last chance to believe me. 'Your father didn't want me to come,' I said quietly. 'He was going to leave you here to...' My voice trailed off. Byron's imagination was probably more vivid than mine; he'd had plenty of time chained to that post to think about what was going to happen to him.

His jaw tightened. 'My father did the right thing. Other people cannot be sacrificed because of me. You should have left me.'

'Would you have left me if our roles had been reversed?' He didn't answer. 'Byron,' I persisted. 'Your father admitted that my father didn't massacre his own Clan. Aifric engineered it because the Fomori wanted more land and the only way he could stave them off was to give them the Adairs. He thought that would stall the prophecy.'

'But they already have all the land they could possibly need,' he returned.

'I know but that's what your father said. He...'

There was a sudden screech from overhead. Without meaning to, my hand snapped out and clutched Byron's. He squeezed it sharply and then we both froze, awaiting inevitable discovery.

'You have to go,' he whispered.

'Hush.'

We waited. Five seconds. Ten. Almost a full minute passed before the screech sounded again. This time it was further away fading into the distance. I let out the breath I'd been holding. 'We both need to go,' I said firmly.

'Leave me,' he insisted. 'I'm too weak. I can't feel my Gifts but if I rest some more I'll recoup enough energy to bring them back. Then I can fight.'

'We're not fighting, Byron. We're fleeing.' I stood up and tugged at his hand. 'Can you stand?'

'I'm not coming.'

I rolled my eyes. 'Then I'm not going. We're at an impasse.'

'Integrity...'

'Look at me. I'm not leaving you behind.' I grinned. 'Otherwise it's a complete waste of a day.'

'You're the most bloody stubborn woman I've ever met. Even Tipsania is more amenable than you.'

'Yeah,' I said, 'but you love me really.'

Something flashed in his eyes. 'Integrity,' he said again.

'We're leaving.' I tied back my hair and pulled him to his feet. 'Now.'

Thankfully he stopped resisting. The rest had done enough to allow him to walk, although I remained close in case he fell again. We limped our way forward, the sunny Highlands beckoning to us. I kept the thought of hills covered in blooming purple heather, the smiling faces of my friends and even the half-derelict Adair mansion in the forefront of my mind. The dark, scarred landscape we were in was almost too much to bear. Even with the knowledge that their skin was too sensitive to sunlight to withstand the world beyond the Veil, I couldn't fathom how the demons and their captives managed to live in this godforsaken land. I'd barely spent a day there and I already felt like I was going insane.

After an hour of relentless plodding, I asked Byron if he needed another rest. He shook his head grimly, the heaviness of the Lowlands affecting him as much as me. He was looking paler, so I put my arm round his shoulders to support his weight. We struggled on like that – and it was just as well we did. Not ten minutes passed when the expanse of the Veil finally came into view.

I felt Byron's muscles sag with relief. Finally the end was in sight.

'We made it,' he said, as if he couldn't quite believe his eyes.

I pulled my own gaze away from the streaks of lightning which, for once, were a pleasure to behold. He reached out and cupped my face. 'Thank you. I owe you my life.'

I tried to smile. I knew what was coming next. 'You're welcome.' I looked ahead. It was probably only another twenty minutes before we'd pass back through again. There were still no demons in sight.

I stiffened and Byron's expression turned abruptly to alarm. 'What is it?'

'I can sense them,' I whispered. 'They're coming.'

He whipped his head round. 'I can't see anything.'

The landscape behind us was utterly bare. I couldn't even see the silhouette of Edinburgh any more.

'Illusion wasn't the only Gift I stole,' I urgently – and vaguely. 'We don't have long.'

For once, he seemed to believe me. 'Can we make it?'

'I don't know. It's an army of Fomori and the vanguard is close. We need to do something to keep them back long enough for us to escape.'

'Where are they?'

'Due south.' I put my hand over his. 'Can you find any magic inside yourself? Anywhere?'

'There's a trickle, nothing more.' He shook his head in dismay. 'Not enough to put up a decent defence.'

I ignored the surge of panic in my belly. 'Enough for one fireball?'

'Maybe. It'll be weak. And I don't know where to send it.'

'Straight ahead.' I pointed towards the city we'd just left. 'They won't know you're using up all the magic you've got. It'll throw them off and give us enough time.'

'Or tell them our exact location.' His expression tightened. 'I can run. We can get to the Veil.'

I was adamant. 'No, we can't.'

If Byron hadn't been in such a bad state, he would probably have refused me. But I had just rescued him and he had to trust me. He nodded and bit his lip. I felt him shudder. I shouldn't be asking this of him while he was in this condition but I didn't have a choice.

He drew in a deep, shaky breath and a little ball of fire sprang into life. It was weak but it was the perfect beacon. Like moths to a flame, I thought grimly.

'That way,' I urged, before he lost the energy or changed his mind.

Byron threw it out. The fireball arced into the air then sprang forward, lighting up the darkness. I had to hope it was enough. I needed some Fomori to follow us through the Veil.

'It's not going to do anything more than singe their eyebrows.'

It didn't have to. 'They don't have eyebrows,' I said. 'Come on. Let's get out of here.'

We turned and ran as quickly as we could. I prayed to whoever was listening that Byron's magic had worked. I didn't want an actual army, I only needed one demon.

The Veil drew closer. At one point, Byron started to lose momentum but I hooked his arm round me and we managed to keep going. Less than fifty feet from the Veil I finally heard them. Thank goodness.

'They're here!' Byron croaked.

'I know.' I crossed my fingers, hoping that this would work. 'But we're almost home free.'

There were three of them of the winged variety, their huge leathery appendages helping them gain on us with unerring speed. One swooped over my head and I ducked just in time to avoid being yanked up into the air. It snarled and spun into a somersault.

'Run!' I shrieked as the demons landed behind us, their wiry bodies making the transition from air to land in a heartbeat. They pelted after us. Somehow Byron found the strength and, together, we surged towards the Veil.

There wasn't time to take a breath. The three Fomori were almost close enough to touch us and I swear that I felt the scratch of curved claws snatching at the back of my shirt. 'Hold on tight,' I said through gritted teeth. 'We're almost there.'

'Fabulous,' Byron gasped in response before the swirling clouds of the Veil made speech impossible. 'Except they are too.'

Golden Boy had a made valid point. As I hauled him through, step after painful step, worry about what was coming next clenched at my gut. If this didn't work, I was out of options. The trouble was that the alternative – certainly in the long term – would probably be far, far worse.

We fell out on the other side of the Veil, heaving in the fresh air. I heard Jamie shouting and, within seconds, Angus was by my side. 'We have to get away from the Veil,' I said, gasping heavily. 'There are three demons coming through.'

I barely had time to register Jamie blanching before Angus took Byron's weight from me and looked at me meaningfully. I nodded once and he looked away. Half stumbling, half running, we moved from the edge of the Veil towards the waiting cars, parked fifty feet away and shrouded in darkness. This would be a damn sight easier if it was daytime. Now we had no advantage against the trailing demons.

'You take Byron in yours!' Angus called to Jamie. 'I'll look after Integrity.'

Angus and I pulled ahead of the other two; with his limp, Byron wasn't going anywhere fast. I twisted slightly; my toe caught on a stone and I went flying, taking Angus down with me.

'Integrity!'

'I'm fine,' I called out, getting to my feet and helping Angus up. 'Just get to the bloody car!'

Byron didn't want to. I could see the desperation on his face. Fortunately for all of us, Jamie yanked him away, wrenching open his car door and ushering him inside. A heartbeat later, I heard a cacophony of snarls. The demons had joined us.

'Integrity,' Angus warned, his voice rising in panic.

'Hang on,' I told him. 'Just hang on.'

A dark shape flew out from behind the nearest car. Chandra, her eyes glittering in the weak moonlight, stretched out her arm. In her hand was a gun with a long, lethal-looking barrel.

'Sorry, Tegs.' Her words rang out in the cold air and made even the demons pause. 'It's nothing personal. You understand that.' She smiled and pulled the trigger.

Pain exploded in my chest; I hadn't expected it to hurt so damned much. My world slid sideways and I collapsed. Dimly, I heard Byron shout. My gaze fell on him struggling to get out of the car. You idiot, I thought. Just stay put and everything will be fine.

Angus screamed my name. He fell to his knees beside me, his hands fumbling.

'The demons,' I whispered.

'Don't die, Tegs.' He grabbed the lapels of my dark blouse. 'Don't you dare fucking die!'

With my peripheral vision, I spotted Chandra throw the three demons a nervous look before she spun on her heel and ran, escaping into the cold Highland night. The fashion-forward assassin knew when she was out-matched.

I coughed, tasting blood in my mouth. 'Get out of here, Angus.'

He shook his head violently. 'No.'

Everything was starting to feel hazy. Byron was still shouting and I heard a crackle as a fireball whizzed past my head. There was a shriek from the demons. How Byron had found the strength to call up his Gift once more, I had no idea.

'He can't kill them,' I whispered. 'Don't let him kill them.'

Angus stared into my face then nodded. He leapt to his feet and waved his arms frantically at Jamie. 'Get him out of here!'

I reached down into myself. A long, rippling shudder ran down my spine.

'Integrity!' Then, 'Fuck off, Jamie!' With more strength than I thought he could possibly have, Byron bounded over and collapsed beside me. I felt his hands on my face. His breathing was coming in short, sharp gasps and he started to moan. 'No. No. You can't. Integrity. Tegs, don't do this to me. Don't...'

Jamie's arms pulled him backwards. 'We have to go.'

'I am not leaving her for those monsters!' Byron's cheeks were glistening and I realised that he was crying. Pain stabbed through me. Not for me, Byron. Don't do that for me.

'It's too late,' Jamie hissed.

Angus ran to his car as Jamie manhandled Byron away. In normal circumstances, he'd never have managed it; Byron's body was built for strength and those muscles weren't just for show. But he was weakened by his ordeal and our escape and he couldn't put up a fight. When I heard the car door slam once more, I breathed a sigh of relief.

Two engines revved and headlights streamed onto my body. The demons took their chance, loping towards me, cackling. The nearest one bent down. This was the most dangerous part. He prodded me with his finger, peering into my eyes and stretching a cold, bony finger to my wrist to feel for a pulse. There was the gleam of a blade. Shite. That wasn't good.

'Get away!' I heard Angus yell. He hit the horn and his car lurched forward, making it clear that he'd run both them and me over if he had to. 'Get back to where you came from and leave her the fuck alone!'

The demon stood up slowly. 'Vern tack Adair. Var?'

'Vas.' His companions said in apparent agreement. They grinned, laughed - and then turned and went back to where they'd come from. The Veil hissed and spat as it swallowed them, resenting the intrusion and welcoming them back at the same time.

Jamie gunned his engine, the tyres spinning as he reversed and speeded off. I could still hear Byron yelling at him to stop. Good boy, Jamie. Keep going and don't look back. Angus did the same, following immediately in Jamie's wake. I stayed where I was, less than fifty feet from the continuously sparking Veil. At last, I was completely alone. I was dead. Finally.

I didn't move for a long time. To be honest, I was more worried that those damned demons would come back and chop off my head as a trophy than anything else.

'Tegs?'

With difficulty, I propped myself up onto my elbows and squinted. Chandra, with Bob perched on her shoulder, came towards me. I rolled away, blinking as the illusion of my corpse started to fade.

'It worked.' I shook my head in amazement. Then I winced; I had a hell of a headache from the way I'd thudded down. And that was without mentioning my chest. 'That bloody hurt,' I complained to Chandra. I spat out a gobbet of blood.

She shrugged amiably. 'It might have been a rubber bullet but it was still a bullet. It's supposed to hurt.'

'I can kiss it better, Uh Integrity,' Bob piped up, puckering his lips.

I didn't answer. Instead, I let Chandra to help me up to my feet.

'Those demons were pretty scary,' she said. 'It's just as well they left when they did. I don't fancy my chances against one, let alone three.'

'We got lucky,' I agreed. 'At least now they think I'm dead. But we should get out of here in case they decide to come back.'

Bob sniffed as we limped away. 'I thought your Byron would have been more heroic. Ranting is one thing but he didn't do anything helpful. If it had been me, I'd have done *something*. I'd have thrown myself in the path of the bullet. Then I'd have tackled the shifty assassin and...'

'Hey!' Chandra protested. 'Who are you calling shifty?'

'If the shoe fits,' Bob dismissed. He flicked a disdainful look at Chandra's footwear but, when he clocked her silver knee-high boots, his expression changed. 'Nice,' he said approvingly before returning to his original topic. 'All Byron actually did was cry your name a few times and then start weeping. What kind of man sheds tears? Pah!'

Chandra and I exchanged looks. 'The kind of man,' she said icily, 'who has a heart and is in touch with his feelings.'

Even through the Gift of Illusion, which made me appear dead, I'd seen the anguish in Byron's face. I wished desperately that there could have been another way but we needed the breathing space that my supposed death offered. Aifric wasn't going to stop trying to kill me, no matter what happened, and my luck would only have held out so far. Sooner or later he'd have hit his mark.

Now Byron would carry the news of my death back to his father – and his father would believe it because Byron had seen it with his own eyes. The three Fomori demons had, too. If what Aifric said was correct and they were attacking the Highlands because of my existence, they would now withdraw and leave everyone in peace. As far as the both the Highlands and the Lowlands were concerned, every single member of the Adair Clan was very, very dead.

**

We regrouped back at the mansion. Sorley was grinning from ear to ear. 'It was perfect,' he said, clapping his hands. 'You should have seen it, Chieftain.'

'Oscar-worthy,' Angus agreed.

I leaned back against the reassuringly solid wall of the Adair house and smiled. 'Tell me.'

'The MacBains got here about midday. All they managed to do was start clearing out some of the rooms with Tipsania ordering them around like she was queen of the castle. We lit a campfire for them and Taylor opened up some of tins of beans...'

I groaned slightly. 'More beans?'

'They were well behaved, those MacBains,' he said. 'No farting.'

I rolled my eyes.

'Anyway,' Angus continued, 'I came flying through right after I left you.' He threw me a look. 'I wasn't faking my panic, those demons were seriously scary. I screeched about how you'd been killed and there were demons at the Veil, and the MacBains went into a blind panic.'

Sorley jabbed at his chest. 'That's when I stepped in. Told them that with the last Adair gone, we were claiming the land ourselves. The trolls were taking over and the MacBains could do nothing about it. They vamoosed before we could even shake our spears.'

'I cried,' Speck said proudly. 'I rubbed Vaseline under my eyes.' In fact, his eyes were still streaming tears. With our apparent victory, however, he no longer seemed to notice.

'Taylor?' I asked.

'I did exactly as you said. Made a big song and dance about how we were going through the Veil ourselves after the demons. We ran out at the same time as the MacBains, then doubled back when they'd all gone.'

Lexie bobbed her head. 'If they look for us, they won't find a thing. They'll just assume we've been killed.'

'And if anyone tries to investigate these lands, they'll find an army of squatting trolls in their way,' Brochan rumbled. 'It was a good plan, Tegs. The last-minute inclusion of that lot worked perfectly.'

'It's not a permanent solution,' I warned. 'Sooner or later someone will discover the truth.'

'Yeah.' Taylor came up and put his arm round me. 'But we're all safe for now. The Fomori will stop attacking and Aifric will think he's won.'

'Except he won't know what's hit him,' Lexie said, rubbing her hands together in glee.

My smile didn't quite reach my eyes. I still couldn't erase the look on Byron's face when he thought I was dead. I'd find a way to reveal the truth to him and I'd just have to hope he didn't hate me too much when he realised what I'd done. It was a necessary evil. Short of actually dying, I couldn't think of an alternative.

'It's a shame the MacBains weren't here for longer to help sort out this place,' I said, gazing up at the high walls.

'I can stay for a while,' Morna said. She wagged her finger. 'I'm not swearing fealty, mind, but I'll help put some life back into this place.'

'And we don't need the MacBains now we have the trolls,' Brochan said. 'There are more than enough hands to get everything shipshape.'

Tipsania appeared in the doorway. May shuffled in behind her, with a shy smile on her face. Chandra's eyes lit up. I knew exactly what she was thinking: there might only be one Fomori demon in the whole of the Highlands but if the wily assassin had her way, she'd be that demon's fashion designer. Before I could say that we needed to keep May's existence as much of a secret as mine, Tipsania spoke.

'What are you cretins doing?' she shrieked. 'I'm not your slave! There are floors that need scrubbing and rooms that need to be emptied. Get a move on!'

Everyone turned and stared at her.

'It's four o'clock in the morning,' Speck complained.

'You're up, aren't you, Four Eyes?'

I winced. Tipsania still needed some work to become a functioning member of our tiny society. We'd get there though. Somehow we'd all get there. I couldn't stay dead forever but for now everyone was safe. I had to separate the part of my heart that yearned for Byron and focus on what we'd achieved. He was safe – and so was my country. We'd won the battle, if not the war.

Epilogue

Neither Jamie nor Byron said a word until they reached the outskirts of Perth. Jamie's hands gripped the steering wheel so tightly the entire way that he had cramp but that was nothing compared to the pain that Byron was feeling. He ignored the blood which continued to seep through his clothes and the sapping weakness which drained his body. The physical pain was nothing and the cuts would heal. His power would return. Not everything else would, though.

Byron stared out of the window when Jamie stopped at a petrol station to fill up. This was all his fault. Integrity, with her laughing violet eyes and smile that would light up the entire country, was gone.

'That MacQuarrie bastard,' he ground out, when Jamie returned. 'Coward.' He cursed and his shoulders drooped. 'So are we. We should have stayed. We should have done something.'

Jamie stayed silent for a long moment. 'We couldn't have done anything. You barely had the strength to lift your head and I have no useful Gift. Not against Fomori demons, anyway.'

'She's dead.' Byron spoke in a strangled voice. 'Integrity is dead.'

His friend gripped his hand, squeezing it tightly. He didn't say anything else.

The gaping chasm inside Byron grew until he was overcome by a void of grief and pain. He kept seeing her face over and over again, that cheeky grin, the way she flipped her hair over her shoulder when she was trying to make a point. Her godawful jokes. He went over and over it in his mind. It had happened so quickly. Who the hell was that woman who'd shot her? What could he have done differently to prevent it from happening?

He clutched his head. It didn't feel like she was gone but he'd seen her die right in front of his own eyes. He'd chase down that woman – and anyone else who'd had a hand in Integrity's death - and make them rue the day they'd crossed Integrity's path. If he couldn't have her, he'd have vengeance instead.

'Here.' Jamie reached into his pocket and pulled something out, tossing it into Byron's lap.

He shook himself and frowned. 'This is the old Adair emblem.'

'Yeah. Integrity gave it to me before she went through the Veil. She wanted me to use my Gift on it.' He sighed. 'I don't suppose it matters much now.'

Byron turned it over in his fingers. He lifted it up to see if her scent still clung to it but all it smelled of was old metal. It wasn't much to remember her by but he held it up to his chest, pressing it tightly against his heart.

'What did you see?' he asked dully. Jamie didn't answer. 'What did you see when you used psychometry on it?' Byron asked again.

Jamie's jaw tightened and a muscle ticked in his cheek. 'It's antique,' he said finally. 'There's a lot of history to it. It was forged by a blacksmith before anyone in Scotland had even heard the word Fomori.'

'And?'

He sighed heavily. 'It was passed down through generations. The Chieftain usually wore it.'

'So Gale Adair was wearing it when he died? Integrity's father?'

'No.' He swallowed. 'It was stolen before that. It was passed to the Fomori demons as a symbolic part of a promise to wipe the Adairs from the country.'

For the first time since they'd left the Veil, Byron sat up straight. 'What?'

Jamie gave an awkward shrug. 'That's what I saw.'

'Who stole it?'

Jamie looked away. Somehow Byron already knew the answer but he still waited to hear it. 'It was your father,' Jamie said so quietly that Byron had to strain to hear.

He breathed in deeply. 'Okay,' he said. 'Okay.' There could be all sorts of reasons for that. Even if there weren't, it didn't mean Aifric was guilty of everything that Integrity had accused him of. He squeezed the brooch.

'Your bag is there,' Jamie said softly. 'Angus MacQuarrie gave it to me.'

Byron pushed away the flash of anger at further mention of Mac-Quarrie and reached down to drop in the emblem. He'd keep it safe for now and speak to his father about it later.

Unfortunately, as soon as he unfastened the clasp, a strong smell escaped. It reeked of rot and death. Jamie recoiled. 'What the hell is that?'

Byron shook his head. 'I don't know.' As terrible as the smell was, at least it was a momentary distraction from the searing pain of his own thoughts. He peered inside. 'It's a haggis,' he said finally. 'A dead haggis.' Big deal.

Jamie frowned. 'Eh?'

'Apparently Morna Carnegie has been using her Gift for less than salubrious reasons.' Byron managed a weak shrug. What did one dead fur ball mean now?

'Was it smothered by the bag?' Jamie asked. 'I thought magically imbued creatures were supposed to be tough.'

'They are.'

Byron reached in and drew out the tiny creature. It lay limply in his hand, its features contorted as if it had died in agony. Something was caught in one of its tiny front paws. He gently pulled it free, holding it up as the first evidence of dawn began to appear across the sky.

Byron's muscles bulged and, curling his fingers into a fist, he lashed out and punched the windscreen. It immediately shattered, making Jamie yell in alarm. Byron paid him no attention. His eyes were fixed on the dead creature.

The haggis was holding the vial which had contained the sleeping draught intended for Integrity. The one his father had given him. Except there wasn't any of the liquid left. The little haggis must have drunk it; the little haggis that was now dead.

An inarticulate howl rose up from deep inside Byron's chest while the sun continued to force its way upwards, signalling a brand new day.

About the author

After teaching English literature in the UK, Japan and Malaysia, Helen Harper left behind the world of education following the worldwide success of her Blood Destiny series of books. She is a professional member of the Alliance of Independent Authors and writes full time, thanking her lucky stars every day that's she lucky enough to do so!

Helen has always been a book lover, devouring science fiction and fantasy tales when she was a child growing up in Scotland.

She currently lives in Devon in the UK with far too many cats – not to mention the dragons, fairies, demons, wizards and vampires that seem to keep appearing from nowhere.

CPSIA information can be obtained
at www.ICGtesting.com
Printed in the USA
FSHW010501270320
68529FS